The Libertines Motorcycle Club

Episode One: An outlaw is born

Max L. Billington

The Libertines Motorcycle Club; Episode One: An Outlaw is Born
Copyright © 2011 by Max L. Billington

ISBN-10 (0615542093)
ISBN-13 (978-0615542096)

Dedication

To my family; especially my loving wife Lisa and my three wonderful children, Olivia, Connor, and Jake.

To my friends; some of whom have known about the creation of this book from the beginning, and some knew only after it was finished.

And to those who helped in the contribution of the story line, when I would get stuck and need a little bit of help moving the story in the right direction.

Without your unconditional love and support, this book would not have been possible.

Preface

The idea for writing this book started from a simple challenge from a friend of mine, Ray Carter, who told me that I should take some of my creativity and just go write a book.

After thinking about it, I decided to accept the challenge. When I first started writing, I mapped out the tale to be a very short story, one that could be read at one sitting in about an hour or so.

Then a tragedy happened, which caused the creation of this book to be put on hold. Due to this tragedy, I wanted to include some details of the tragedy into the story line. As the story developed, I realized that I was enjoying the creation of this world so much, and the turn the story took made it apparent that one book would not be able to complete the tale.

While this book and the books to follow are works of fiction, I have tied in some "based on a true story" items which I have witnessed in my life, then skewed the details to fit the story. For those of you reading who know me personally, you will see the connections.

What started out as a simple tale of a regular guy turned biker grew into a complex account of a lifestyle change, proving that it is never too late to change lanes on the highway of life.

Special thanks to Jake Lee for his photograph on the front cover.

Chapter One – Commute

Another Monday morning arrived on the calendar of life. The key of the less than reliable pickup went into the ignition and brought the engine to life. The same typical banter on the sports talk station was heard through the aging speakers. That same buzz when the truck was cold sent the same shivers through Connor's body.

"Why should I even go into the office again today?" Connor asked himself. "It will be another day of typical useless work getting to no end."

Connor was quite the accountant. He had studied hard in school and graduated near the top of his class. He didn't have any trouble finding a job with quite a decent salary just starting out. His salary was good enough to buy him his nice work clothes, which has became his daily uniform. His white long-sleeved shirt and khaki pants, which were lightly starched and fresh from the dry cleaners down the road from his rental house he lived in.

Connor was your typical suburbanite. He was another washed down version of a man. He couldn't change his own oil in his car. He could operate a drill, but no other power tools. If anything broke in his house, he couldn't fix it. Connor pays to have his grass mowed at his house, just as everyone in his typical suburban neighborhood full of similar track houses does.

That morning was a bit warmer than normal. Connor rolled the windows down in the pickup and shut off the air conditioner. The fresh air pouring in the cab of the truck was awakening. That air made Connor seem to wake up even more than the cup of coffee he had which was already beginning to get cold. Pouring milk and adding the sugar to the coffee didn't help with its temperature at all.

As Connor changed lanes on the freeway, his mobile phone began to ring. It was his friend Terry. Terry hadn't called Connor in quite a while and Connor felt bad for not keeping in as good of contact as he should have been.

Terry and Connor had known each other since college. They were dorm mates their freshman year. Terry decided to do more partying than studying in college and ended up dropping out his sophomore year, but Terry and Connor continued to hang out together. Terry was that friend that made Connor enjoy life.

Connor and Terry were similar on so many different levels in college. They both decided to grow their hair long. They both hung out at all the same places, they ran around with the same crowds, they drank the same beer, and listened to the same music. The only difference between the two was Connor's focus on the future.

Terry lived for today. Connor lived for tomorrow. But, in their younger years, Connor partied just as hard as Terry did.

"What's up, Terry!" Connor answered.

"Trying to sober up a bit so I can get to work" responded Terry. Terry worked for the city as a maintenance man. When Terry interviewed for the job two years ago, he got a haircut. He hasn't since.

Connor laughed. "Sounds like you had a good fucking time last night. Wish I could have been there." You could slice the jealously with a dull plastic knife. Terry always had a good time and it made Connor extremely jealous. Terry was the type of guy that never grew up according to everyone else in Connor's life.

Terry sighed. "You should have been there, man. It was one hell of a party, at least for a Sunday night. What the hell are you doing tonight?" Terry asked.

"No clue" responded Connor. "I wish I had something to do other than the same ol' shit I do every day."

Since Connor had his white collar nine-to-five job, a fairly straight-laced wife, and his new and improved group of friends, he didn't get to use foul language all that much. So anytime Connor had a chance to talk to Terry, he let curse words fly that would make a sailor proud.

"Well, I was wondering if I could borrow you and your truck tonight chief."

"What the hell for?" Connor retorted with a hint of sarcasm. "You've got that fancy motor-sickle you ride every damn day, you outlaw son-of-a-bitch."

"It's like this. I met this dude at the party last night. He's got an older bike that he is looking to get rid of. His old lady doesn't want him to have it anymore since she's got a bun in the oven. I think I will be able to get it for a song and a dance, but I don't trust the bike to ride it home so I was hoping to strap it down in the back of your truck and take it from the local shop if I buy it."

"Is it a Harley?" Connor asked.

"Of course it is dipshit. Why the fuck would I want to ride something other than a Harley-Davidson. I just hope I can scrape the cash together today to buy it. Since the dude's ol' lady is making him get rid of it, it's a great deal. I'm thinking I'm going to be able to get it for about half of what it's worth. The plan is to grab it, fix a couple of things, and sell it."

Connor always wondered why Terry never referred to a Harley-Davidson motorcycle as a "Harley." He would always say "Harley-Davidson."

"Just fucking with you," Connor said. "What type shit does it need?"

"Not a lot," Terry answered. "The dude said that the tires are shot so she needs new tires and both holes filled. I can do the oil change but I don't feel like mounting tires. If I get this bike, I will put a couple of used tires on there and do the oil and she will be good to sell."

"Sell?" Connor asked.

"Yeah, just going to flip it man. I don't need two bikes. I can make at least a grand off this in less than a week. I've already got a buyer lined up and I ain't going to pass up making some quick cash this easy."

Connor paused. Connor had always envied Terry for that Harley he had. Every weekend Terry would go here and there, bar to bar, hitting on women and living the life of a biker. When Terry would come by Connor's place, Connor knew Terry was almost there when he heard the sound of that bike rumbling closer and closer. However, those visits had become far and few between the past few years. The mystery of why these visits had become sparse was one that Connor couldn't solve. He narrowed it down to two different possibilities: Julie or booze.

Terry had a bit of a drinking problem according to Connor. As far as anyone else was concerned, Terry was a full-blown alcoholic. Everyone who knew both Terry and Connor looked at Terry's drinking problem as a sign of a loose lifestyle. Terry would never back down from a challenge, whether it was a drink, a race, or a fight. Even though Connor and Terry were the exact same age, and their birthdays were only a few days apart, Terry looked like he was 10 years older than Connor.

Connor had a red sport bike in college. During his college years the ownership of that sport bike was able to land Connor quite a bit of chicks. Riding a sport bike was soon a part of Connor's past and he had never really thought about owning another one, but the sound of Terry's motorcycle made Connor think about that old red Ninja every once in a while.

"What time were you thinking?" Connor asked.

"Whenever you get out of that lame office, dude!" Terry always prodded Connor about his yuppie lifestyle but would love to have the kind of cash that Connor always carried with him.

"Cool deal." Connor responded. "I will call you once I'm headed home. I haven't got shit to do tonight anyway and hopefully Julie won't mind since we haven't hung out for a while. Later."

Now all Connor had to do was convince Julie to let him out of the house. Ever since Connor and Julie moved in together, Connor had been under the lock and key of Julie. Terry was the only single friend of Connor's that still talked to him on a semi-regular basis. Every other person Connor knew was married, and they all lived the same bull shit life as Connor did.

"Fuck me running," Connor said to himself. "I wish I could get out tonight to hang out with Terry but that raging bitch I married isn't going to let me do it."

The sad thing was Julie was not a raging bitch. Julie had sacrificed quite a bit to be with Connor. Her family didn't really care too much for Connor, even though he was a good husband. Ironically, the old red sport bike was what initially attracted Julie to Connor.

Julie never really made Connor sell the bike, but Connor didn't ride the bike at all and had the bike in storage along with other junk that they were never going to use. Connor needed the money and the bike brought them a few thousand bucks, so he sold it. However, Julie didn't realize how much Connor did miss riding.

Nervously, Connor picked up his phone to call Julie. Since he was only a few minutes away from the office, he knew that once he asked her she would not have too long to argue or yell at him.

Connor started to push the speed dial button and the phone began to ring. The caller ID let him know that it was Julie.

Connor thought, "That bitch. It's almost like she knew that I was going to call her and ask for something, so she's calling to yell at me."

"Hey, babe." Connor always answered the phone that way when she would call. No matter how much disdain he held for her, he did love her. He never even once thought about leaving her or living his life without her. Julie was the type of woman that could be considered a trophy wife by most. Connor knew she was hot and Julie knew she was hot. Since they had been together since that chance meeting in college, Connor wanted no other woman in his life. However, as happens to most married couples, the spark was gone. Connor and Julie were basically roommates now who had sex about twice a month.

"Lisa called me this morning and wanted me to help her pick out bridesmaid dresses tonight for the wedding, so I won't be home until later on tonight. I'm going to make her buy my dinner."

"Sounds good to me, honey," responded Connor, with a devilish grin on his face. "I guess I will see you whenever you get back home.

"Since we are not eating dinner tonight, don't go drive through some fast food place for your dinner. You need to stick to your diet. No fried foods. No pizza. You got me, mister?"

Connor sighed. "Of course not. I think I will stop by the deli and have them make one of those big salads for me."

"That sounds yummy," said Julie. "I will see you later on tonight. I love you."

"Love you too, babe" Connor hung up the phone.

So there was Connor's out. He just had to make sure that he got home before Julie did and he wouldn't have to tell her that he saw Terry. He would be able to hang out with him for a bit and not even ask for permission.

Connor's pickup had arrived at his typical parking spot about 5 minutes earlier than usual. Those two conversations, coupled with the thoughts of hanging out with Terry had allowed him to make up a few minutes. Connor began to talk to himself as he sat in front of his office building.

"So, here's what I do. I will text Terry and let him know that I will leave work early to come by his place and pick him up. Julie will not be home until at least ten so I should have plenty of time. Only thing I need to do is make sure to buy a six pack of beer to put in the fridge when I get home. Hell, I know. I will get some and pour it all out and put the empties in the trash. That way I can say I drank them while watching Monday night football."

Connor glanced at his clock on his phone and saw that he still had a couple minutes before he needed to walk in. He began to type a message to Terry:

"Hey Fuck Stick! I will be at your place around 5. I got to be home by 10. Buy beer!"

Chapter Two - Bill

Connor had spent all day watching the clock. The hours seemed like days and the minutes seemed like hours. Connor couldn't remember the last time he had been out of the house and especially out of the house with Terry. Four-thirty finally came and Connor could start his escape.

Connor pushed the button on his key fob and unlocked his truck. His hands were shaking from the excitement of heading to Terry's place so much that he dropped his keys by the door of his truck. He reached down to pick them up and noticed that there was a quarter on the ground next to his truck. Connor grabbed his keys and the quarter, opened the door to his truck, put the ignition key in and roared the old beast to life.

After a very uneventful commute to Terry's, Connor pulled up into his driveway. Connor put the truck in park and shut the truck off. He looked up as the garage door at Terry's place opened and there stood Terry.

As the garage door opened, the various treasures in Terry's garage began to appear. There were two bike frames sitting on the floor, surrounded by motorcycle parts and old tools. The two neon beer signs hanging in the garage were turned off. Right next to the entry door into the house was a trash can that was completely full of mostly pizza boxes and beer bottles and next to it was the almond beer refrigerator covered with stickers. But the true treasure was backed in and sat right at the front, Terry's bike.

Terry rode an old Shovelhead Harley. Terry spent all of his free time and what little spare change he had keeping that bike in tip top shape. That bike was a biker's bike. She had 18 inch ape hangers, loud drag pipe exhaust, and tons of chrome. Connor always loved watching Terry kick that bike to life.

Terry came walking out of the house into the garage. He still had his work clothes on, which were permanently stained with grease and dirt. No matter how much he would wash them, those stains weren't coming out, and Terry could care less. His sleeves on his shirt were rolled up just below the elbow, which revealed two of his many tattoos.

Terry's left arm had a tattoo of a mermaid and his right arm had an eagle with wings wrapping all the way around his arm. These two, along with the rest, were not the new school fancy type tattoos, but they were of the prison variety either. Terry's age and constant time in the sun had faded them quite a bit.

"What's up, Connor!" shouted Terry, as he crushed a beer can that he had just finished.

"Same ol' same old," Connor answered. "You ready to head out?"

"Yeah, let me grab another beer. You want one?"

Connor thought about it for a second. If Julie found out he actually had an open container in his car, she would be pissed. "What the hell? Grab me one."

Terry grabbed two beers from the almond fridge and hopped in Connor's truck. They both cracked open their beers and Terry hit the garage door opener button to close the garage.

"So, where are we headed, man?" asked Connor

"The bike shop right off Elm Street," Terry replied.

Connor had driven by this bike shop several times. This shop was no modern style dealership. It was an old school mechanic's shop. At any time you would see a few motorcycles parked out in front and some bikers hanging around. The shop was strictly a service and parts place so Connor was a bit surprised that they were going to look at a bike to buy there.

Connor said, "I thought you told me that Bill didn't sell bikes."

Terry replied, "He don't, but he lets folks leave them there."

Connor had always heard great stories from Terry about Bill, but had never met him, and really had no reason before to go up to that shop. Connor knew that Terry hung out at that shop every now and then and knew who Bill was, but Connor knew that Bill had no idea who he was.

"So I guess I'm finally going to meet this Bill dude," Connor said, with a hint of excitement in his voice.

"Yeah," Terry answered. "Don't worry though. He's cool. Just because you don't have a bike doesn't mean he won't like you, but if I were you I wouldn't mention that you used to have a metric. He's not really a big fan of those type folks."

Since Terry and Connor had known each other for quite a while, it did not matter to Terry that Connor once rode a Japanese bike. Besides, Connor didn't have it anymore. Terry would always make comments about metric bikes and how they were inferior to the American made bike that was Harley-Davidson.

Connor made the turn onto Elm Street and pulled up next to the shop.

"Park over there," Terry explained as he pointed to another pickup parked beside the building. There was no specific parking for cars or trucks, but there was a specific area roped off for motorcycles.

Terry walked towards the open sliding door at the front of the building and Connor continued behind him by a few steps.

The shop looked deserted. There were no bikes parked outside the shop and just the lone pickup, which looked like an abandoned vehicle, was parked beside the shop. As Terry walked into the shop, a small, black, mixed breed dog greeted him with a loud, growling bark as to try to convince anyone that he was more Doberman than a Terrier mix. The dog bounced up and down like a basketball. Terry finally reached down and put his hand gently on the dog's head. Then a voice came from around the corner of the shop:

"Get that son of a bitch, Chief. Get him. Bite his fucking nuts off."

That was Bill. Connor rounded the corner behind Terry and took his first look at Bill. Bill stood about 6 foot tall and probably weighed in the 250 pound range. He had on a black T-shirt with the sleeves cut off that had a phrase in white lettering on the front reading "Would you like a nice 'Fuck You' with those fries?" Bill's jeans were covered in oil and grease stains, and the boots that he was wearing looked like they were black at one time in the distant past. He wore a black bandana on his head, wire frame glasses on his nose, and had the remnants of a cheap drug-store cigar hanging out of the side of his mouth.

Terry reached into his shirt pocket, took out a cigarette, gave the smoke a light, took a drag and breathed out a puff of smoke as he spoke to Bill.

"So Bill, where's the bike that dude has for sale?"

"You mean the dipshit whose ol' lady won't let him have a bike?" Bill responded.

"That's the one I came to have a look see at." Terry answered.

"It's over here," said Bill.

Connor followed Bill and Terry as the made their way toward the back of the shop. Connor stepped over the grease and oil spills on the floor, as well as the smeared dog shit that was a few feet from a pile of old tires. Bill and Terry didn't seem to care as they walked without paying any attention to what was on the floor.

"Well, there she is Terry. She don't lack much. Hell, if I didn't have so many fucking bikes right now, I would buy her myself."

"Cool deal," said Terry. "It's pretty much as I expected. Oh shit, I forgot, this is my old friend Connor."

"Nice to meet you," said Bill as he extended his filthy grease covered hand out to shake Connor's hand.

Connor gave him a firm grip back, even though he hesitated to get his hand dirty. "You, too." Connor replied.

"So which one of you is going to buy this, Terry?" Bill asked.

Connor laughed. "Julie would kill me if I brought a bike home."

Bill then turned to Terry. "So, you want it?"

Terry scratched his head for a few seconds. Then, he crossed his arms and leaned back against the wall and seemed to disappear into deep thought. Connor was looking at Terry with baited breath as he was hoping that Terry was going to buy the bike. Connor always enjoyed seeing people make large purchases and when it came to things that he knew Julie would not let him have, he took every opportunity to live vicariously though whomever was getting to make the purchase.

"Man, I don't fucking know," said Terry. "Let me grab a beer. It will help me think."

"Help yourself," said Bill.

Connor looked befuddled. "Beer," he thought, "at a place of business. That's cool as hell."

Terry opened the refrigerator and grabbed three beers from the cardboard beer case inside. He tossed one to Connor, one to Bill, and cracked open the third. Rather than slamming down the first drink out of the can, as Terry normally did, he just took a small sip and swished the beer around in his mouth. This was exceedingly strange, as Terry never made a decision in his life with any thought. Terry lived for the moment, for today, not tomorrow.

"Connor, you should buy this bike and start riding again."

Connor laughed again. "Dude, Julie would kill me, you know that."

"Man," Terry replied, "Julie ain't as bad as you think she is. She didn't marry a pencil pushing sissy like she has made you into. Maybe if you put a little bit of bad ass back into yourself, then Julie would bang your brains out more often."

Terry's line of logic was typical of Terry, and Terry knew that Connor had the money. Terry knew that Connor knew how to ride and that knowing how to ride a motorcycle is something that you never forget how to do. Terry assumed that Julie would be a little bit frustrated with Connor if he bought the bike, but Terry figured that she would eventually get over it.

"Dude, your birthday is coming up. Why don't you just buy this bike and tell Julie that it's your birthday present and she doesn't have to buy you anything? Look, you buy the bike and I will fix her up a bit, get her nice and shiny, and come riding up on the bike in your driveway on your birthday with a big bow tied to the forks. You will never forget that birthday. Think about it."

The idea that Terry presented was very tempting for Connor. Connor took a drink of his beer and contemplated the feasibility of him getting a bike as the various scenarios were racing through his head.

"Bill," asked Connor, "what's the guy asking for it?"

Bill looked at Connor a bit surprised that Connor even wanted to know. "The dude said he wants $3500 but I bet if you gave him 3 grand cash he would take it. You want me to call him?"

Connor hesitated. Terry and Bill were staring at him, each one holding their almost empty beer cans, anticipating a negative response from Connor.

"Sure. Tell him I will give him 3 grand cash today only. If he won't take it, then I ain't going to do it tomorrow. Terry, if he takes the offer, we will do what you said. Can you have it ready by this weekend?"

Terry couldn't believe what he had just heard. This was definitely not a typical spur-of-the-moment decision that Connor would make.

"Dude, listen, Julie doesn't care that much for me as it is. I was just fucking with you." Terry continued, "Bill, I'm going to have to wait a week or so before I have the scratch to buy it so…"

Connor interrupted. "Dude, Terry, I'm serious. I want it. Bill, call the guy up and see if he will take 3 grand."

Bill walked away as he was dialing his cell phone. Terry looked at Connor as he crushed his beer can with his hands and proceeded to throw it into the trash can next to the refrigerator.

"It's your funeral," said Terry, "but I will hang on to it for you until the weekend. That should give me time to get the stuff done to it."

"Can Bill do it for me?" asked Connor.

"Yeah, but it will cost you some money."

"That's fine," said Connor. "I can't rely on you to always fix the bike so I might as well have Bill do the work on the bike since I'm guessing that I will be having him do all the service on it. I don't know how to do any of that shit."

"Okay," Terry replied, "Let's see what Bill says when he gets off the phone."

Terry reached into the refrigerator and grabbed two more beers. Connor had about ¼ of a can left and he quickly downed the beer so as to keep up with Terry. They both cracked open the beer cans and watched as the dog brought in a plastic coke bottle that he was attacking like a stray cat.

Just as the dog decided that he was bored chewing on the plastic bottle, Terry and Connor heard a voice behind them.

"What's happening, Big T?"

Connor and Terry turned around. Terry reached out his hand and shook the man's hand.

Terry greeted the man. "Hey Ratchet. What do you know good?"

"This and that and everything else."

Ratchet was a man of fairly slender build. He had long salt and pepper hair and a full beard that hung down past his neck. He was wearing a pair of blue jeans, brown work boots, a black T-shirt with no sleeve, and a black leather vest.

Connor took note of this black leather vest. The vest had three patches sewn onto the front of it. One patch had "Ratchet" embroidered on it, while one patch had a skull with broken wings on the side of it and the last patch said, "In memory of Trigger."

As Ratchet turned away from Connor to reach inside the fridge for his beer, Connor noticed the back of Ratchet's vest. There were three patches on the back of his vest. The bottom patch had "Kansas" on it, which was the state that they were in, the patch in the middle was a skull with a liquor bottle in its mouth, and the top patch read "Libertines."

Connor knew that there was a bike club in town called the Libertines. He had seen them riding on the roads, usually 4 or 5 bikes at a time. They all rode loud bikes and seemed to always be going to a bar. Connor envied their lifestyle as he considered his life dull.

Connor stuck out his hand to introduce himself to Ratchet. Before Connor could open his mouth, Terry grabbed his hand and immediately made eye contact with Connor. Terry gave Connor a gaze with his eyes as to telepathically tell Connor to shut his mouth and stand still.

Ratchet turned back around and opened his beer.

"Ratchet, this is a friend of mine, Connor. Connor, this is Ratchet."

Connor said, "Nice to meet you, Ratchet."

"Same here." Ratchet extended his hand and Connor took it and they shook hands. Ratchet then wandered off and went back outside.

Terry grabbed a hold of Connor and whispered to him, "Dude, there is a whole etiquette thing with club members. You basically don't exist to them until introduced."

About that time, Bill came walking back into the shop with a manila folder in his hand. He walked up to Connor and opened up the folder. Inside the folder were a few pieces of wrinkled up paper and a Kansas motorcycle title.

"Gimme three grand bud. She's yours."

Chapter Three – Maiden Voyage

Connor left the bike at Bill's shop. Connor liked the idea of having Terry come up riding on the bike. Now Connor had to decide how this was going to go over with Julie.

The drive back to Terry's house to drop Terry off was quick. Terry hopped out of the truck and turned to Connor as he shut the door.

"Dude, I can't believe you did this, but I'm real happy for you. Hopefully Julie won't completely flip her lid and let you keep it. I guess it's always better to ask for forgiveness than permission."

"Thanks for the reassurance," Connor responded. "Hopefully I won't have to live with you after this weekend."

Terry waved at Connor as he disappeared into his garage. The last thing Connor saw was Terry grabbing a beer from the beer fridge as he walked into his house. Connor thought that it will be great to see Terry come riding up on his new-to-him bike, but then Connor's stomach began to turn.

Connor had not made a decision on any kind of purchase without Julie's input or rather approval, and a purchase of a motorcycle might just set her completely off, but Connor thought that he was a grown man and he should be allowed to do whatever he wanted. If it was buying a bike, then so be it.

Connor pulled into his driveway just as the sun began to go down. He opened the garage door and saw that Julie's car was not in the garage, so she had not made it home. This bade well for Connor so he could go inside, take a shower, brush his teeth, and get all of the beer smell and dust and grime off of his so Julie would not be the wiser.

After Connor did his thorough cleansing, he went into the kitchen and made himself a sandwich. He grabbed a bottle of water out of the refrigerator and went into the living room and turned on the television, in hopes of finding some kind of sporting event on the sports channel, which was never on in his house while Julie was home. However, there was no game to be found.

Connor hit the DVR button on his remote to see if there was anything he could find to watch that was recorded. Nothing there either. Frustrated, Connor set the remote down on the couch beside him and took a bite out of his sandwich. Just at this instance, he heard that familiar sound of the garage door opening. Julie was home.

The pass-through door opened and there was Julie. Julie was a little bit younger than Connor and was extremely attractive. She was an avid shopper and knew how to buy clothes to compliment her perfect figure. Julie also made sure to wear low cut shirts to show off her breasts, which always made men turn their heads, and the shirt that she had on that night was no exception. Her jeans were so tight that you could not tuck a shirt into them if you tried, but Julie never tucked her shirt in since her shirts never were long enough to touch the waist line of her jeans.

"Hey babe!" said Connor as Julie walked in.

"Hi. How was your night?" asked Julie.

"Pretty uneventful," Connor said. "Nothing much to report. What did you and Lisa do?"

"Well," she answered, "I think we have the dress narrowed down now. While we were shopping I got to thinking. Your birthday is coming up and you haven't told me what you want for your birthday. Have you thought about it?"

"I know exactly what I want this year. A Harley-Davidson!"

Julie exploded into laughter, laughter so violent that she bent over at the waist and almost fell to the floor.

"You have got to be kidding. You will kill yourself on one of those!"

"Babe," retorted Connor, "when you met me I rode a bike. I have missed having a bike for quite a while and I would really like to have another one. Remember when you used to ride on the back of my old Ninja. Those were great times. I just…"

"Yeah," interrupted Julie, "I remember. We were much younger then. Besides, you are not a biker like Terry and look at him, always broke, always drunk, a worthless piece of…"

"Hey!" shouted Connor, "First off you asked me what I wanted for my birthday and now you turn it into another attack on Terry. You know just as well as I do that Terry would do anything for me and just because he lives that biker lifestyle doesn't mean that if I got a bike I would get all tattooed up and turn into a greasy biker."

Julie stared Connor down. An uncomfortable silence filled the room. After 15 seconds of nothing but silence Julie said, "Well, keep thinking. You're not getting a stupid motorcycle for your birthday."

Julie left the room and went into the bedroom. Connor wasn't surprised by the way that conversation turned out, but that was typical. Connor knew that he only had a few days to soften the blow of the motorcycle purchase, if that was going to be possible.

Connor got up from the couch and headed into the bedroom after about an hour sitting in the living room. There was no way that he could come up with a descent idea of how to get this plan to work. Before Connor could get to the bedroom, his cell phone rang. It was Terry.

Connor thought to himself if he should answer or not, but he knew the sound of his ringtone had already been heard by Julie so she would want to know who called anyway, so he figured that he might as well answer.

Connor answered, "What's up, Terry?"

"So, did ya tell the ol' lady yet?"

"I haven't had a chance to think about it yet." Connor didn't want to give Julie any reason to ask what the conversation was about so he tried his best to disguise his answer.

"Well," said Terry, "Good luck with all that. If I could help you with it I will, but I still can't believe you bought that bike and she doesn't know about it. She is going to shit her pants when she finds out!"

Connor laughed. "Dude, I got to go. I have to get up early. I will talk at you later."

"Who was that," Julie shouted from inside the bedroom.

Connor walked into the bedroom and answered, "That was Terry. He was wanting to know what's been going on and if I could take some crazy trip with him. You know that I'm not going but I don't want him to think that I am just going to blow him off."

Connor plugged his cell phone into its charger and climbed into bed.

Julie was still in the middle of her nightly going to bed ritual of removing her makeup, brushing her hair, and putting on old worn out comfortable pajamas to get into bed. After several more minutes, Julie finally finished, grabbed a fashion magazine and got into bed.

"So, really," Julie whispered, "What do you want for your birthday? I need some advance notice as I am busy."

Before Connor answered he let out a resounding sigh for two reasons. First, Connor knew that Julie was not busy. She didn't do anything around the house during the day except watch TV and talk to her friends on the phone. The second reason was Connor knew what he wanted. Connor already had made up his mind that there would be no sex tonight since they had already had one argument and Julie had on her old pajamas, so Connor threw caution to the wind.

"A Harley-Davidson."

Julie laughed again, but this time not as before. This was Julie's evil laugh.

"You are not going to get a motorcycle so get over it."

Connor rolled over on his side facing away from Julie and started to fall asleep. The picture of the bike was in his head. Connor began to imagine himself riding that bike along side of Terry and feeling the rush of wind in his face as he rode down the street, feeling like an outlaw, hoping to have a dream about it. He then fell asleep.

\#

Bright and early the alarm woke Connor up from his slumber. He sat up on the side of the bed as the local talk station was still on the alarm clock.

"Turn that off!" said Julie as she was still half asleep.

Connor reached over and switched the radio off. He arose from his bed and began preparation for yet another day of his toilsome life. He walked into the bathroom, placed his hands on the vanity, and looked at himself in the mirror. Then the thought of the motorcycle came across his mind which led to a devious smile coming across his face.

"How in the hell am I going to pull this off?" he thought to himself. "There is no way she is going to go for it."

After Connor finished his normal morning ritual, he began to walk out of the bedroom and he gave his normal farewell to Julie. "Bye babe. I love you."

Julie just let out a half asleep groan. She heard him, but she was too tired to respond since she sat up most of the night watching women's programming on cable TV.

"Hey, one quick thing, I need to get the oil changed in the truck after work, so I will be home after that. Love you. Bye."

Connor walked briskly out of the house so as to not cause an issue with his tardiness home. He didn't have to get the oil changed after all.

"So this is the plan," Connor said to himself as he drove to work, "I will go get the oil changed on the truck during my lunch break and swing by the motorcycle shop after work and talk to Bill for a bit."

So this was the plan, and Connor figured that he would be able to get away with that. Telling Julie that he had to get the oil changed in his pickup would buy him at least an hour at the motorcycle shop to gawk over his new purchase and hopefully get to know Bill a bit more.

Connor had a busy morning at work, hurried to get his oil changed over his lunch break so he would have a fresh sticker on the inside of his windshield proving that the work was done, and then his afternoon went dead. During a break at work, Connor made a phone call to get insurance put on the bike and had the bill sent to his office address so Julie would not see any paperwork on the bike. The clock could not move fast enough. All Connor could think about was getting to the motorcycle shop and looking at his bike.

A slow moving commute commenced as Connor drove to the motorcycle shop. With only a few days until his birthday, he could not wait to mount that iron pony and take it for his maiden voyage, but just getting to gawk at the bike sitting inside Bill's bike shop would satisfy his needs for now.

As Connor pulled up to the bike shop, he saw that the bike shop was as dead as it was yesterday. There stood Bill with a cigar hanging out of his mouth and a beer in his hand. Bill saw Connor pull up to the shop but didn't acknowledge his arrival as Connor would have thought he should.

Connor opened the door to the truck and greeted Bill. "Hey Bill, what's going on?"

"Nothing," responded Bill. Connor was hoping for more of a welcome than that, but other than Terry, he had no other connection to this world of motorcycle folks.

"I came by to stare at my new bike," Connor said.

Bill said, "You know where it's at," and then turned around and walked around to the side of his building to relieve the stress on his beer-filled bladder.

Connor walked into the shop and there sat the bike. The bike had new tires on it and looked like it was just begging to be fired up. Connor threw his right leg over the bike and sat down. He put both hands on the handlebars and rocked the bike upright. Then his mind started to wander.

Connor imagined all of the nice rides that he could share with his new bike. He imagined riding down the road with Terry. He even pictured Julie on the back of his bike, with her arms wrapped around him and her hair blowing in the wind behind him. The smile on Connor's face was ear to ear and he could hardly contain himself.

Bill walked back into the shop and crushed the empty beer can in his hand. He then turned to Connor and yelled at him from across the shop, "Why don't you fire it up and take it down the street? After all, it's your bike man. I bet that would make you happier than an itchy pig at a leaning post."

"Cool," said Connor, after wiping the enormous grin off of his face and attempting to not show what a big deal this was for him. He reached down and turned on the ignition and hit the start button. The engine turned over and turned over but it would not come to life.

"Stop! Stop! Choke it, dammit!" yelled Bill.

Connor's face began to turn red. It had been so long since he had actually started a bike and had been so used to the fuel injection in his truck that he had forgotten all about carburetors and chokes.

"Right," replied Connor as he reached down to the side of the engine where the choke was on his sport bike and was pleased to find that the choke was in the same place on his Harley. He gently pulled out the choke knob and hit the starter button again. A loud roar of straight pipes bellowed in the shop as Connor's new beast came to life. Connor couldn't help but pull down on the throttle and make the engine rev up and down.

Connor walked the bike out of the shop door and pushed in the choke, causing that great "Potato Potato" sound to come out of the shiny chrome pipes on the right side. He kicked up the jiffy stand with his left foot, fed some fuel to the motor, grabbed the clutch, and threw the bike into gear. Connor took off from a stand-still and all of his motorcycle riding skill immediately came back to him. He shifted through the gears effortlessly as he rode about a mile away from the shop before pulling into a parking lot to turn around. As he did, he noticed a familiar site, someone whom he had seen before.

It was Ratchet, heading down the other side of the street, right toward the shop. Connor wondered to himself if Ratchet was going to stop at the shop or not. Connor hurriedly turned back around and headed back to the shop. As he pulled the bike in, he noticed that Ratchet was just now dismounting from his bike.

Connor pulled his bike up next to Ratchet's, but didn't park all too close. You could have easily parked a pickup truck in between them.

"Hey Ratchet, good to see you," exclaimed Connor, who was still railing from his maiden voyage.

"You are Terry's friend, right?" asked Ratchet.

"Yeah, Connor," Connor answered as he extended his right hand to shake Ratchet's. Ratchet returned with his hand as well and gave Connor a firm handshake.

"Right, Connor, so what do you think of the bike, man?" asked Ratchet.

"I freaking love it, man. Freaking love it! Best decision I have made in a long time."

Ratchet smiled at Connor and said, "Yeah, I remember my first bike."

"Well," said Connor, "It's not my first bike. Had a rice rocket years ago and rode the shit out of it, but I got married and I sold it. I figured it was time to get back on two wheels."

"Right on, right on." said Ratchet, as he walked into the shop and opened the beer fridge, and to Ratchet's surprise the beer fridge was out of beer.

"Damn," he said, "I guess I drew the short straw."

Ratchet began to walk across the street when Connor said, "Hey, where you going?"

"I got to get beer, man. That's the rule. If you open the fridge for a beer, and there ain't any beer there, you got to fetch beer and restock."

"Wait," said Connor, "I got it." Connor walked across the street to the local convenience store and made a purchase of 30 cheap beers as was the common beverage of choice for the bike shop. As he returned from across the street, Ratchet and Bill were standing there patiently awaiting his arrival.

"Beer?" asked Connor as he approached the two men. Bill and Ratchet both held out their hands as to non-verbally answer and Connor handed them each a beer can and grabbed one for himself. They all cracked open their beer cans and drank in silence.

Connor wanted to break the silence so he thought and thought about what to say. Before Connor could come up with anything to say Bill broke the silence.

"So," said Bill, "How long have you known Terry?"

"Since college," answered Connor, "We go way back. He kept his interest in bikes and mine kind of fell out, but I have always wanted to get back into riding, and I'm not getting any younger. Besides, it's high time I get my balls back from my wife and do some shit that I want to. If I watch any more TV, I'm going to go fucking nuts."

Bill and Ratchet laughed. Connor wanted to leave on a high note, but at the same time he really wanted to hang out there all night. He knew that he couldn't so he shook both of their hands and said that he would see them soon. Connor then got into his truck and drove off.

Ratchet looked over at Bill and said, "He seems to be an alright guy. I talked to Big T and they have known each other for a while. Big T says he can ride and logged a bunch of miles with him years ago. He said that he would be a fit, but his ol' lady probably won't be too keen on the idea."

"So," said Bill, "if he hangs around, is Big T going to sponsor him in?"

"Well," said Ratchet, "Big T is willing to sponsor him in. He just didn't want to talk about it until the whole bike deal got finished. Hell, Connor's ol' lady might make him sell the bike. I hear that she's pretty good looking."

"If this dude pulls this off," Bill explained, "it shows that he wears the pants, whether his ol' lady is good looking or as ugly as homemade soap. The rest of it we can learn if we decide to prospect his ass."

Ratchet reminded Bill, "Been a fuck while since we had a prospect."

"Yeah," said Bill.

"And," Ratchet replied, "I'm sick of walking across that fucking street and fetching beer."

Chapter Four - Pickup

Connor's birthday was finally here. He woke up that morning without the assistance of his alarm and within a few brief seconds realized the day was here to pick up his bike. Connor wondered to himself how Julie was really going to react to all this. He knew that she would definitely be pissed, but how pissed was she really going to be?

After Connor rolled out of bed, he awoke Julie from stirring up the blankets. Julie slowly sat up, rubbed her eyes and looked at Connor.

"Happy Birthday," she said, "What do you want to do today?"

"Well," said Connor, "Terry said that he had a surprise for me this morning. It hopefully won't take that long. After I get back let's go do something."

"Okay," said Julie with a heavy hesitation in her voice. "It is your birthday and you haven't seen Terry in a while, so go, have fun. I will see you when you get back."

Connor was in a bit of disbelief. He knew that in a very short while things were going to change at his house. Julie was going to go off her keel when she saw Connor ride up on that bike but he decided that he would at least relish in his victory this morning.

After he got dressed, Connor grabbed his cell phone and sent a text to Terry that he was ready. Terry texted back and told him that he was on his way. It only took Terry 15 minutes to get to Connor's house, but to Connor it seemed like an eternity.

Terry pulled up to Connor's house and honked the horn twice to alert Connor. Connor opened the front door, told Julie "Bye," and did not receive a response as he left. Connor walked briskly toward Terry's car and hopped in.

Terry said, "Let's roll, buddy! It's time for you to get back on two wheels."

"I'm so ready. I barely slept last night."

Terry backed out of the driveway and pulled onto the street. It was almost 10 o'clock in the morning, which was the opening time of the shop. As Terry pulled into the shop parking area, Bill had just finished opening the sliding gate. Terry and Connor exited the vehicle, Bill cracked open a beer and tossed one to Terry.

"It's kind of early for you Big T, but I'm sure you're ready for one," said Bill.

Without hesitation, Terry passed the beer to Connor and said, "Toss me another, it's time to celebrate."

Bill laughed and replied, "Get your own; I'm not a fucking bartender."

Terry laughed back and entered the shop, opened up the refrigerator, and cracked open another beer.

"Cheers," said Terry, as he tapped his beer can against Connor's. "Today is the first day of the rest of your life."

Terry, Bill and Connor all took a drink from their beers and walked over to Connor's bike. Connor stood there and took a very long look at it. Bill and Terry stood there as Connor gawked at the bike and kind of smiled at each other. They knew the feeling and remained silent as Connor took it all in.

"Well," said Bill, "you just gonna stare at the bitch all day or are you gonna ride her?"

"Hell yeah I'm gonna ride her," said Connor as he straddled the bike and rocked her up off of the kick stand.

"Wait a second," said Terry. "Not just yet. I have to go grab something. Don't start that bike until I get back."

Before Bill or Connor could even ask Terry what he was doing, Terry was in his car and gone. So all that was left was Bill and Connor, standing there, next to Connor's bike, and an uncomfortable silence ensued.

"Well, shit," said Bill, "Guess I better get to work. That shovelhead over there ain't gonna fix herself." Bill started to walk towards one of his lifts in the shop.

Connor followed behind Bill and replied, "You need a hand?"

Bill stopped and turned around, looking at Connor in a pleasant surprise. "Sure thing, bud. Grab a ½ inch wrench and drain the oil."

As Bill walked into the retail portion of his shop, Connor walked over to Bill's tool box and started to open the drawers, looking for a wrench. Each drawer was filled with oil-soaked tools and appeared to be in no particular order. After opening 5 drawers he found a wrench. Connor walked over to the old shovelhead and started to loosen the drain plug when he heard a familiar voice.

"What's happening?"

It was Ratchet. Connor thought to himself that he must live there or something. He didn't hear Ratchet pull up since the air compressor was running right next to him. Ratchet put a six pack of Budweiser in the refrigerator and took one of the bottles from the pack, twisting off the lid, and taking a nice long drink.

"So, man," said Ratchet, "Bill has you working here already, huh?"

Connor replied, "Guess so. I haven't worked on a bike in a while but I think it's all coming back to me. Changing the oil isn't rocket science."

Ratchet laughed and replied, "You hang around here for a while and you will get put to work, but it's all good. If Bill told you to wrench that means he likes you."

Connor felt pretty good about himself at that point. It seemed like Ratchet liked him and now he thought Bill did too, and all the while he thought that these bikers would look at him as a yuppie outsider and would not give him the time of day.

Connor finally removed the drain plug from the motorcycle and the old black oil began to pour out into the drain pan. He grabbed a rag from the front of the bike and wiped off the wrench and his hands of the dirty oil when he heard a bike pull up out front and a familiar voice.

"Hey Ratchet, what's happening?"

Ratchet replied, "Big T, what's up?"

Connor thought to himself, "Big T? What the hell is Ratchet calling Terry that for?"

Terry came walking into the shop with a leather vest on just like Ratchet's vest and the same patches on the back. Connor had no idea that Terry was also a member of a club.

"So Bill already has your boy working I see," said Ratchet.

"You know how it is," said Terry.

"Hey Terry," said Connor, "Where did you go?"

"I had to go get my bike, man. I didn't want to follow you home in my car."

Bill came walking back out from inside the shop. He looked over at Terry and Connor.

"Well," Bill said, "you boys should roll."

"We will be back in a bit," replied Terry.

Connor and Terry hopped on their bikes and went for a ride. Terry rode in front of Connor in the left side of the lane and Connor hung back a bit. Connor could not help but stare at Terry's back and the 3 piece patch that was on his back. Connor wondered why Terry never said anything about being in the club to him, but he knew that he and Terry had lost touch over the last couple of years and this must have happened during that.

Terry motioned back to Connor to pull over at the gas station. They both flipped on their turn signals and entered the parking lot of the gas station. Terry pulled up to a gas pump and shut down his bike as he pulled out his wallet to find his credit card. Connor pulled up right behind him and opened up his gas tank to find that it was full and was in no need of gas.

Connor sat silently on his bike as Terry filled up the gas tank, still staring at his black leather vest.

"Dude, why are you staring at me?" said Terry.

"What's up with the leather vest?" asked Connor.

"You mean I never told you? I patched into the Libertines about 6 months ago."

"Patched in? What the hell is that?" asked Connor.

Terry finished fueling up his bike and returned the gas hose to the pump. He screwed on the gas cap quickly and walked over to Connor.

"It's a long story. I started hanging out at Bill's bike shop about two years ago. Most of the guys up there know a little bit about wrenching on bikes but not as much as Bill. So, I was up there one day and Bill had a problem with a bike that he just could not figure out. I offered to take a look and figured out the problem.

Since I had been hanging around for a while and most of the guys from the club knew me, Bill asked me if I wanted to prospect for the club."

Connor interrupted. "Prospect?"

"Yeah, prospect," replied Terry. "When you prospect it's a chance for everyone in the club to get to know you and decide whether or not you would be a good fit. Prospecting is basically a trial period where the club works your ass off and determines whether or not you can be trusted.

Typically the club doesn't prospect anyone unless they see and actual need that someone can fill. For me, it was wrenching and my ability to fix stuff.

"Take Ratchet for instance. He can build anything. Give him tools and some wood, and he can build you a fucking house. Everyone in the club has something that they are really good at and it helps to contribute to the good of the club."

"So," said Connor, "Bill is a member of the club?"

"Yeah," replied Terry. "He is the vice-president and one of the founding members of the club. Thing is, dude, he's asking about you."

"Asking about me?" asked Connor in complete surprise.

"Yeah," said Terry, "It's like this, no one in the club is college educated like you. Everyone is a blue collar guy like me. They have asked me some questions about you and think you might be able to fill a need. I probably shouldn't tell you this but I think they are going to invite you to a party as a hang-around so the club can get to know you. If all goes well, I will be asking you to prospect."

Connor was taken aback by all of this. Last week, Connor didn't even own a bike and now just a week later he might be able to join a motorcycle club. Connor was elated, but he knew that Julie wouldn't go for it.

"Dude," said Connor, "I doubt Julie will go for that. She doesn't even know about the bike yet."

"Well," replied Terry, "That's going to have to be your battle. Let's head back to the shop. I have a feeling that there will be a few members there if not all of them this morning. I have a feeling that Bill has asked them to be there this morning to be there to meet you. Don't let on that you know any of this, it would be my ass."

"Sure, no problem," replied Connor, as he roared his bike to life and Terry's followed. They both pulled onto the road and headed back to the shop. Connor stared even more intently at the patches on Terry's back. He thought to himself that it would be so cool to wear that vest but was afraid that he didn't have what it would take to join.

As Connor and Terry returned to the shop, Connor noticed that there were 5 bikes parked outside. One bike he recognized as Ratchet's but he knew the other 4 bikes were not there when he and Terry left. Connor and Terry pulled up to the shop and shut their bikes down. Upon hearing the noise of bikes pulling up, Connor saw 6 people exit the shop.

Two of the six people he recognized as Bill and Ratchet. The other 4 were wearing black leather vests with the Libertines patch on the back. Connor thought to himself to remain cool and just go with the flow.

Connor stood by his bike and watched as Terry approached each of the four who were not there before, shaking their hands and hugging them. After the greetings were exchanged, Terry turned around towards Connor.

"This is Connor. He's a friend of mine."

Terry proceeded to introduce the four men, stating their road names as he pointed to them.

"This is Cobbler, Pepper, Nutcase, and Knuckles."

As each man was introduced, they extended their hands and shook Connor's hand. Connor repeated his name to each member.

"Good to meet all of you guys," said Connor.

Terry walked into the shop to grab a beer out of the refrigerator only to find out that the beer supply had already been exhausted.

"Dammit," exclaimed Terry, "why is it always me?"

Terry started to walk across the road to the convenience store and as he walked by Connor, Connor stopped him.

"Dude, let me get it," Connor told Terry. Connor walked across the street to go get beer.

"So this is the dude, huh?" said Nutcase.

"Yep, that's him," said Terry. "He's just a regular Joe. No ties to law enforcement, good job, real smart mother fucker. He does accounting work. He's real good with numbers and computer shit."

"Computers huh?" said Ratchet, "Is that one of those typewriters attached to a TV set?"

Everyone laughed. Ratchet always had a way of making a joke at just the right time. As the laughing died down, Terry decided to feel out the club about Connor.

Terry explained. "Well, assuming that his ol' lady doesn't kill him over buying the bike, does anyone have a problem with me inviting him to the party tomorrow?"

Everyone looked at each other and shook their heads when Bill spoke up.

"As far as I'm concerned," said Bill, "he is welcome at the party. It is up to each one of you to get to know him at that party. For the shit that we are about to get into we need someone who can run numbers and work computers and take care of that techie stuff for us. Anyone got a problem with that?"

Everyone shook their heads in agreement with Bill, with one exception, Cobbler.

Cobbler spoke up. "I don't think we need to fast track a hang-around to prospect so fast before we know that we can trust him. I know he is your friend Big T, but that's all anyone knows about the guy. Just because he offers to fetch beer doesn't mean that he will make a good patch and I don't want...

"Hey," Bill interrupted, "we are not fast tracking shit. Calm your big ass down, Cobbler. Your signature on his card would be required just like mine, and your vote will be required to give him his bottom rocker. Don't jump the fucking gun just yet. Now, shut your fucking mouths, here he comes."

Connor walked up with a 30 pack in his hand and walked past the members of the club to put the beer in the fridge.

"Who wants one?" asked Connor.

Everyone replied with their hands held out as to let Connor know that they expected him to bring them a beer, which Connor did. After Connor handed each member a beer, he grabbed one for himself and all the men cracked open their beers. As they drank the cold, cheap beer, they all stood in silence. Bill turned around and quietly walked back to the bike that he had began working on. Ratchet, Cobbler, and Nutcase walked off to the side of the shop while Pepper followed Bill into the shop and Knuckles remained standing there, in silence.

"So...," said Connor to Knuckles as he pointed in the direction of the bikes parked in front of the shop, "Which one is yours?"

Knuckles pointed to a black Harley-Davidson FXR with tall ape-hangers and hardly any chrome on it whatsoever. "That one."

"Cool, man. Nice bike. I picked mine up just now. I bought it a few days ago and I have had it here. It's that one over there."

"Gotcha," replied Knuckles. "I have seen it parked in the shop for a while. It's a good looking scoot."

Knuckles reached into his vest and pulled out a cigarette. He held it up to his mouth and lit it with an old chrome Zippo lighter that had obviously been dropped over a hundred times. He then turned his back to Connor and walked away.

Terry looked over at Connor and said, "Let's go."

Even though Connor wanted to hang out there all day with these bikers, he knew that it was time to head home and face the music with Julie. He couldn't delay it any longer. Connor and Terry mounted their bikes and both bikes roared to life.

The ride from Bill's shop to Connor's house was extremely quick for Connor. He enjoyed riding the bike for that short distance so much that he had not put any thought into what he was going to say to Julie when she saw the bike.

There would be no hiding this purchase, as two Harleys pulling into Connor's driveway would not go unnoticed by Julie, but even if they would have pulled in with the motors not running, it would not have mattered, because as they pulled into the driveway, Julie was standing outside, looking at the mail that she had just removed from the mailbox.

Chapter Five - Doghouse

"What in the hell is that?" yelled Julie as Connor and Terry parked their bikes in Connor's driveway.

"It's my birthday present. What do you think?"

Julie was less than enthused.

"I cannot believe that you did this Connor. What is going through your mind? Did you think that I would just let you get a fucking motorcycle for your birthday? How old are you, you mindless, selfish piece of fucking shit. Get the fuck out of here and don't come back on that fucking motorcycle."

Julie turned around and walked into the house, slamming the door as she entered.

"Well," said Terry sarcastically, "that went pretty good."

Connor laughed and said, "That's pretty much what I expected to happen. She will calm down. Like we have said before, it's always easier to ask for forgiveness than permission."

"I think I better come in with you in case Julie wants to murder you so at least you will have a witness."

"I don't think that's a good idea, Terry. I better handle this one on my own."

Terry chuckled and said, "Suit yourself, dude. Before I go I need to ask you something. I know that you are most likely going to be in the doghouse now, but I've been asked to invite you to the club party tomorrow. You can even bring Julie if you want but I doubt that she will go."

"I'm going to have to get back to you on that one, dude."

"Yeah," said Terry, "I kind of figured that. Just send me a text either way. If you do go, I will come over tomorrow shortly before noon so we can ride over there. You can't get in without being escorted in."

Connor nodded his head in acknowledgement and said, "Gotcha. I will shoot you a text when I know."

Terry got on his bike, fired it up, walked it backwards to the end of the driveway, and watched Connor walk toward the house slowly as he tried to muster up the courage to go inside. He walked up to the door and turned the door knob only to find out that Julie had locked the door. Connor put his key into the lock to open the door and walked inside to find Julie standing in the kitchen with a birthday cake in front of her. On top of the cake was a motorcycle.

"Happy Birthday! Gotcha!" exclaimed Julie as Terry walked in behind Connor.

"What the hell?" exclaimed Connor in disbelief.

Julie explained. "Terry and I had you going. It was all a set up. I knew the whole time that you were getting a bike."

Terry grabbed Connor's shoulders from behind, laughed, and replied, "Yep. Your ol' lady is a lot cooler than you think. I called her about doing this for your birthday two weeks ago and got the okay from her. Man, this was tough to keep a secret, but we both wanted your birthday to be special."

Connor walked up to Julie and wrapped his arms around her, hugging her ever so tightly and kissing her on the forehead. He began to shake with excitement knowing now that he had absolutely nothing to worry about.

"I'm so sorry that I didn't say anything to you, but I have really wanted a bike for a while."

Julie said, "I know. I know you have for quite a while and you never buy yourself anything. You do work really hard and provide for us really well.

Terry spoke up, "Well, you two kids have a good day. I've got some stuff I have to do today. Don't forget to let me know about the party tomorrow."

"Will do," said Connor, "I will text you later."

Connor reached out his hand and shook Terry's and gave him a hug with his left hand as Terry returned the farewell. Terry walked out the front door and left on his motorcycle.

"Now," said Julie, "I want to talk to you about this motorcycle. While

I want it to be enjoyable for you, I think we need some ground rules."

Connor thought to himself, "Here it comes. She's gonna take all of the fun out of it."

"I don't want you to ride this thing stupid like you used to ride your other bike. No speeding, no tricks, no stunts. None of that shit. Secondly, I don't want you to go out with Terry or anyone else and get drunk on this thing. I don't want to get a call from the hospital that you were in a wreck or get a call from the cops saying that they picked you up for a DUI or something like that. Agreed?"

"Absolutely, babe. All that goes without saying. I am so happy that you are cool with this. I am so excited. In fact, Terry invited me to a party with his club tomorrow."

Julie had a puzzled look on her face and replied to Connor, "You're not a biker. Don't forget that. Just because you have a Harley now doesn't automatically make you a bad ass. You don't even have a tattoo. You can't hang with any of those bikers and don't pretend that you can. That's a good way to get your ass kicked."

"I've already met 4 or 5 of the guys from Terry's club. They all seem to be good guys. They all work blue collar jobs and are stand up guys. It's kind of important that I at least go to the party since I was invited. If I don't go I doubt that I will get invited again."

"So what?" responded Julie, "What difference does it make whether or not you get invited to another party? What's the big deal?"

"The big deal," answered Connor, "is that the Vice President of the club is the guy that owns the bike shop in town. I don't want to get on his bad side right from the start. Look, it's no big deal. I will go to the party with Terry tomorrow. Besides, you have stuff you have to do tomorrow for Lisa's wedding tomorrow. You go with her and have a good time and I will go to the party with Terry."

Julie hesitated and thought for a minute. She knew that she was a little hard on Connor most of the time and that she wanted him to enjoy his new birthday present, so she decided to compromise with him.

"Okay," said Julie, "Go to the party tomorrow but like I said, no getting drunk, you hear me?"

"Of course, babe. One or two beers, tops. I'm sure that most of it will be just watching football which is what I was hoping to get to do tomorrow while you were helping Lisa."

"So, where is this 'party' at?" asked Julie.

"It's at the club's clubhouse. I'm not sure where that is exactly but Terry is going to come by to get me. He said he has to bring me to the party."

Julie laughed. "It sounds like a bunch of little boys pretending that they are bad-asses or something. I guess if you really want to go, then go."

Connor paused for a moment, and then replied, "Don't make fun of it. Those guys seem pretty cool and down to earth, not like any of your stupid friend's husbands that you make me hang out with."

"Hey," said Julie, "Remember, that I am trying to be supportive of this motorcycle thing, so I suggest that you don't shit all over me right now."

"You're right," said Connor. "I'm sorry. Just don't pass judgment until you know everything. Okay?"

"Fine," said Julie, "Now, go get ready. You are going to take me out to the movies and dinner for your birthday, and before you even ask, we are not going to ride on that motorcycle."

Julie left the kitchen and went into the bedroom to change her clothes. Connor walked out the front door and looked at his new bike, shining in the sun in all of its glory. He could not wait until tomorrow to go to the Libertine's party. He started up the bike and pulled it into the garage, parking it as far away from Julie's car which resided on the other side. He dismounted himself from the bike and noticed a small mud spot on the gas tank, which he wiped off with the t-shirt he was wearing.

Connor reached into his pocket and pulled out his cell phone. He scrolled through his contacts and found Terry and sent him a text message:

"I'm in! See you tomorrow at noon."

Connor walked into the house and went into the bathroom to start getting ready when his cell phone went off. It was a return text from Terry:

"Cool. See ya then."

Chapter Six – The Clubhouse

Connor and Julie decided to sleep in that Sunday morning after their date night. Connor had taken Julie out to a romantic comedy movie and a nice candle lit dinner. After a night of passionate sex, they both needed some rest.

Connor was the first to wake up. He looked over at the alarm clock which read 10:30. He rolled over and noticed that Julie was still sleeping and had not put anything on after their love making last night. Connor still was infatuated with Julie and was severely attracted to her. Connor slowly moved the sheets off of her and admired her naked body as she slept.

As Connor tended to do now and then, he reached over, grabbed his cell phone off of the charger and took a picture of Julie as she slept in the bed. He then took another picture in which he zoomed in on her bare breasts. The sound of this second picture began to cause Julie to awaken. Connor hurriedly put the phone on the nightstand and stretched out his arms above his head and let out a large yawn.

Julie's eyes opened and looked at Connor and said, "What time is it?"

"It's 10:30," answered Connor. "What time do you have to meet Lisa?"

"Shit. At 11. I'm going to be late. Hand me my robe."

Julie rushed into the bathroom and started to throw on make-up. Connor was still sitting on the side of the bed when he reached down on the floor to grab his jeans that he had worn the day before. He put his jeans on and grabbed a pair of socks from the dresser. He put those on and his boots and walked into the bathroom to grab a t-shirt out of the closet.

Julie then said, "So what time is this party of yours again?"

"Right around noon. Terry said that he is going to be by the house to ride with me to the clubhouse."

"I bet you are excited aren't you?" said Julie in her normal sarcastic tone. "You get to hang out and be a biker today. Just remember, no bullshit. I don't want you to come home drunk. Just because this is your birthday weekend doesn't mean to go get fucked up with a bunch of white trash bikers."

"Hey now," said Connor, "Don't fight with me about something that hasn't even happened yet. I won't get drunk. I promise. Besides, I don't think that it would be smart to get trashed the first time I hang out with these guys."

Julie finished getting ready as Connor put on a plain black t-shirt. That was the best that Connor had to offer as far as looking like a biker. Connor started to stare at himself in the mirror as he tried to personify a biker-like person, but to his dissatisfaction, he didn't look the part at all with his short hair cut and his clean shaven face which he shaved the night before to go out with Julie.

Julie and Connor heard a horn honk outside. It was Lisa, who had arrived right at 11 o'clock to pick up Julie.

Julie said, "Hey, run outside and tell Lisa that I will be there in a minute."

Connor left the house through the front door and waved at Lisa. He walked up to her car as she rolled down the passenger window.

"Julie will be out in a minute. We got in a bit late last night and slept in and I forgot to set the alarm."

"Oh yeah, you went out for your birthday last night, didn't you?" asked Lisa.

"Yeah. We did. Did Julie tell you what I got?"

"Nope. What did she get you?" asked Lisa.

Connor was a bit shocked, but he replied, "I finally got a bike."

As Connor finished answering her question, Julie came up from behind him and gently pushed him aside so as to enter the passenger side of the car when she said, "Don't forget what I said about today. I will see you later on."

Lisa and Julie drove off. Connor watched as they turned the corner and left the neighborhood. Connor reached into his pocket and sent a text message to Terry:

"Ready whenever you are."

Connor walked back toward the house and punched in the garage door code. As the garage door opened, Connor's bike came into view. He stood there are stared at the bike as it sat there in the garage, like a sleeping beast waiting to be awoken. Connor was trying to figure out what to do with his time while he waited for Terry's arrival.

He threw his leg over the bike and walked it backwards into the driveway. Connor then went back into the garage and took some cleaning supplies off of the shelf in the garage along with a towel and began to shine every nook and cranny of his bike, from the handlebars, to the mirrors, to the engine, to the pipes.

As he finished cleaning the seat off, Terry pulled up into the driveway. Terry got off of his bike and left it running as he walked up to Connor and said, "You ready for this?"

"Hell yeah. Let's hit it."

"Okay," replied Terry. "Now, today, I don't want you to ride behind me like you did yesterday. I want you to ride side by side like we used to. When we pull into the clubhouse I want them to see that you can ride side-by-side. It's important."

"No problem," replied Connor, "I can handle that."

"One thing before we go, keep to yourself, but don't keep to yourself. In other words, don't just walk up to guys from my club and start talking to them like you have known them forever, but keep yourself available for them to approach you. The thing is, dude, it's all about respect in the MC world. There's a bunch of rules, but I'm not going to go into that shit with you right now. Just be yourself and be respectful, but don't be a kiss-ass and make it seem like you are trying to brown-nose your way in."

"Okay, fucker, okay. I get it. Let's just get going. I'm ready to ride."

Terry and Connor backed out of the driveway and headed toward the clubhouse. As Connor rode on the right side of Terry, he imagined himself already in the club, heading toward a party or toward Bill's shop, or wherever the road might take them. It was as if they were 10 years younger and the feeling brought a smile to Connor's face as he turned to look at Terry. However, when Connor noticed that Terry did not have a smile on his face, but a look like he was angry at the world, Connor wiped the smile from his face and looked straight ahead.

Terry and Connor turned off of the main road through town and drove past Bill's shop, when they took yet another turn by the shop and went about 2 city blocks and arrived at a chain link fence. Terry reached over to a keypad and typed in a code, which caused the gate to open and they both drove through the gate where about 20 motorcycles were parked in front of a cinderblock building.

The building was not much to look at from the outside. It was grey in color and had a black door. There were quite a few people standing outside, with beer in their hands, which Connor did not recognize. None of the men standing outside had a black leather vest on like the one the guys from the club wore. Terry and Connor parked their bikes along with the other motorcycles there and shut off their engines.

Terry looked at Connor and said, "Hang on a sec, there must be something going on inside. You hang out here and I will be right back."

Terry walked up to the clubhouse door and pulled on the door handle, only to find that it was locked. He knocked on the door three times and a small window slid open, and then quickly closed. The door opened and Terry walked in.

Connor walked up to the other people standing outside and nodded at them. They nodded back. Connor found himself looking around the complex. He saw a couple of storage sheds, an outdoor smoker grill, and a small stage which looked like it could accommodate a small local band or a DJ. On the side of the club house building was written in spray paint: "L.F.F.L."

Before Connor could say anything, the club house door opened, Ratchet came outside and yelled at everyone outside, "Okay, you guys are good to come in."

Connor made sure that he would be the last one to enter the clubhouse. Everyone walked in front of him as Ratchet was holding the door. Connor reached out to grab the door and motion Ratchet to go in after him when he noticed a sign on the inside of the door which read: "Don't touch the Fucking Door." So, Connor lowered his hands and walked in with Ratchet right behind.

Connor could not believe his eyes. The outside of the clubhouse might have been comparable to a junk yard or an industrial site, but the inside was plush. There was a long granite topped bar at the far side of the room, with "Libertines" painted on the wall. The furniture was all leather and nice and there were 6 flat-screen TVs hanging from the wall.

As Connor was taking in everything that the clubhouse had to offer, Terry walked up to him and said, "Okay, I need to introduce you to the president."

"Now?" said Connor.

"Right now," said Terry. "Before anyone can be in this clubhouse, they have to have been introduced to every member present. I am responsible for you while you are here, so it's my ass if I don't do this now."

"Whatever you say, Terry," replied Connor. Connor followed Terry through the clubhouse and went towards the bar, where he saw 4 members of the club standing at the bar with their backs to him as Terry began to speak.

"Brother Pres, this is Connor. Connor, this is Jackal, our club's president."

Connor reached out his hand to shake Jackal's hand and said, "Nice to meet you, sir"

Jackal returned the handshake and said, "So you're Connor, huh?" and then turned around to grab his beer.

Terry looked at Connor and said, "Grab us a couple of beers, huh?"

Connor went a few barstools away and saw the bartender, who was a short woman wearing a very low-cut top and extremely short shorts. Trying not to stare at the bartender's breasts, Connor tried as best as he could and looked at the bartender in the eyes and said, "Can I have a couple of cold ones?"

The bartender replied, "Who are you here with?"

"Terry, I mean, Big T."

The bartender looked down the bar towards Terry hoping to get an acknowledgement from Terry in which Terry nodded his head and the bartender handed Connor two bottles of beer.

"What's the damage?" asked Connor.

"It doesn't work that way, sweetheart," replied the bartender.

Befuddled, Connor took the beers over to Terry and handed him one. Terry took a drink from his beer and let out a loud breath of relief, as a person would after their first drink upon a desert crossing. He then took his beer bottle and clanked it against Connor's and said, "Cheers."

Connor nodded his head and took a drink from his bottle. Before Connor could even ask, Terry began to explain what the bartender meant.

"We don't really sell the beer since we don't have a liquor license so it's put on a tab under a member's name. The member has to settle up with the club each week."

"Got it," replied Connor. "I will settle up with you when we leave."

"Let's go for a walk," said Terry, as he motioned Connor with his head to follow him.

Terry and Connor walked to the other side of the clubhouse and Terry opened a door which led into a room with a small desk at one end and a bunch of chairs lined up in a semi-circle around the desk. Terry motioned Connor to go into the room in front of him and then he closed the door behind his and slid a lock across the door.

"Have a seat," said Terry.

Connor sat down in the middle of the semi-circle of chairs and Terry sat right next to him. Terry's face then changed to a very serious look as he began to explain a few things to Connor.

"So," started Terry, "Here's the deal. When you got here and had to stay outside, the other members of the club were waiting for me to have a quick meeting. That's what we do in this room. We call it "church". Usually we have church once a week on Thursdays, but they wanted to talk about you."

"Me?" said Connor.

"Wait, don't interrupt me."

"Sorry," said Connor.

"No problem. Just listen. I've been talking to Jackal and Bill about you and they are willing to prospect you, but I have to warn you, it's a big commitment. We have got some really promising shit coming down the pipeline and to be quite honest, the club needs a smart mother fucker like you to help work some of this shit in the background with computers and books and shit. Obviously I can't tell you what it is until you are accepted in as a prospect, but I will tell you that it is some money-making shit and it's going to be good for our club. But right now, what I need to know out of you is, whether or not you want to prospect?"

Connor sat in silence. This had happened quite fast for Connor and was not really expecting to be tapped as a prospect so quickly. He remembered thinking about how he didn't hear much from Terry during the last year and a half and wondered if that had anything to do with him joining the club.

"Well," said Connor, "What would be expected out of me?"

"Good question," said Terry, "Everything and anything. This is a no shit commitment to something great. The people in this club are my brothers. I would do anything for them and they would do anything for me. You have to be willing to show that you would fit that mold.

"As a prospect, you are going to be doing whatever the club needs, whether it is running errands, or taking out the trash, just basically whatever a patch holder tells you to. The only excuse that you can use as to not do an errand is that you are at work or with your family. We don't interfere with your job, because we know you have to pay your bills, and family is important, but you can't pull the family excuse like you can the job excuse."

Connor took a slow, long drink from his beer, and swished the beer around in his mouth as he absorbed what Terry just told him.

"So," said Connor, "How long does the prospect period last?"

"Another good question," said Terry. "It will depend on you and how long it takes the club to get comfortable with you, but it's a minimum of 6 months. When I think everyone is ready for you to patch out, then I will take it to a vote to get your card. Once you get a card, you will have until the next meeting to get every member to sign it. Then you give the card to the president to get your patch."

"How long did it take you, Terry?" asked Connor.

"Took me about 8 months or so", replied Terry. "Bill was my sponsor and he wore my ass out, but he knew that it was time to patch me out."

"Well," said Connor, "not to sound too selfish or anything, but what's in it for me?"

"Aside from the brotherhood, which is worth it by itself, you would not believe the perks. I don't want to give all of it away because it's well worth the surprise. Let's just say that what happens in this club house stays in the clubhouse and what happens between brothers stays with them. Your sacrifice is the ever-loving commitment to this patch."

Connor took another drink of his beer, and swished it back and forth in his mouth before swallowing it. He looked at Terry as Terry stared back at him patiently waiting for Connor's response.

"I'm in," said Connor, "with one condition."

"Condition?" said Terry, "There are no conditions, man."

"No, wait;" retorted Connor, "My condition is this. You have got to help me get this past Julie. I want to be all in but she might flip her lid about it."

"Look, dude," replied Terry, "All you got to do is tell Julie that it's a Harley riding group and that we just like to hang out and talk about bikes and have a few beers now and then. Nothing more. Don't get into details with her. There are parties that we have the family here and then there are closed parties where the families are not here. The family parties keep all of the ol' ladies happy and the closed parties keep all of us happy, but you will just have to wait and see. I will help you with Julie, dude. Don't worry."

Connor took a deep breath and said, "Let's do this."

Chapter Seven - Introductions

Connor and Terry walked out of the small room and rejoined the party. Terry grabbed Connor by the shoulder and said, "Hey, go grab us a couple more."

Connor walked up to the bartender again and before he could say anything, the lady behind the bar reached into the ice chest below and handed him two beers, winked at him, and smiled. Connor returned the smile, thanked the bartender and turned around to find Terry. Connor wondered to himself why her attitude had changed so much since the last beers that he took from her.

By this time there were approximately 40 people inside the clubhouse. The cigarette smoke was beginning to create a haze toward the ceiling and Connor's eyes were finally beginning to adjust to the less than adequate lighting inside the clubhouse. Connor spotted Terry on the other side of the room and walked the beer bottles over to him. He handed Terry his beer and they clanked their beer bottles together as before.

Connor stood there among Terry and two other members of the club, Knuckles and Nutcase. Connor could easily figure out why they called Terry "Big T" but he wanted so badly to find out the back story behind Knuckles and Nutcase. However, Connor knew not to ask any questions. Connor took a drink from his beer and noticed that the president of the club had started walking toward the three members and himself.

Jackal said, "I need you fellas in the room," and walked past them toward the room where Connor and Terry had just left. Knuckles motioned to the other members of the club and they all followed Jackal into the room.

Terry looked at Connor and said, "Stay right here, drink your beer, and watch for me to stick my head out of that door. When you see me poke out my head, come over there. Got it?"

"Got it," replied Connor as he swallowed with some anticipation.

All of the members of the club retired into the room with Cobbler being the last one to close the door. They all sat down in the semi-circle with the exception of Jackal, who sat behind the desk. Jackal reached into the desk drawer and took out a black wooden gavel and struck the desk with it. He then began to speak.

"Okay, you all have had a brief chance to meet Connor. Big T gave me the nod that he has talked to him and Connor does want to prospect. Anyone have an objection?"

Then, Cobbler spoke up, saying, "Look, no one really knows this guy all that well. Big T says he can vouch for him, that's fine by me, but I am not for fast-tracking this guy's patch just because of the deal we have going down. I want some assurance from this room that you will not back me into a corner to sign his card over our deal. We have to protect our charter."

Terry then spoke up, "Cobbler, Connor is good people. He will fit in just fine. I will be sure not to bring his name to this room for a patch until he is ready and I will go to Bill for any guidance that I might need during his prospecting period. Like I have said before, I have known him forever but I know that I have to protect our club and our charter and that comes before my friendship with Connor."

Jackal then turned to Bill and said, "Well, V.P., what's your take?"

"Look," replied Bill, "He's a fucking yuppie, and none of us are yuppies are we?"

Everyone in the room laughed, but Bill continued.

"With what we are about to embark on, we need a yuppie type fella like Connor to do the shit that we all know none of us can do. My fear with Connor is that he is too straight-laced and he won't be able to make the requirements to patch out."

Terry spoke up, saying, "It's on me, V.P., I got it. I will put him through the ringer hopefully as good as you did me."

Laughter filled the room again.

Jackal said, "Okay, let's vote it. All in favor?"

Everyone in the room raised their hands.

"No opposed?"

No one raised their hands in opposition. Jackal then turned toward Terry and said, "Well, Big T, go get your prospect."

Terry stood up from his chair and opened the door. As the door began to open, Connor immediately noticed the movement as he had not taken his eyes off of the door. Terry stuck his head out the door and nodded at Connor to come over there as he had described he would. Connor walked over to the door and entered the room. He walked inside and stood just inside the door. Terry shut the door behind him and returned to his seat.

Jackal looked at Connor and said, "Alright, Connor, from now on, you are a prospect of this club. Do you accept this?"

"Yes, sir," replied Connor.

Jackal reached under the desk and took out a plain black leather vest and threw it at Connor. Connor caught the vest, which was wadded in a ball, and allowed the vest to unfold itself as he held it out in front of him.

"Come over here to the desk," commanded Jackal.

Connor walked over to the desk and awaited instructions from Jackal. Jackal reached into his pocket for a set of keys, which he removed from his pocket and unlocked a drawer of the desk. Connor could not see what exactly was inside the drawer as Jackal removed a patch from the drawer. It was the bottom piece of the club patch which read "Kansas." He then removed a small plastic box and opened it up. The box contained several sewing needles and spools of black thread.

"Sew this on, prospect," said Jackal. "You have 10 minutes. Go."

Connor began to sew on the Kansas bottom rocker patch. Connor had not sewn anything since he was a little kid and never had he sewn a large patch to a leather vest. Connor was nowhere close to halfway done before Jackal reminded him that he had 5 minutes left. Connor began to sew quicker, taking broader strokes to get the patch sewn on. With about 1 minute to spare Connor was done sewing and tied the end of the thread on.

"Done," said Connor.

Jackal grabbed the vest off of the desk and pulled on the Kansas patch. It stayed on to Connor's relief.

Jackal then said, "Ok. Your sponsor is Big T. He will answer any question you will have. Ask questions. Don't assume anything. Now, a few ground rules. One, you don't say anything to anyone about this club. You are not a member, you are a prospect. No one should ask you anything, but if they do, you don't answer any questions other than the fact that you are a Libertine prospect and that's it.

"Two, you are a servant of this club. You better show your face as much as possible. You do what you are told when you are told. You don't speak unless spoken to. The only exception is your sponsor. If you fuck up, it's not only on you but it's on him.

"Three, you will be a prospect for a minimum of six months. You are going to earn this patch. We are not going to just give it to you.

"Four, Church is on Thursday. Your ass is here. You understand all of this, prospect?"

"Yes, sir," answered Connor.

"Good," said Jackal, "We're done." Jackal hit the black gavel against the desk.

As everyone left the room they shook Connor's hand until the only ones left in the room were Jackal, Terry, and Connor. Terry shut the door and Jackal turned to Terry saying, "He's your responsibility now. Get it done."

Terry responded, "Will do," and Jackal left the room.

Connor was still taken aback from all that just happened and his head was spinning. Terry looked at Connor and said, "Well, prospect, you better get your ass out there, but before you do just remember to enjoy yourself today, keep your mouth shut to patch holders unless you are spoken to first, and remember that inside the walls of this clubhouse is a different world. Anything that happens here is never repeated outside these walls, and I have a feeling that before you leave, you will understand that.

Connor looked at Terry and nodded his head in acknowledgment as they both walked outside the room into the main area of the clubhouse. As they walked out, the bartender was standing there with two beers in her hand. She handed one to Terry and one to Connor and said, "Here you go sweetheart. Let me know if there is anything you need, and I mean anything." She then winked at Connor as she gently bit her bottom lip and then made a kissing motion with her lips toward him before she turned and walked away.

Connor walked behind Terry and before he could start asking Terry any of the numerous questions that he had, every non member started coming up to him and introducing themselves. For every man in that clubhouse without a patch on their back, there were two very attractive women. The men would come up to Connor and introduce themselves with the utmost respect and the women would introduce themselves with a very tight hug, purposefully pressing their breasts into Connor's chest.

"Hi, I'm Sally," said one of the many women at the clubhouse. She wrapped her arms around Connor, pressing her chest against his, but then kissed his neck during the hug and whispered into his ear, "I want to take care of you before you leave." Sally then walked off and went back toward the bar.

Connor thought to himself, "Holy shit, what did I just do?"

After all of the introductions, Terry wandered his way back over to his old friend and new prospect. With a laughing grin on his face, Terry said, "Well, prospect, welcome to the first step. Cheers!"

They clanked their beer bottles together and as Connor started to bring his beer bottle down from his lips, he noticed that Terry had not stopped drinking and was attempting to finish the whole beer in one drink. So, as to not break that off, Connor slammed back his beer bottle and drank all of the beer down in one pour as Terry did.

After the beers were emptied, Terry put his arms around Connor and gave him a big hug. Connor hugged Terry back in total joy and couldn't wait to get another beer in his hand.

Connor told Terry, "Let me grab us another one."

Terry replied, "Get to it, prospect.

Connor walked towards the bar to retrieve two more beers, except he didn't quite make it to the bar before he was abruptly stopped by a hand gently touching his chest. It was Sally.

"Let me get you a beer, honey," said Sally as she ran her hand down his chest and past his navel almost touching his crotch. Sally waltzed up to the bar, retrieving two beers from the bartender, adjusted her top so as to reveal more cleavage, and returned to where she had stopped Connor.

"Here you go, babe," said Sally, "and don't bother going up to the bartender to get your beers. I have you all taken care of."

Connor hesitated for a minute. He realized that he did have his wedding ring on and he also knew that he had just entered a different world. Maybe these folks were just friendlier than anyone he had met before, but Connor didn't want to cause any confusion.

Connor walked up to Sally and said, "Hey, Sally, can I borrow you for a minute."

"Yes, you can!" replied Sally in a very cheerful voice. Connor and Sally walked over to a quiet corner in the clubhouse to a leather couch. Connor sat down at the very end and turned his body toward the middle of the couch, in hopes of creating a barrier so Sally could not sit right next to him. Rather than sitting on the couch, Sally climbed into his lap and wrapped her arms around Connor's neck.

Sally asked, "What can I do for you, babe?"

"Look," replied Connor, "I just want you to know that I am very flattered by the attention. You are obviously a very gorgeous woman and I would be very lucky to be with you, but I have to tell you that I am a happily married man, and if my wife saw you right now sitting in my lap like this, I would be headed toward divorce court in a heartbeat."

Sally looked upset. She said, "What did I do wrong?"

"Nothing. Nothing at all. You are great." replied Connor. "Like I said, I'm married and…"

Before Connor could say another word, Sally had begun kissing Connor with absolute brute force. Her tongue was so far down Connor's throat that he could barely breathe. Sally grabbed Connor's hand and placed it on her breast as she began rocking back and forth on top of him. As she removed her lips from his you, Connor looked at everyone in the clubhouse watching. Before Connor could even begin to explain, every patched member in the clubhouse raised their beer bottles in the air and exclaimed, "Way to go, prospect!!!"

Connor looked at Sally and said, "Excuse me for just a minute; I need to go do something."

Connor got up off of the couch and walked over to Terry and said, "I need a minute."

Terry and Connor walked into a hallway that had 10 doors, five on each side. Connor followed Terry down the hall to the last door on the left and they walked in. Inside the door were a neatly made bed and a picture of the Libertines patch hanging on the wall above the bed.

Connor drank all of that room in for a second and then asked Terry, "Dude, what the fuck is going on?"

"Dude," replied Terry, "Like I said, what happens here, stays here. Sally is a friend of the club. She knows that you are married, just like half of the club. That's the thing, though. Even though you are a prospect, she belongs to you. She has been hanging around here hoping to get hooked up with one of us, but we all already have a bitch. She's been waiting to be someone's bitch and today is her lucky day."

Connor was in utter disbelief. "A bitch? Dude, if Julie finds out…"

Terry interrupted. "Connor, dude, she won't find out. Here's how it works, there are parties that you can bring Julie to and parties where you shouldn't. For instance, if you would have brought Julie today, then you wouldn't be here still. You would have been asked to leave after you got your vest and we would be partying with all of the bitches. There are specific parties where the ol' ladies come and the bitches are here, but they know not to say a word. Trust me. You will be okay. It's all part of being in the club. It's your first perk."

"That's quite a perk, in more than one way if you know what I mean."

They both laughed, and then Terry said, "Look, man, if you don't want a bitch, I will tell her to lay off, but I suggest you give it a try before you just turn it away. For now, I will tell her to cool it and let you start it, cool?"

"Yeah," said Connor, "that's cool."

"Now," said Terry, "get your ass back in there prospect. No hiding in the hallway."

Chapter Eight – Sparky's

The next Thursday had come. Connor had made it home from the party with no questions asked since Julie had not arrived home from helping Lisa with her wedding plans. While Connor sat at his desk that afternoon, he was trying to figure out just how he was going to get out of the house tonight, and furthermore, every Thursday night. There was no way in his mind that he was going to be able to swing this and he did not want to miss the first church meeting as a prospect.

Since Julie was not home that past Sunday afternoon, she had not seen his new vest with his Kansas bottom rocker on it. Connor knew that Julie was familiar with the Libertines in town but just saw them as a bunch of guys who like to ride their Harleys around, nothing more.

Connor decided to use this to his advantage. Connor picked up his phone from his desk and decided to do what he considered the right thing and tell Julie about his new club. After 3 rings, Julie answered the phone.

"Hey babe, what's up?"

Connor answered, "Not much. Hey, I was wondering if you care if I go out with Terry riding tonight. We will probably end up at the Libertine's clubhouse for a while and then I will be home. Terry said that the best night for him to be able to ride would be Thursday."

Connor was pleased with how clever this scheme was.

"Well," said Julie, with a bit of hesitation, "I guess that's fine. I want you to enjoy the bike. Have fun. I will see you later on at home. Love you."

Connor hung up his desk phone and could barely contain his excitement. He finally had his out. Connor looked up at the clock and saw that it was almost 3:30. He only had an hour and a half to go before it was time to head out of work when his cell phone rang. He looked at the phone number and didn't recognize it.

"This is Connor"

A familiar voice sounded off on the other end of the phone. It was

Knuckles.

"Prospect, get your ass to the clubhouse, now!"

Knuckles hung up the phone. Connor was trying to figure out how in the world he was going to get out of work without his boss finding out, especially since he had the only motorcycle in the parking lot and everyone would hear the resounding rumble of that V-twin engine as he started his bike.

Connor reached under his desk and removed the duffle bag that he had hidden his vest in and walked out the door. He walked outside to his bike and took out the vest from the duffle bag, threw it over his back, stuffed the now empty duffle bag into his left side saddlebag, started his bike, and rode off.

"Fuck it," he thought. "I have worked there forever. If I catch any shit, I will deal with it then."

Just by wearing that vest on his back, Connor felt a new sense of toughness. It was as if he had received a Kung Fu lesson just by being a prospect for the Libertines. In the small town of Clark, Kansas, the Libertines were highly respected and Connor knew that. Luckily for him, he was for the most part unknown in the circles that the Libertines frequented so he could pull off a "Billy Badass" attitude while he wore his vest and he figured no one would dare challenge him.

Connor rode quite aggressively to the club house and arrived at the chain link gate when he realized that he did not possess the code to open the gate. As he stared at the numeric key pad, wondering just how he was going to open the gate, he felt his phone vibrating in his pocket. As he reached in his pocket and flipped open his phone, he had received a text message from Knuckles that read: 'LFFL#.'

"What in the hell does this mean, LFFL#?" Connor thought to himself.

He continued to stare at the numeric keypad when a thought crossed his mind. Connor reached over to the key pad and pushed in the numbers 5-3-3-5 and pressed the pound sign on the key pad. Three beeps came from a small speaker located inside the key pad and the gate began to open. Connor thought pretty highly of himself for solving this little riddle.

Connor pulled his bike inside the gate and parked it close to the front door of the clubhouse. His bike was the only motorcycle in the parking lot. The place looked deserted except for a few vehicles parked inside the gate. As Connor shut off the motorcycle, Knuckles walked out from the clubhouse.

"What the fuck took you so long, prospect?"

"I got here as fast as I could. I came from work and had to sneak out."

Knuckles laughed and said, "Yeah, work, I remember that. I need you to run an errand with me. Start your bike back up and follow me. And, take off that fucking polo shirt. Don't wear a fucking polo shirt underneath your colors. You look like a faggot."

Connor removed his polo shirt. As standard practice for Connor, he always wore a white t-shirt underneath his dress clothes, so he did not have to ride wearing his vest and nothing else underneath it.

By the time Connor had neatly folded his polo shirt and placed it in his saddlebag, Knuckles had rolled out his motorcycle from one of the storage sheds in the club's complex. Knuckles fired up his bike and took off with Connor following right behind him.

Knuckles riding style was a bit different than Connor was used to seeing as he had only ridden with Terry before. Knuckles had no regard for speed limits, stop signs or had any use for turn signals. It took everything that Connor could muster up to not only keep up with Knuckles but maintain his concentration while riding a motorcycle he had owned less than a week.

As the two were flying past the town limits and on a state highway with very little traffic, Connor was amazed at how not one single car honked at them for their discourteous driving habits or their lack of respect for any traffic laws. He then looked down at his speedometer and noticed that they had been going just under 100 miles per hour out on this two lane state highway.

Within a few minutes they had crossed the border of a neighboring town. Knuckles made a gesture towards Sparky's, the town's saloon located in an old building on the town's square. Knuckles pulled up to the corner and backed his bike toward the curb and Connor followed suit. As they both shut off their bikes, Connor noticed 4 motorcycles parked outside Sparky's.

Knuckles grabbed a hold of Connor by the shoulder, put his arm around him and said, "Come over here."

The two went around the corner where they were able to speak in relative privacy considering that they were outside at the main intersection of this little town.

"So, it's like this, prospect," explained Knuckles, "There are 4 fucking jokers inside this place that thought it would be cute to start a club without permission. They must be from somewhere north of here and have watched too much fucking TV. Now they want to play biker.

"Phil, the barkeep, who is a friend of the club, called and said they have been in here since this morning and are causing some problems with a couple of the waitresses. We are here to educate these fuckers in a bit of protocol. Understand?"

There was not a single part of this explanation that Connor understood, but he nodded in acknowledgment. Connor and Knuckles walked toward the front door of the seedy establishment and Connor opened the door for Knuckles. Knuckles proceeded into the saloon first and Connor followed, closing the door behind them.

In the back of Sparky's was a coin operated pool table and four men standing around it, all holding pool cues in one hand and beer in the other. They appeared to be having quite a good time and were being just a bit louder than the other patrons in the bar. When Knuckles and Connor walked into the bar, the group of men at the pool table did not notice their entrance.

As Knuckles walked toward the bar, with Connor following close behind, a short, stocky man walked from one side of the bar to the other to meet Knuckles.

He said, "Knuckles, here's a beer for you. Thanks for coming. I hate to bother the club with this type of shit but I knew that you would want to know."

"So what exactly is the problem, Phil?" asked Knuckles.

"Well," replied the man behind the bar, "It's like this. These four guys came strolling in here earlier wearing colors. I have never seen or heard of this club. I didn't acknowledge the fact that they were patch holders. They were pretty tame for a while but now that they have a few beers in them they are starting to bother the other folks in here and they are really disrespecting the waitresses. When I didn't know the patch and also noticed a Kansas patch on their back, I figured the club needed to know."

"Got it," replied Knuckles. "Prospect, go over there and tell them to give you their cuts."

Connor gasped. "You want me to do what? How in the fuck am I supposed to do that?"

"Walk over there and tell them who you are and tell them to hand over their cuts. It's that simple, prospect."

Connor nodded his head and swallowed. As he slowly moved towards the four men at the table, he realized that the bad ass feeling that he had on his bike when he was on the way to the clubhouse had left and a giant dose of fear and reality had set in. After walking past tables of nervous looking patrons and past three waitresses with disheveled looks on their faces, Connor came face to face with one of the four men.

"Help you with something, friend?" said the man in a condescending tone.

"Actually, you can. I'm a prospect for the Libertines. I'm sure you know who we are."

Before Connor could finish his introduction, the man interrupted Connor, saying, "Nope, not a clue. Should I?"

"Yes, you should," continued Connor, "It seems that you and your buds here have started a club without permission. I need you to hand over your vests to me and all will be good. I don't want any trouble."

"You don't want any trouble?" replied the man. "Sounds like you are looking for an ass kicking and I'm just the one to do it."

This unfriendly exchange had made the bar become completely silent and the man's other three friends had now walked up behind the man in what appeared to be a show of force.

Connor felt the fear churn his stomach as well as the stare of Knuckles, who was still on the other side of the bar. The last thing Connor wanted to do was start a fight, and then the adrenaline began to flow through his veins. Connor's fist began to tighten up. His eyes began to grow larger as his eyebrows raised up and he gritted his teeth. With all of his anger and fear he could muster, Connor threw a right-handed punch which landed with perfection on the chin of the man who stood in front of him.

The power of the blow knocked the man backwards into his three friends, which caused them to stumble backwards and crash into the wall behind them, with beer spilling all over the pool table, the floor, and the four men. Connor then grabbed a bar stool, which was sitting to his left, picked it up, and threw it at them before they could regain their balance.

"Give me the fucking vests!" yelled Connor, as his heart raced at twice its normal pace.

The four men pushed the side-laying barstool to the side and got to their feet. As the man drew his fist back in a motion to punch Connor, a life-saving voice yelled, "Wait!"

It was Knuckles. Somehow, within an instant, Knuckles had made it across the bar and was right behind Connor.

"Now," explained Knuckles, as his sheer size and commanding appearance seemed to instill the fear of God into the four men, "there might be four of you, and you might think that you are some kind of MC, but I am here to tell you that your days of playing biker club are over. You can either hand those cuts to my prospect here, or I will cut those mother fuckers right off of your backs. Your call, fuck sticks."

The man lowered his fist and said, "Look man, we don't want any trouble. If this is a gang thing or whatever, we are sorry, but we paid good money for these. Just let us go and we promise that we won't cause any trouble."

Knuckles let out a creepy chuckle and said, "Boys, it don't work that way. Don't make me ask you again. I don't like to repeat myself."

The four men traded glances with each other and slowly removed their vests. Connor reached out his hand and the four men placed their vests in Connor's hand.

"Now that that's out of the way," said Knuckles, "I think you owe this bar and some of the waitresses an apology."

"We're sorry," said the self-elected leader of the group.

Knuckles showed his disapproval of the apology and retorted, "Not to me, dip shit, to the bar and the waitresses. Pay your fucking tab, apologize, get the fuck out, and don't ever come back."

The four men walked up to Phil and all of the waitress and apologized. They left a wad of cash on the bar and exited. Phil looked at Knuckles from across the bar and gave him a nod of acceptance of their tab.

"Prospect," commanded Knuckles, "go outside and watch them leave."

Connor walked outside and watched as the four men mounted their motorcycles and rode off into the distance, heading north as Knuckles had predicted. When Connor lost sight of the 4 men, he turned around and returned into the bar, where he saw Knuckles sitting on a bar stool at the end of the bar apparently finishing the beer which was given to him by Phil upon their arrival.

"Have a seat, prospect," said Knuckles, as Connor came within a few feet of him.

Connor sat down on the barstool next to Knuckles. Before Connor could ask, Phil placed a beer in front of him and a fresh beer in front of Knuckles.

Phil said, "I haven't met you yet. I'm Phil."

"Nice to meet you. I'm Connor."

Knuckles seemed to disapprove of the exchange. He grabbed Connor by the shoulder and decided to educate him a bit.

"When you wear that cut, you're not Connor. You are 'Libertine Prospect Connor.' You got that."

Connor sighed and replied, "My bad."

"Do it right," said Knuckles.

Connor stood up from his barstool, reached out his hand to Phil, and said, "I'm Libertine Prospect Connor. Thanks for the beer."

Phil let out a slight chuckle and he returned Connor's handshake and said, "Good to meet you. Thanks for taking care of that little problem for me. If there is anything I can do for you, just let me know. You are always welcome here."

Knuckles and Connor sat in silence as they drank their beers. Connor made sure to drink his beer at the same pace as Knuckles drank his, and after 5 swallows both of their beers were empty. Knuckles arose from his seat at the bar and Connor followed suit.

"Let's go, Prospect," said Knuckles as he motioned toward the door. Connor followed behind thinking that they didn't pay for the beers, but just assumed that this was normal and the free beers were a method of payment for ousting the 4 assholes.

Knuckles and Connor walked outside to their bikes. After Connor had stuffed the 4 sets of colors from the men inside his saddlebag, they both mounted up, rocking their bikes off of the kickstands. Knuckles just sat there, not starting his bike, as if he was in some form of deep thought, or even just spacing out. Connor waited patiently for Knuckles to start his bike, and it never came. Knuckles rocked his bike back over to the kickstand and looked at Connor.

"Well, Prospect," explained Knuckles, "you did good in there. Not everything we do has to result in violence but now I know that you are not scared. I had my doubts. When you clocked that one asshole, I was proud of you."

"Thanks, Knuckles," replied Connor.

Knuckles rocked his bike back off of the kickstand and fired up his engine, with Connor following suit afterwards. The two bikers rode off from Sparky's as quickly as they had arrived and headed back to the Libertine's clubhouse.

As they arrived back at the clubhouse, several people had begun to gather outside the Libertine compound which Connor had recognized from the party a few days before. Connor had purposely ridden by the compound every day this week and never saw any activity inside the compound since the party on Sunday. Connor made sure that Knuckles went in front of him and parked his bike in front of the clubhouse and Connor did the same.

Connor dismounted from his bike and Terry walked up to him and said with a chuckle, "Where ya been, Prospect?"

Connor, noticing Knuckles had already walked inside the clubhouse, replied, "Holy shit. Holy fucking shit. You wouldn't believe me if I told you."

Terry walked around to the right side of Connor's bike and opened his saddlebag. He removed the four colors from there and threw them into a large metal fire pit outside the clubhouse. He then poured lighter fluid on the cuts and handed Connor a pack of matches, laughed, and said, "I will see you inside, Prospect."

Chapter Nine - Church

The time had finally come for Connor to attend his first Church. Connor was excited to see what exactly went on in the inner workings of the club.

Connor entered the clubhouse. He had not been there since the party on Sunday and was relishing the thought of another good time at the clubhouse. Right inside the door stood Cobbler, whose job as the club's Sergeant of Arms was to watch that door and keep a sense of order inside the clubhouse.

"Hey, Prospect," announced Cobbler, "Stand here and watch the door. I got to take a piss."

Connor stood at the door as Cobbler had asked and surveyed the room. He recognized all of the members of the club as well as several folks from the party on Sunday, especially Sally, who turned around from the bar and noticed Connor standing at the door.

Sally was wearing a low cut shirt that evening, with her large breast protruding from the shirt as if they were attempting to escape their white cotton prison. Her denim shorts that she was wearing were so short and tight that part of her ass was hanging down below the material. She had on a pair of black high heels which had scuff marks on them.

Sally took a beer from the bartender and started her walk across the clubhouse. Connor knew by the look in her eyes as they made eye contact that the beer was for him and he was in for another night of trying to keep his marriage vows intact.

"Hey sexy! You want a beer?" asked Sally as she put her arm around Connor in a more than friendly embrace.

"Thanks," replied Connor, as he took the beer from her.

"Hey, don't worry," said Sally, "I know that you're married and I think I might have caught you a bit off guard the other night. I'm here for you, though. Just ask sweetie."

Sally then walked back to the bar where she continued the

conversation she was having when Connor walked in. Connor stood at the door, sipping on his beer as he awaited Cobbler's return to relieve him from his bouncer duties. As Connor continued to look around, he noticed Cobbler exit the bathroom, walk up to the bar and grab a beer, and make his way toward Connor.

Cobbler approached Connor and said, "I hear you got your first taste with Knuckles today. How was it?"

"Well," replied Connor, "to be honest it was exciting."

"Good to hear," said Cobbler, "because I'm sure that it won't be the last time you have to do shit like that. It comes with the territory. These bitches think they can do whatever the fuck they want and don't have to answer to anyone."

As Cobbler finished his comment, the door opened and Jackal walked in. Cobbler reached out his arms and hugged Jackal. Jackal returned the gesture and then tapped Connor on the shoulder in a friendly sort of way.

"How are we doing, prospect?" asked Jackal.

"Good, sir," respectfully responded Connor.

Jackal smiled and then told Cobbler and Connor, "I need to get a beer in me and then lock her down for Church."

"Understood," replied Cobbler.

Jackal strolled across the room slowly as everyone from guests to the other patched members greeted the president of the charter. As Jackal made his way to the bar, the door opened.

A man standing about 6 foot 5 inches tall walked in wearing a Libertine's cut whom Connor had not seen. As the man grabbed Cobbler in a brotherly embrace, Connor noticed that his Libertine cut was a bit different than the rest because of the bottom rocker, which read "Missouri."

"How the fuck are you doing, Cobbler?" exclaimed the man.

"Fuck me running! Where in the fuck have you been, Sampson?" asked Cobbler.

"Here and there. Here and there. I figured I need to come pay you fuckers a visit. It's been too long."

Sampson finished his embrace with Cobbler and took a step back. He turned and looked at Connor with a glaring glance as if he was sizing Connor up. A short uncomfortable silence followed before Connor broke the silence and stretched out his hand to introduce himself.

"Libertine Prospect Connor."

Sampson did not immediately return Connor's handshake offering. Instead, Sampson looked at Cobbler and said, "New blood, huh? Looks to me like they are making them a bit smaller these days."

Sampson and Cobbler shared a laugh at Connor's expense. Sampson then grabbed Connor's hand with his massive gorilla-like mitts and pulled Connor in for a huge bear hug. Connor's breath was knocked out of him in the amazing strength of the hug.

"Just fucking with you, prospect," exclaimed Sampson, as he released Connor from the embrace and chuckled. "Now, get me and Cobbler a beer."

Connor nodded to Sampson and approached the bar. From across the room the bartender heard Sampson's request and had three beers waiting for Connor on the bar before he could make his way across the room. Connor took the three beers, assuming one was for him, and started to make his way across the room back to the door where Cobbler and Sampson were standing when Bill entered the clubhouse. As the door closed behind Bill, Connor arrived at the doorway with the three beers in hand. He handed one to Sampson and one to Cobbler. Without hesitation, he handed the third beer to Bill.

"Now that's some fucking service right there," responded Bill to his cold beer in his hand. "Now, go find a broom or something, prospect."

Connor turned and started to walk back to the bar when Jackal stood up from his barstool and said, "Okay, to the room."

The patched members of the club started making their way to the other side of the clubhouse where the meeting room was where Connor had received his vest and had officially became a prospect. Terry made his way toward Connor and put his arm around his shoulder and whispered in his ear.

"Okay. Go into the room and don't sit down. Stand by the door. Don't say a fucking word about anything unless you are asked. Got it?"

Connor replied, "I got it."

Connor was now really excited. He was going into the room for the second time now, and for the first time he would hear about the business of the club. Terry was the last patched member of the club to walk into the room and Connor followed behind him and closed the door.

Jackal reached into the desk and took out the same black gavel and slammed it against the desk. He then began to open the meeting.

"This meeting of the Libertine's, Clark charter is now open. I want to thank everyone for being here. Now, we all know our new prospect, Connor, who is attending his first Church. In case you haven't been told, keep your mouth shut, prospect, unless me or another patch asks you a direct question. Understood?"

Rather than responding with a verbal response, Connor nodded his head acknowledging his understanding.

Then, Jackal continued, "Let's get on to business."

The meeting began with reading the minutes of the past meeting. The club member discussed some ideas for a few parties. They talked about purchasing a different grill for cooking outside. Connor started to become very disappointed in the discussion as it was tedious and boring and knowing that he could not speak, he was becoming bored. That was, until the first topic of what he considered "club-type business" came up.

Jackal led the discussion, "Cobbler, I understand we had an issue earlier today. Was it handled?"

Cobbler responded, "Handled. Knuckles took the prospect with him and it's all good. Phil sends his thanks."

Connor patiently awaited either Cobbler or Knuckles to explain how Connor courageously took on the four bikers and, with Knuckle's assistance of course, removed the four cuts and burned them in front of the clubhouse just a few minutes earlier.

"Good," said Jackal, "Anything else we need to talk about?"

A silence filled the room. Jackal picked up the gavel and struck it on the desk again and said, "Adjourned."

Everyone stood up out of their chairs and returned to the main room in the clubhouse as Connor stood there in disbelief that he was left out of the story about Sparky's and that not much was said. Connor stared at the wall for a minute, shook his head, and shrugged his shoulders.

Connor walked out into the main room and approached Terry as he stood around a few of the guests, laughing and drinking a beer already.

Connor tapped Terry on the shoulder and said, "Hey sponsor, I need a minute."

"Yeah, sure," responded Terry and the two of them went back into the meeting room.

Connor then began to explain his disappointment, saying, "Dude that sucked. I got into a fight today and it wasn't brought up. I want everyone to know…"

Terry immediately interrupted Connor and said, "Hang on a second. We don't talk about shit like that in detail in Church. Don't worry. They know. It went like this today. We got the call from Phil and Jackal told Knuckles to handle it. Knuckles told Phil he would call you to come along just to see how you would handle it. He could have easily done it by himself. They don't call him Knuckles for nothing. It was a test."

"So," replied Connor, "why do they call him Knuckles?"

"Why don't you ask him yourself?"

"What about the whole don't speak unless you are spoken to rule?" asked Connor.

"Man," replied Terry, "The club expects you to get to know the members. If you don't ever say anything, you won't get to know them and they won't get to know you. The rule is more so when there is business going on or we are in a situation. That's when you keep your mouth shut. You and Knuckles now have a past and he is probably expecting you to talk to him a bit more now that you have shared some road time. If two or more patches are having a talk, just get within eye shot of who you want to talk to, make sure that he sees you, and wait. Don't ever interrupt."

"I just don't want to get you or myself into any shit," explained Connor.

Terry laughed and said, "Don't worry about it."

Terry and Connor exited the room and Connor felt that he now had somewhat of an understanding as to why the story wasn't shared in

Church. Terry returned to the table where Connor had removed him from, which did not have any patched members sitting at it, which relieved Connor that he had not interrupted a patched member's conversation as Terry had warned him about.

Knuckles was now talking to a couple of guests that were partying in the club house. There were no patched members around Knuckles so Connor decided that it was a safe time to approach Knuckles and have a talk. Taking Terry's advice, Connor walked toward the wall beside the bar where Knuckles was standing and looked at Knuckles, awaiting an acknowledgment from him so he could talk.

Knuckles saw Connor standing there and excused himself from his current conversation, asking the guests for a minute. He then motioned Connor over with his head and neck.

"You need something, prospect?" asked Knuckles.

"Yeah," said Connor, "if you don't mind, I was wondering, how did you get the name Knuckles?"

Knuckles raised an eyebrow at Connor and an angry grin came over his face. He grabbed Connor by the shirt collar with his left hand and balled his right fist tightly, then slowly moved his fist touching Connor's upper lip and covering both of his nostrils.

Connor exclaimed, "Sorry, man, I didn't mean to..."

"Just fucking with you prospect," said Knuckles with a grin. "So you want to know how I got my road name. You know, your sponsor gives you your road name and usually other brothers in the club help to name you, right?"

"Yes," replied Connor, even though he was not aware of that fact, but he didn't want Knuckles to know that and he didn't want to bring heat on Terry for not informing him of that.

"Right," continued Knuckles, "so, Jackal first met me at a little bar about five or six years ago. I had been riding around independent for quite a while and had run in to several Libertines here and there, but never knew how to get in.

"I was sitting in this place minding my own business when Jackal and a few other Libertines walked in and started drinking beer. Later on that night, some jokers decided that they were going to challenge the bikers and be Billy Badasses, so this asshole broke a beer bottle and threatened Jackal.

"It was nine of them and 4 of the brothers. Outmatched two to one you know. When the swinging started, I decided to jump in. I'm still not sure why I did.

"The broken beer bottle caught me across my knuckles on my right hand and cut me wide open."

Connor looked down at Knuckles' fist as he showed him the scar, which Connor had never noticed until that moment.

Knuckles continued, "I took out three, maybe four of them by myself. It's all in the military training, ya' know? When the fighting finished, the blood was pouring from my knuckles.

"I got invited to the clubhouse after that and people knew me as the guy with the bloody knuckles, so then it ended up Knuckles for short."

Connor replied, "Cheers to that, Knuckles," as he tilted his beer bottle towards Knuckles and Knuckles returned the toast.

Connor then walked away and headed toward the bar and thought to himself, "Well, shit, Knuckles has a fucked up name. I know about Ratchet, and Big T. I'm not sure that I want to know how Nutcase was named."

As the hours went by, the party started to fade off a bit, since it was a Thursday night, and most of the guests had left. All that remained of the Libertines were Jackal, Cobbler, Terry, and Connor.

Jackal began his exit toward the door of the clubhouse. Before he exited, he gave Cobbler a farewell hug and turned back around.

In a loud, commanding voice, he said, "Prospect! Make sure this shit is cleaned up before you leave."

Connor decided that he was going to go ahead and get a jump start on cleaning so he would be home at a descent time. With no help from anyone, he had emptied all of the ashtrays, swept up the floor, and took out the trash bags as they clanked together with the sound of empty beer bottles.

In the midst of his cleaning duties, all of the other guests had left,

Terry was waiting outside for Connor, and all that remained was Cobbler.

Cobbler had retired from his post at the door and was drinking a beer at the bar. Connor returned from taking the last bag of trash out.

Connor turned toward Cobbler and said, "All done, man. Anything else?"

"Nope," said Cobbler, "I will lock the door behind you."

"Okay," said Connor, with a bit of a questioning tone in his voice.

Connor walked out of the door of the clubhouse and heard Cobbler lock the door from the inside. Terry was sitting on his bike, finishing up a cigarette when Connor walked up to his bike.

Connor looked at Terry and said, "Isn't Cobbler going to go home?"

Terry laughed and said, "Cobbler lives in the clubhouse right now. He's going through some shit with his ol' lady. It's just another one of those perks, you know?"

"You can live in the clubhouse?" asked Connor.

"Basically," said Terry, "That's what all those rooms in the back hall are for, either someplace to crash when you are fighting with the ol' lady, or when you're fucking your girlfriend."

Terry laughed and fired up his bike and Connor did the same. As both of them finished backing their bikes up and pointing them towards the gate, they nodded at each other and headed home.

Chapter Ten - Pepper

The sunlight started to peek through the blinds in Connor and Julie's bedroom on a Sunday morning. Connor felt Julie move the covers off of her and get out of bed. Connor sat up and rubbed his eyes. He was tired from going out with Julie, Lisa, and Lisa's fiancé last night.

Now that Connor had been a prospect in the Libertines for quite a while, he had developed a disdain for what he called "Yuppie Bars," which was the only thing that Julie did not approve of so far in his relationship with the club. Julie loved getting all dressed up in fancy outfits and going out for a night on the town. Connor had changed his wardrobe to mostly blue jeans and black t-shirts, most of which had club sayings written on the front of them, such as "Support your local Libertines."

Connor also did not look forward to nights with Julie for another reason. She had still not ridden on the back of his bike. When Julie went out with Connor, they took her car. Connor had tried and tried to get her on the back, but she refused every time. This made Connor jealous of all the other club members, as they frequently had their ol' ladies or other random women on the backs of their bikes. Connor had as of yet to have a passenger.

To make matters worse, Julie and Connor were spending less and less time together. Julie seemed to always be off with Lisa, doing wedding preparation errands, and Connor was spending more and more time with the club. Connor enjoyed himself while he was with the club, but he started to get a bit sexually frustrated as his marriage seemed to lack any kind of affection anymore, which has led Connor to increase his alcohol consumption.

Connor never was completely drunk, but he had an almost continuous buzz outside of his office hours. If Connor was not at work, or home with Julie, he was either at Bill's shop, the Libertine clubhouse, or some dingy bar with Terry and guys from the club. Since the time spent with Lisa had increased, Connor had also noticed that Julie had made a few new friends. Connor didn't have a problem with that, as Julie tended to not be too social and also didn't have all that many friends to begin with, while at the same time Connor now had a new circle of friends with the club.

Julie had also become a bit more protective of her cell phone, which she never used to do. Half the time, Julie had no idea where in the house she had left her phone and had Connor call her phone so she could find it. Now, her phone never left her pocket or her purse except at night, which she now kept her phone under her pillow while it charged. But, Connor's focus was on the club and he knew that Julie's focus was on Lisa's wedding. Connor figured that after the wedding was over, which was in three months, Julie would get back to focusing on him a bit more, so he let it go.

Julie had just finished getting ready and had walked out the door to meet Lisa and some of their new friends for a Sunday brunch. Connor had put on the blue jeans that he wore the day before and took a clean black t-shirt, which had a picture of a fist on the front and the letters L.F.F.L. below the fist, out of the drawer and put it on.

He walked into the kitchen to drink a cup of coffee from the pot Julie made before she left when his phone rang. He looked at the Caller ID and noticed that it was Pepper.

"Hey, Pepper! What's up?"

Pepper replied, "You got anything going on this morning, prospect?"

"Not a damn thing. You need something?"

"Yeah," said Pepper, "Can you meet me at Bubba's?"

"I'm on my way," said Connor as he hung up the phone.

Bubba's was your typical bar, which Connor had learned to love. Bubba's was known to have the best bar-be-cue for miles around. They slow smoked all of their meats in an old style outdoor smoker that they kept behind a ten foot wooden stockade fence. When you got within a few blocks of Bubba's, you could smell that smoker and it almost immediately made most folks around there hungry.

It was also known that there would be bikers in that bar, and it was a known hang-out for the Libertines. Whenever Connor was in Bubba's, everyone knew him and treated him with the utmost respect, especially the staff. Due to the presence of the Libertines, there was never any trouble that didn't get handled swiftly and violently. That trouble usually never stemmed from a regular, unless someone had too much to drink. So, Connor assumed that he was not going on a mission similar to what had happened with Knuckles a few months back.

Connor pulled up to the motorcycle-only parking at Bubba's, parked his bike, and walked inside. As Connor walked inside, he saw Pepper was sitting at a table by himself and the waitress was busy trying to not succumb to Pepper's charm and advance. Connor had witnessed this before.

Pepper was the womanizer of the club. There wasn't a woman ever safe from Pepper's charm. He was the quintessential bad-boy and a gold-medal winning flirter. Women in the club house were always hanging all over Pepper. Pepper wasn't married, and didn't have a girlfriend, but he rarely slept alone.

Connor walked up to the table and Pepper stood up and gave Connor a hug and said, "Good to see you, prospect. Have a seat."

Then, after they both sat down, Pepper said, "Debbie, this is Connor. Bring him a beer and a sandwich."

"Whatever you say, honey," replied Debbie, as she patted Pepper on the shoulder.

Pepper smiled back at Debbie and gave her a wink, which gave Debbie a full body shiver with ecstasy. As she walked out of eye shot from Pepper, who was staring at her butt as she walked away, Pepper turned to Connor.

"So, bud, I got some club business to do and I got the okay from the president to include you on this job."

"Whatever you need, Pepper," replied Connor, trying to hide his enthusiasm.

Connor had not done much more than fetch beer and clean the clubhouse since his escapade with Knuckles, so anything related to the club was a welcome distraction from his normal prospect duties. This would be the first opportunity for Connor to see some of the inner workings of the club and find out what all they did, except drink beer and ride motorcycles.

Pepper pushed a mug shot towards Connor. The photograph showed an obvious meth addict with long brown hair and a bushy moustache.

"This asshole jumped bail on a bondsman from Missouri, who is a friend of the club. The bondsman has already had to pay up and he wants some pay back. You think you can get your hands dirty, prospect?"

Connor instantly thought to himself, "Well, I wonder what "Get your Hands Dirty" means?"

Connor nodded his head. Pepper then continued.

"A chapter in Missouri heard that he made his way over here, and was supposed to be somewhere close to Clark. I called in a favor and this dipshit is supposed to meet a friend of the club's up here so they can talk about a job for him. When he comes in, just follow my lead. Until then, relax."

As Pepper had finished his less-than-adequate explanation, Connor's beer and sandwich arrived at the table.

"Can I get you anything else?" asked Debbie.

Pepper chuckled and said, "How about some company later?"

Debbie smiled and said, "I get off work at 10. Pick me up."

"Will do," said Pepper.

Debbie sashayed off with an ear to ear smile. Connor shook his head in disbelief.

He took a swig out of his beer, swallowed it, looked at Pepper, and said, "How in the fuck do you do it, Pepper?"

"It's simple, prospect. I have the three things that all women want and they just can't refuse in a man, so I don't have to really try."

Connor, a bit puzzled, shrugged and said, "What three things?"

Pepper leaned forward, as if he was about to let Connor in on the secret and seemingly magical way that he was able to win over women, and whispered, "Confidence, good looks, and a huge cock."

Connor and Pepper continued their conversation over a few more beers when the man they had been waiting on entered though the side door. Pepper immediately made eye contact with him and he stopped in his tracks with an abrupt halt. Casually, the man turned back around and walked back outside.

Pepper jumped out of his seat, knocking the chair over in the process, which made all of the patrons of Bubba's turn their heads and look. Pepper took off running out the door and Connor ran after him.

As they got outside, the man was opening the door to an old white Chevy pickup when Pepper slammed his left shoulder against the door and stretched out his arm, similar to a football player performing a stiff-arm move, and forced the man backwards. The man stumbled backwards, but did not completely lose his balance. Pepper continued toward the man and in another football-style move, tackled the man, bringing him down hard on the asphalt parking lot.

"Get his legs!" yelled Pepper.

Connor reached down and, with all his strength, wrapped his arms around the man's legs so he could not get up. Pepper then pinned the man's arms down with his knees and began to punch the man repeatedly in the face, alternating his hands. The man begged for Pepper to stop, but Pepper continued until the man lost all ability to struggle and went limp.

Pepper then stood up as the man was lying there with his eyes swollen almost shut and blood running out his nose and mouth.

"Pick him up," ordered Pepper to Connor as they carried him away from the truck. Pepper was walking backwards with his arms wrapped underneath the arms of the man and Connor held his legs. They made their way through the stockade fence and dropped the man by the smoker, which was radiating so much heat that you could see the distortion in the air surrounding it.

Pepper then reached into a small leather holster that he carried on his belt and removed a multi-purpose tool from it, which looked like a pair of pliers and a Swiss army knife all in one. As the man began to come back into consciousness, Pepper handed the tool to Connor.

"Pull off his fingernails," said Pepper to Connor.

Without hesitation, Connor took the tool and using the head of the pliers, removed the man's thumbnail. The man began to let out a blood curdling scream when Pepper put his hand over his mouth and then delivered a viscous head-butt, returning the man to unconsciousness.

"Keep going. I want them all off," said Pepper.

Connor continued his medieval surgical removal of the man's fingernails. As he did so, he was trying to figure out why Pepper wanted the man's fingernails removed, but he did not dare question a patched member.

Blood was now spewing from the 10 places on the man's hand where the fingernails had once been. Pepper had taken the bandana off of his head and stuffed it into the man's mouth. He then took another bandana which he had in his pocket and tied it around his mouth to keep the man from making any more noise.

Pepper then looked up at Connor and said, "Go into my saddle bag. There's a roll of duct tape in there and an extension cord. Go get them and come back."

Connor did as he was asked. He went into Pepper's saddlebag and saw the half used roll of duct tape and an old extension cord. He fastened his saddle bag latch and returned to the smoker. Pepper had turned the man on his stomach and had his hands behind his back.

"Tape his hands and legs together, and take off his shoes and socks," said Pepper.

Connor once again did as Pepper asked, wrapping several layers of duct tape around the man's wrists and ankles. He then took off the man's shoes and socks and threw them beside the man, and once he did, Connor watched as Pepper would do something that he would never forget.

Pepper grabbed the man's legs and dragged him beside the smoker. Pepper then lifted up his legs and aggressively forced the bottoms of the man's feet against the side of the firebox of the smoker.

"Hold him still!" muttered Pepper as he struggled to keep the man's feet pressed against the fire box.

Connor put his knee in the man's chest, who now had a look of desperation in his eyes as tears flowed from them due to the excruciating pain the man was enduring. Once Connor had the man completely immobile, Pepper continued the torture to the man's feet. The smell of burning flesh was present, but due to the size of the smoker, the smell of the meat smoking inside was masking the flesh smell.

After two minutes of the man enduring sheer agony, Pepper released his feet from the fire box. The man's feet were charred black. The man tried desperately to catch his breath and calm himself from the pain he had just endured as his eyes began to close as if he was going to drift into unconsciousness again. Pepper appeared to be catching a bit of a breather himself, when he surprised Connor yet again.

Pepper reached between the man's legs and crushed the man's genitals with his hand as he gritted his teeth. The veins in Pepper's arms were pulsating has Pepper would squeeze with all his strength and briefly release his grip before he would squeeze again. Pepper then stuck his hands inside the man's pants and pulled them along with his underwear down around his knees. He then grabbed the extension cord off of the ground and handed one end to Connor.

"Cut the end of the extension cord off and fray the wires."

Connor did as he was told. After he finished, he handed the cord back to Pepper. Pepper then took the frayed end and rubbed in on and around the man's head, covering it with blood.

"That 'ought to be enough lube," said Pepper as he violently shoved the frayed end of the extension cord inside the man's anus. "Go plug it in over there."

Connor began to get sick to his stomach. He also began to feel sorry for the man, who had endured so much torture, and worse, Connor had participated. Reluctantly, Connor walked over to the power outlet and plugged in the cord. The man's head snapped back in pain.

After about 10 seconds Pepper yelled, "Pull it!"

Connor pulled the plug.

"Again!" commanded Pepper.

Connor plugged the cord back into the outlet. This continued six more times. Due to the excruciating pain, the man had urinated and defecated all over himself.

"Open your fucking eyes and look at me mother fucker!" commanded Pepper to the man, as the man's eyes slowly opened. "Now, I bet you won't fucking jump bail again will you?"

The man shook his head from side to side, as to non-verbally communicate "No."

"Good," said Pepper. "Now, your debt is settled. Don't fuck up again, dipshit. You never know who is connected to us. I'm going to take the gag out of your mouth now. If you so much as try and scream, I will end you. Got it?"

The man nodded. Pepper reached down and removed the bandanas from the man's mouth. The man turned his head to the side and spit out a mouthful of blood and snot.

He then turned and looked up at Pepper and said, "Man, I'm sorry. I'm fucking sorry. Please don't hurt me anymore."

"I'm done if you're done," said Pepper toward Connor, who nodded his head in agreement that he was done as well.

Connor handed the tool back to Pepper and Pepper took out one of the knife blades from it and cut the duct tape loose, freeing the man's hands and legs. The man let out a sigh of relief as he believed that the pain had finally ended.

"Now what?" asked Connor.

"Well," answered Pepper, "I guess it's time to go."

Pepper went over to a water spigot on the outside of the building and washed the blood off of his hands. Connor followed suit. They both wiped their almost clean hands on the backs of their jeans and began to walk outside the fenced in area. Pepper opened the gate and walked out. Connor turned around and took one more look at the man, lying there in his own blood, urine, and feces, still trying to collect himself.

Connor walked over to Pepper and said, "I will go in and take care of the tab."

"Don't worry about it;" said Pepper, "I will take care of it tonight when I pick up Debbie."

Connor and Pepper got on their bikes and headed to the clubhouse where Cobbler was standing outside with a beer in his hand and a fresh dip of snuff in his lip. As Connor and Pepper pulled up to the clubhouse and got off of their bikes, Cobbler looked at them and let out a little laugh.

"Looks like the two of you have been having fun today."

Pepper replied, "It was pretty uneventful. I need a shower though before I go choke Debbie with my dick."

Chapter Eleven - Card

Several months had passed by and Connor continued to be the good prospect for the club. As the wedding of Julie's friend Lisa neared, Connor was able to get away from the house much more often than usual, since Lisa could not make a decision without Julie right there by her side.

Julie seemed to be accepting of the fact that Connor had some new friends. Although she had not met anyone from the club, with the exception of Terry, Connor's mood seemed better all the time and Connor was focusing on making Julie happier since she was supportive in the purchase of the motorcycle.

Connor had also spoke to his boss and received permission to change up his work schedule to where he came in earlier and was able to leave earlier. This decision had both a positive and a negative effect on Connor. While he was able to leave earlier to swing by the shop during the work week, the loss of two hours of sleep was starting to catch up with him.

It was a Thursday, and Connor was looking forward to his night out during the week to go to Church. Usually, Connor would swing by the shop on his way home from work on Tuesday and Wednesday for a few hours or so, but would be sure to be home shortly after Julie arrived home from work. However, Thursday, he could go straight from work to the shop and then to the clubhouse.

Connor was also familiar with the rumors that had begun to swirl around his office. Most of the employees knew by now that there was a Libertine prospect working there and most of them didn't really understand what that was all about since Connor had the only motorcycle in the parking lot. However, there were a few that were very familiar with the Libertines, and they began to treat Connor much differently since his introduction into the club.

Connor's hair had become a bit longer than he used to keep it and he had the beginnings of a thick goatee, which he had not grown since college. He had put on about 20 pounds, mostly from the beer that he now drank on almost a daily basis. The skin on his hands had also began to get rougher, from not only riding his motorcycle on a daily basis, but from the manual labor at the clubhouse and the assistance that he continuously gave at Bill's shop once he left work.

Connor was sitting at his desk that Thursday morning, staring at spreadsheets and going through memos. Time seemed to always go by slow on Thursdays. This day was no exception. Connor looked at his calendar and realized that he had now been a prospect of the Libertines for 5 months. He remembered that his prospecting period was supposed to be a minimum of 6 months, so he knew he had to put in at least one more month as a prospect.

Throughout the last five months, Connor had begun to learn about the club, and what it took to be a patched Libertine. However, since he was still just a prospect, he did not know everything that was going on and all that the club was mixed up in.

Several times upon arriving at Bill's shop, there would be Libertines there, and it always seemed that the topic of conversation changed when Connor arrived. Connor could not prove it, but he had his suspicions. So, Connor plugged along with his normal routine.

#

At the clubhouse, Jackal sat behind the desk in the Church room. The members had came in and taken their seats. Every member of the charter was there.

Jackal slammed the gavel down on the desk and began to speak.

"Okay. Before we have Church tonight, I wanted to bring something up before the membership. I didn't want to do this during the typical Church tonight with other folks outside the room.

"I have the deal set up now. Everything for the most part is ready to roll. The offshore accounts are there. We just need to get someone who can do the books and run the computer shit.

"Connor has been prospecting for 5 months. So we have a decision to make here. We can either give him his card now with a month to get his signatures and patch him in at the six month mark, or we can let him in on the deal now, as a prospect. Discussion?"

Terry spoke up, saying, "As far as I'm concerned, as his sponsor, he has done everything the club has asked out of him. He's never bitched once to me. He gets shit done when asked, and has, on more than one occasion, stepped up to the plate and drew blood for the club. I say we give him his card. Once he gets his signatures, let him in on the deal, and we patch him in at the six month mark."

Nutcase and Pepper shook their heads in agreement, as well as Bill, who followed up Terry's statement, saying, "Connor turned out to be a good idea. I had my doubts, thinking this yuppie was going to be as fucked up as a football bat, but, for a yuppie, he ain't afraid to get his hands dirty at my shop, and since he's been around, there's always beer in the fridge."

The room filled with laughter. Everyone in that room knew that one of the most important needs in Bill's life was his cheap, pilsner beer.

"If you ask me," said Cobbler, "I still have my doubts about the guy. I mean, he hasn't been inside any conversations except Church. What happens when he gets in deeper and freaks out? What happens when he gets some kind of bull shit threat from the cops or the feds? It could bring us all right the fuck down in a fucking hurry."

Jackal answered, "Cobbler is right. Big T, or anyone else for that matter, is there anything you can think of in talking to Connor that would make you think he would turn coat or rat?"

"I know," said Ratchet. "His goatee ain't as pretty as mine."

Everyone laughed. Ratchet always knew when to throw in a joke to lighten the mood.

"I know that me and Knuckles both have stories with Connor that to me says he's going to make a good patch," said Pepper. "If he was going to quit, I think he would have done it by now. I say we give him his card and get started on this deal. The sooner we get started, the quicker we're going to get some cash."

"Dammit," replied Cobbler, "look, I will sign his card, but if something fucking happens, I just want everyone to remember, I had some doubt."

"Duly noted Cobbler," replied Jackal. "I think Connor has made a good fucking prospect and I think he will be a good addition to this charter. So tonight at Church, I'm giving him his card. Anything else?"

No one in the room spoke up. Jackal hit the gavel on the desk to adjourn the meeting. Everyone arose from their seats and started to make their way out of the room.

"Cobbler," said Jackal, "Hang on a second."

Everyone exited the room except Jackal and Cobbler. Jackal shut the door and put his right hand on Cobbler's left shoulder. He looked him in the eye for a minute.

Cobbler then said, "What's up, brother? Did I piss you off or something?"

"No," replied Jackal, "but what I don't get is, why, from the start, you have been questioning this prospect?"

"Brother," answered Cobbler, "I've just got one of those feelings about him. I know everyone else doesn't, but I do and I can't help it."

Jackal looked down at the ground, and then back up at Cobbler and said, "You do realize that if we don't do this, then we can't do this deal. This deal can get us out of all the bull shit errands that we have been doing for so many years."

"And," retorted Cobbler, "if we do this and the prospect turns out to fuck us, this whole club goes down. Not just this charter, all the charters."

"It's a calculated risk, brother. If you don't vote at Church to give the prospect his card, you bring down the deal. It is what it is."

\#

Thursday night had arrived and the members had congregated in the clubhouse for another weekly Church meeting. Connor, who was unaware about the vote that would soon take place, had become more comfortable in the club setting. He got along with the entire membership well and he made sure to keep up the work of keeping the clubhouse looking good and doing all of the bull shit errands that the club members asked him to do.

Jackal, who was sitting at the bar on his usual barstool, turned around to the room and said, "All right, everyone to the room."

The members, along with Connor, entered the room and took their seats as Connor stood just inside the door, as he had to do at every Church. The normal business took place as it did at every meeting, going over the bar supplies and such when the moment Connor had no idea was coming, happened.

"Last thing we need to vote on," explained Jackal, "is the prospect getting his card. Now, prospect, just because you get this card, and if we vote to give you this card, don't mean that everyone will sign it, which they have to do so you can get your patch."

Connor nodded his head in understanding.

"Anyone in here opposed to the prospect getting his card?" asked Jackal as he seemed to stare directly at Cobbler.

No one raised their hands. Jackal reached into the locked desk once again and removed a 3X5 note card from the drawer which had the Libertine's center patch embossed on it. He motioned for Connor to approach the desk, and Connor obliged, and then Jackal handed Connor the card.

He then said, "You have to get the signature of every member of this charter on this card within 30 days from today. Once you get them all, you bring this card to me. I'm the last to sign it. Once I see that you have all the signatures, I will then decide whether or not I want to sign your card. Got it?"

Connor once again nodded his head in understanding. Jackal slammed the gavel down on the desk again adjourning the meeting.

As the members filed out of the room, Connor walked up to Terry and said, "So, how exactly do I go about this?"

"Well," answered Terry, "You have to go up to the members and ask them for their signature. It's that simple."

"Okay, can I get yours?"

"Absolutely!" replied Terry. He took Connor's card and wrote "Big T" on the card and then gave Connor a hug. He then said, "You're one step closer."

Connor walked out of the room and into the main part of the clubhouse. The party had begun and the beer was flowing. Connor figured that since he had Terry's signature, he only had six more to go before he turned his card into Jackal for his signature. Rather than approaching the members that night, Connor decided to be the good prospect that he had been focused on and ran petty errands for the members, never asking a single one of them for their signature.

After the party had ended, Connor went home. Julie was sitting on the couch watching a fashion television show. Connor walked into the living room and sat down next to Julie.

"How was the club thing?" asked Julie.

"It was good. I'm tired though. What did you end up doing tonight?" replied Connor.

"Just had a night out with the girls."

Julie's cell phone rang and she looked at the phone and answered as she got up from the couch and went into the other room. Connor sat there on the couch, trying to keep his eyes open. Within less than a minute as Connor's eyes were beginning to close, Julie came back in the room and sat back down on the couch.

"Who was that?" asked Connor.

"It was Chrissy."

"Chrissy, huh? I guess I don't know her," said Connor with a questioning tone in his voice.

"No," said Julie, "I don't guess you two have met. Chrissy is friends with Lisa and the other girls. We met not too long ago."

"That's good," replied Connor. "I'm glad you are making friends. I'm going to jump in the shower and head to bed. I'm beat."

Connor took a shower and prepared himself for a much needed night's sleep. As he crawled into bed, he heard Julie on the phone in the other room. He couldn't quite make out what she was saying, but he did hear the sound of her voice and her unmistakable giggle, but he could not fight his sleepiness anymore and faded off to sleep.

Chapter Twelve - Sign

The club seemed to have satisfied themselves with Connor as a prospect. Upon the required unanimous vote to present Connor with his card, Connor had spent time with each member of the club individually getting to know them a bit better and the obtained their signature.

Connor was now two signatures short. One of the signatures that he lacked of course was Jackal, who told him that his signature would be his last. The other signature was Cobbler.

Connor felt the Cobbler had something against him, but he could not quite figure out exactly what Cobbler's beef was. Connor had watched the door for Cobbler at the clubhouse several times. Connor had fetched beer for Cobbler. Connor had been on rides with the club and been to bars with Cobbler. However, Cobbler just never seemed to care for Connor or offer Connor any kind of conversation, other than the simple one sentence demands for beer or other various errands.

Cobbler was the only member of the club that didn't frequent Bill's shop. Connor knew that Cobbler was still crashing at the clubhouse more often than not and tended to not be a social type to anyone in the club at all. Connor thought that maybe that's the way he was. Perhaps Cobbler did not have any real disdain for Connor at all. Perhaps he did. Connor was torn.

However, the time was drawing near to get that signature. Connor had only two more days before the next Church meeting which would mark 30 days since he had received his card. He realized that he was going to have to bite the bullet and approach Cobbler for his signature.

Connor needed an excuse to go to the clubhouse, as he did not have a key to get in as a prospect, so someone would have to let him in. He knew that there was a very good chance if he went up there, Cobbler would be there, or would at least be back shortly.

"I guess the best way to do this is to call Cobbler and see if he can let me in to clean up a bit before the meeting," Connor thought to himself, so he flipped open his phone and dialed the number to the clubhouse phone.

Cobbler's voice answered on the other end, "Libertines."

"Cobbler, this is Prospect Connor. If you don't mind, I was going to come by the clubhouse and straighten up before Church on Thursday. Are you going to be there later?"

There was a silent pause and then Cobbler replied, "I guess."

"Thanks, man," replied Connor, "I will see you up there in a little while."

Cobbler, without responding, hung up the phone. Now, Connor had his excuse to go there and see Cobbler. So Connor left work at his usual time and rather than paying a visit to Bill at his shop that Tuesday, he went to the clubhouse.

As Connor pulled in, the clubhouse compound was deserted, as it normally was on a Tuesday, since all of the members tended to hang out at Bill's. Connor got off of his bike and knocked on the door of the clubhouse.

After a few minutes of waiting, Cobbler opened the door. Cobbler looked at Connor and raised his head slightly, as to non-verbally greet him, and then turned around and went back to the back rooms of the club house and shut the door.

"Well, shit," thought Connor, "How am I going to get into a conversation with him? This guy just does not like me at all."

Connor started to clean the clubhouse up a bit. The clubhouse had been kept quite a bit cleaner in the past six months since Connor had became a prospect, which did not go unnoticed, but Connor also did not receive any form of praise for this either. Since Connor had kept this level of cleanliness, it was more expected out of him to continue rather than slack off, and Connor thought that he might have set the bar too high for himself.

As Connor finished up getting everything fixed up at the clubhouse, he decided that the time had drawn near to approach Cobbler for his signature. Connor put away the cleaning supplies that he had been using and went towards the back rooms of the clubhouse, when Cobbler's door opened.

Cobbler exited his room and met Connor face to face in the hallway. As a knee jerk reaction, Connor stepped aside to allow Cobbler to easily pass by. Instead of passing by, Cobbler stopped just short of passing Connor in the hallway and turned towards him. Cobbler stared at Connor in silence and Connor did not say a word.

The uncomfortable silence was broken by Cobbler, who looked right into Connor's eyes, as though he was looking through Connor's head and said, "You need something, Prospect?"

Connor replied, "No, I'm good. Do you need anything?"

Cobbler, looking a bit disenchanted, replied, "I think you do, Prospect."

Connor swallowed and tried to hide his fear as he responded back to Cobbler, "Yeah. There is one thing. I need your signature on my card."

Before Connor asked, Cobbler knew this was coming as well, and said, "Where is it?"

"It's right here in my wallet."

Connor took his wallet out of his pocket and exhibited his card. Cobbler took the card from Connor and briefly looked at all the signatures, as if he was taking an inventory prior to his signature.

"So," said Cobbler, "looks like all you lack is me and Jackal, huh?"

"Yes," replied Connor softly.

Cobbler then took the pen out of Connor's left hand and pressed it against the card and appeared to begin signing it, when he stopped.

Cobbler looked at Connor and said, "Come here for a second, let's have a little chat."

Connor followed Cobbler into the main room of the clubhouse where he took a seat at one of the tables in the middle of the room. Connor stood there as he watched Cobbler stare at his card and patiently waited for Cobbler to speak.

"Have a seat, Prospect."

Connor did as he was told and sat in the chair directly across the table from Cobbler. Cobbler then slid his chair back from the table about a foot so he could prop his feet onto the table, which he did. Cobbler then took Connor's card and placed it in the center of the table and laid Connor's pen on top of the card.

"You know," began Cobbler, "you haven't said a whole hell of a lot to me since you have been a prospect, and whether or not that you know, I have had my doubts about you from the start. I don't think that you are a cop or anything like that, and even though you have proved yourself to Pepper and Knuckles, I just don't know.

"When the shit hits the fucking fan, I have to know, without a doubt, that I can count on you, without question or hesitation. Can I?"

Connor, without any hesitation in his response, said, "Hell yes you can Cobbler. Without a shadow of a doubt, you can."

Cobbler reached across the desk and picked up the pen and put the tip of the pen back to Connor's card and began to sign his name. Connor looked with anticipation and he was finally getting Cobbler's signature. Cobbler finished signing his name, but instead of handing the card back to Connor, he slid the pen across the table to Connor and held the card in his hand.

"Now," continued Cobbler, "I don't know if any of the brothers have told you this, but the easy part of this gig is about to be over. Once that patch is on your back, you have to do a hell of a lot more to keep it then to earn it. You got me, Prospect?"

"I got you," replied Connor.

Cobbler then slid the card back across the table to Connor and said, "Okay, now get the fuck out of here so I can get some sleep."

Connor walked over to the door and left the clubhouse. He stood outside for 30 seconds and heard the deadbolt lock close from the inside. Connor then hopped on his bike and decided to swing over to the shop just before going home.

As Connor traveled to the shop, he noticed that he had about 2 hours until Julie arrived at home, which would give him plenty of time to hang out at the shop. Since it was the night before Church, Connor wanted to make sure that he was going to be home with Julie so she would not balk on him going to the club house the following day.

Connor arrived at the shop and turned off his bike. He reached into his pocket and took out his phone to check for missed calls and texts when he noticed that he had a text from Julie which read: "Last minute plans with the girls. Not going to be home for a while. See you later."

Connor replied to the text: "Ok. Have fun. Who all is going?"

Connor then closed his phone and walked into the shop, where he found Bill, by himself in the shop, working on an oil change to a later model motorcycle. Bill was covered in grease and oil up to his elbows, as usual, and had just lit up one of his cheap cigars when Connor strolled up to the refrigerator to grab a beer.

Connor looked at Bill from across the shop and yelled, "Hey, want one?" as he grabbed two beers from the shelf.

Bill responded, "Yeah, bring me one, prospect."

Connor walked the two beers over to the lift and placed Bill's beer in front of him. He then cracked open his beer and took a drink and began to explain to Bill where he had been.

"Well," Connor began, "I just got back from straightening up the clubhouse and now I am only one signature short. I just have to get Jackal's now."

"That's good," replied Bill, "I don't think you will have any issue with that. Grab that wrench over there and tighten the bolts on that side, will ya?"

Bill asked people to help him in the shop from time to time and since Connor had been hanging out there quite a bit over the last six months, Bill had begun to trust Connor in completing simple tasks on bikes he was working on, while at the same time Connor had began to grow in knowledge about the ways motorcycles were put together.

As Connor finished tightening the bolts, Bill reached into his pocket and took his cell phone out of his pocket, scrolled through his contacts, and pushed send. Bill then started to walk away from Connor and go outside as he began his telephone conversation with the other party on the phone. Connor could not hear the conversation, and it was typical of Bill to walk away from people when he got on the phone, so this was no surprise to Connor.

Bill took the phone away from his mouth and turned around, facing Connor from across the shop and yelled, "Hey Prospect, you going to be here for a bit?"

Connor said, "Yeah, what do you need?"

Bill replied back to Connor, "Nothing," and continued his phone conversation. As Bill spoke, Connor's phone buzzed with a text message alert. It was Julie responding to his prior text. The text read: "Going to have drinks with Lisa."

Connor closed his phone and thought, "Good. I will hang out here until closing time and maybe have some beer afterwards."

Bill returned back into the shop after he finished his conversation and sat down on a stool next to the bike that Connor had finished tightening the bolts on. Bill looked exhausted, as the day was especially hot, and Bill did not have any air conditioning in his shop. He relied on an old water-cooled fan to cool his shop, which at best only worked within standing about 4 feet in front of it. Bill reached over to the beer, which remained unopened on his lift, and cracked it open, taking a refreshing drink, which seem to at the moment cool him off a bit.

He looked at Connor and said, "Well, Prospect, looks like you might not be a prospect much longer once you get 'pres'' signature. There is just one more thing. Just because we vote you in doesn't mean that you have to accept the patch. If you want to walk away from it all, you can now. Once you get that patch on your back, there is no walking away. You understand?"

"I get it," replied Connor, "but, I'm all in. This is what I want. Everyone in this club is good people, well, for the most part."

"What do you mean, for the most part?" asked Bill.

"Well," explained Connor, "everyone is good people. I shouldn't have said it that way, but I know Cobbler has his doubts about me, and I just want him to know that he has no reason to have any doubts about me."

Bill laughed and said, "Of course he has his doubts. We all do in some way. I mean, you are a yuppie. We aren't. None of us have the cash that you do and the education that you do. We are all just regular folk and we don't have as much to lose, I guess, as you do. You have had to do some shit for us already, and that proved to us that you ain't scared to get your hands dirty, but there's also shit you haven't seen that we get into. Once you patch-in, you are one of us, until the day you die. This ain't the fucking lions club."

Connor began to explain his understanding, saying "No. I got it. In case I haven't said it, I have looked for something like this for a long time. I know that there is a part of my life that has been missing for a while. I guess you could call it a sense of belonging and brotherhood that I know I found here."

Bill nodded his head in agreement. Connor seemed a bit surprised that Bill was being as candid with him as he was right now, but in all of the time Connor had been hanging out at the shop, this was the first time that he was able to talk to Bill without either a member of the club there or a civilian just shooting the shit with Bill, as was typical.

Bill and Connor continued in light conversation, telling jokes and having friendly arguments, such as who were the greatest musicians of all time. These were typical topics that were discussed at the shop along with motorcycle speak. After about 30 minutes of these discussions, a motorcycle was heard pulling up outside the shop, which Bill immediately recognized, not by the sight of the bike, but by the sound.

"There's Jackal," announced Bill, to Connor's surprise.

Along with Cobbler, Jackal would not typically hang out at Bill's shop, so his mere presence there immediately excited Connor's curiosity. Jackal dismounted his bike and strolled into the shop in his usual manner, with a posture that one could easily tell he had back trauma in the past.

"How we doing?" asked Jackal to Bill.

"Oh, we're doing," responded Bill, "Up to my asshole in alligators, as usual. I had the prospect wrenching on that Road King over there."

Connor began to walk across the shop to announce to Jackal that he had completed his card with the exception of Jackal's signature. Before doing so, however, Jackal beat him to the punch.

"Let me see you card, Prospect," commanded Jackal.

Connor reached into his wallet and presented his card to Jackal, which now contained Cobbler's long sought signature, as well as each member of that charter, with the exception of Jackal of course. Jackal looked at the card as Bill and Connor stood in silence. Connor watched closely as Jackal took a mental inventory of the signatures on his card.

As Jackal finished his brief inspection, he gave Connor a look of approval. He reached inside the pocket of his colors and removed a pen. He then proceeded to sign Connor's card. After finishing his signature, he handed the card back to Connor.

He then said, "Give this to me tomorrow night. Don't fucking lose it."

Connor laughed and said, "I won't lose it. Don't worry about that."

Connor placed the card safely back into his wallet. A sense of completion had now come over him. It would be about 24 hours before the next Church meeting, where Connor assumed he would be voted on and finally become a full fledged member of the Libertines Motorcycle Club. As that shiver ran down his spine, he tried his best to contain his excitement, when two more bikes pulled up to the shop, both of which were ridden by members of the Club, Ratchet and Pepper.

Ratchet and Pepper walked into the shop and greeted Jackal with the usual club greeting and, after a brief conversation between the three club members, Jackal left. It was apparent now to Connor that the phone call Bill had made earlier was to Jackal and that Jackal had seemingly made a special trip to the shop to complete the signatures on his card.

Pepper went up to Connor and said, "So, Jackal tells me you got all your signatures, huh? You're one step closer, Prospect. I guess I might not have another chance if all goes well for you tomorrow night to ask this again, so I better do it now. Go shine up my bike, Prospect."

"Mine too," said Ratchet. "Make her pretty."

Ratchet and Pepper laughed as Connor retired outside the shop and began to clean the two member's bikes, which Connor had done many times before. Due to Connor's meticulous nature, the member's bikes had become the cleanest since anyone could remember.

Connor cleaned the member's bikes as he heard the laughter coming from inside the shop, as Ratchet, Pepper, and Bill stood in front of the water-cooled fan and traded stories and jokes while they watched Connor clean. When Connor finished cleaning the bikes, he returned the cleaning supplies to where he had found them in Bill's shop.

Bill then looked at Connor, who was now covered in grease and sweat and said, "Now, Prospect, grab yourself a beer and have a seat. I think your bullshit work is done for the day. You probably need to get rested for tomorrow night."

Chapter Thirteen – Patching In

Just as Connor was about to leave work on that fateful Thursday afternoon, he went into the public restroom at his office as he usually did, going through his normal ritual of removing his dress shirt and putting on a black t-shirt, then placing his prospect colors over his t-shirt before exiting the building to ride his bike. Upon placing that leather vest over his shoulders, he stared at himself in the bathroom mirror.

As had now become a habit for Connor, while not always in a mirror, he began to talk to himself, watching his reflection as he spoke, "Today could very well be the day. You have your signatures. You have busted your ass for this club. Today, these guys could become your brothers. Are you up to it? Well, are you? Of course you are. Let's do this!"

Connor had no doubts in his mind that tonight would be the night that he patches in. The fear and excitement that he had contained within himself made his blood pressure rise. Over the last six months, there had been a huge paradigm shift in his behavior, attitude, and personality. He was quick to react, quickly to speak, and even quicker to retaliate against anything that he felt was a threat. He felt that once he had that full patch on his back, he would become essentially untouchable, invincible to any rules handed down by an outsider of his club. He would be a full patch Libertine.

Connor walked out into the parking lot and prepared for his ride to Bill's shop, where he figured he would hang out for just a while before the club's Church meeting that night. Connor placed all of his work items and clothing into his saddlebag and began to start his bike.

Connor rode off from the parking lot and headed to Bill's shop. The feel of the wind in his hair and the adrenaline pumping through his veins overtook him as he began to go faster and faster, heading toward Bill's shop, when he looked into his rearview mirror and saw something that he had yet to see since he had been riding his bike. Connor saw the unfortunate flash of red and blue lights behind him, the same red and blue lights that belong to a squad car of the Clark city's finest.

"Shit," Connor said, as he pulled his bike over to the side of the road. Connor put the bike on the kickstand and shut off the motor. He crossed his arms over his chest and awaited the approach of the police officer to issue what Connor assumed would be his first speeding ticket in almost 10 years.

Connor waited for what seemed to him an eternity and the police officer never exited his vehicle. After the eternity for Connor ended, which realistically amounted to about 5 minutes, another squad car pulled up behind the initial car. Now there were two officers on the scene. Connor thought to himself that the first officer must be intimidated by his presence, with his Libertine prospect colors on.

Upon the arrival of the backup officer, the initial officer exited his squad car and finally made his cautious approach toward Connor, resting his hand on his sidearm. The police officer who approached Connor was between 5'6" and 5'7" and weighed about 150 pounds soaking wet. He was dressed as typical for the new age police officer, complete with his combat style black boots and his Nazi storm trooper style SWAT team pants, in a vain effort to overcome the little man syndrome that the entire Clark Police Department possessed. The officer approach Connor on the right side of his motorcycle after glancing down at his vest.

The officer looked at Connor and said, "Good afternoon, sir. My name is Officer Johnson with the Clark Police Department. May I see your license and registration please?"

Connor obliged the officer. He reached into his back pocket and produced the required documentation to prove that he did have a license and his bike was registered. The officer looked over both of the documents, and after satisfying himself as to their validity, he continued his interrogation.

"Do you know why I pulled you over today, sir?" asked the officer in a respectful tone.

"No, I don't officer," responded Connor.

"Well, you were exceeding the posted speed limit on this road by 15 miles per hour. Is there any reason for the rush?"

"Actually," replied Connor, "there is. If my bike is passing other cars, then the likelihood of a traffic accident involving myself and another motorist is substantially reduced. Therefore, my choice in speed is actually directly connected to remaining safe on the public roads."

The officer looked at Connor with a look of utter surprise. Since the officer had pulled over not only a biker, but a Libertine prospect, he full well expected to have to deal with an uneducated thug. After a moment of pause due to his surprise, the officer continued.

"Interesting explanation. I will be back with you in a second."

The officer retreated back to the second squad car and entered into a conversation with the back-up officer, which only lasted for a few minutes, and them he returned to his vehicle. Connor could see from looking at him that he was writing something down, which Connor assumed was the form he was filling out for his speeding ticket. After a few minutes of writing, the police office exited his vehicle with nothing in his hands and approached Connor again.

"Sir," said the officer, "I am going to let you off with a warning. I noticed that your record indicates that you have had no moving violations for the past several years. Try to keep your speed a bit closer to the speed limit and ride safe. Have a nice day."

The officer turned around and went back to his car. Connor was befuddled and a bit amused at this whole experience. He thought that this would make an interesting story to tell at the bike shop in a few minutes. He also thought to himself that he was glad he did not have any alcohol on his breath, which might lead the officer to attempt a DWI arrest.

Connor brought the motor of his bike back to life and headed to the shop. He couldn't help but laugh the entire way there about the traffic stop. Even though Connor had been polite during his stop, he wished that he would have maybe took an attitude with the cop, but in hind sight, he was pleased that he did not get a ticket on his record.

Connor arrived at the bike shop to find Bill outside on the phone, and Ratchet standing there with a beer in his hand. After the normal greetings were exchanged, Connor reached into the fridge and grabbed a beer. He began to retell the story to Ratchet and Bill and they all three shared a laugh.

"Fucking pigs," said Ratchet, "anytime they get a chance to fuck with you just for a bit, they get happy.

"No shit," replied Bill, "Those mother fuckers are always driving by my shop slowly just looking for a reason to give me shit. One of these days, they are going to catch me in a bad mood."

Connor, Bill, and Ratchet spent the remainder of the afternoon guzzling beer and wrenching on motorcycles when it became time for Bill to close up the shop early, as he always did on Thursday, and head to the clubhouse.

The three bikers rode from Bill's shop to the clubhouse. When they arrived, Connor noticed that the parking lot was quite packed with motorcycles, about 5 times the usual amount. There were quite a few people milling around in the parking area, all with beer bottles in their hands. Connor noticed that just about every other person in the parking lot was wearing Libertine colors.

Connor saw Libertine cuts from Missouri, Oklahoma, and even saw one member's bottom rocker read Arkansas. Over at the outdoor cooker, he saw two familiar faces that were cooks at Bubba's, which looked like they were busy making food. To Connor, this looked like one hell of a party, which even though Thursday nights always ended up to be a ton of fun, there were never this many people there.

Connor looked at the time and noticed it was nearing 7:00, which was Church time. Not wanting to be late, Connor quickly made his rounds through the crowd, shaking hands with patched members, some of whom he had never met. He then entered the clubhouse door, which, as per usual, was guarded by Cobbler.

When Connor entered the clubhouse, he noticed that the only people inside were members of his charter now. There were no guests inside, no women, and no members of other charters. Cobbler closed and locked the door. The loud thud of the deadbolt locking the members within the confines of the clubhouse could be heard quite clearly as there was no music playing and very soft talking taking place inside.

The members of the charter all turned around and faced Connor, who was now standing in between Cobbler guarding the now locked door, and the rest of the membership of the charter, who had now formed a line shoulder-to-shoulder. On the table in front of the members was a skull which had a liquor bottle sticking out of its mouth, in a similar fashion of the center patch of the Libertines.

Upon a closer examination, Connor noticed that this skull was not a store bought prop, but an actual human skull. Connor wondered for a brief second how they got a hold of that. The skull appeared to have what looked like old blood stains on it as well. Connor also noticed that there was a strange looking liquid in the liquor bottle, which looked more like soup than a normal alcoholic beverage.

Jackal took a few steps forward from the rest of the group and hit the black gavel, which was normally used to bring the church meetings to order, on the table containing the skull and liquor bottle.

Jackal then said, "Brothers, listen up. We have here before us a prospect, who has proven to me by his card that he has received the required signatures of the members of this charter. I now ask each of you to verify, on your word as a Libertine, that you did, in fact, give your signature to this prospect."

Every member of the charter, taking turns, repeated the following as the looked at Connor: "I did, for it was I who signed."

"So it is," continued Jackal, "that this prospect has now completed his required time and errands as such, and now the debt lies at his feet. Prospect Connor, step forward towards the Libertine and kneel."

Connor, assuming that the Libertine was the skull, moved toward the table and knelt down on both knees.

Jackal then continued, "Prospect, what you see before you is the Libertine. A Libertine accepts that he hold no moral restraint. We care not about society's rules. We care not about anyone's rules other than our own, and we hold our rules and our brothers higher than anything. In order to become one of us, you must affirm your belief is not only agreeable to ours, but absolute. Do you affirm?"

"I do." answered Connor.

"Then," as Jackal continued, "your days as a prospect are about to come to an end. Before doing so, however, your blood must be joined with the blood of your brothers. Extend your left hand."

Connor extended his left arm out and his hand, facing palm up, outstretched above the skull. Jackal then took a hold of Connor's wrist with his left hand and removed a knife from his pocket with his right hand. Jackal opened the knife and cut Connor's palm open, which caused blood to begin pouring from his hand.

Jackal took the liquor bottle out of the mouth of the skull, removed the cork from the end, and began adding Connor's blood to the contents of the bottle, which Connor now realized was coagulated blood inside the liquor bottle. Connor hoped that he would not have to take a drink out of that.

Jackal took a hold of Connor's hand and applied pressure with his bare hand to stop assist in stopping the bleeding. Then Jackal gave a nod to Cobbler, who had snuck up behind Connor, and Cobbler cut the bottom "Kansas" rocker patch off of Connor's vest. Cobbler then took the rocker patch and wrapped it around Connor's hand. Every member of the charter then approached the table.

All of the members then placed their left hands onto Connor's left hand in a gesture to mimic Jackal's pressure gesture of stopping the bleeding.

Jackal then said, "Should a brother ever bleed for our club or our territory, it is the responsibility of you to come to their aid, just as these brothers have came to yours in an effort to cease your bleeding. You now bleed with all of us."

The other members of the club let go of Connor's hand except Jackal, who pulled Connor to his feet, and continued, "The vest that you now wear represents your past life, before you enter our brotherhood. It has come time to remove yourself from that life to enter your new life."

Connor took his vest off. As Connor was being brought to his feet, Cobbler had brought a large metal bucket and placed it next to Connor. There was a liquid in the bottom of this bucket, which by the smell Connor recognized as gasoline.

Jackal then said, "You will now sever your ties with the prior world in fire and become one of us."

Connor dropped his vest into the bucket. Jackal lit a single match from a cheap 20 paper matchbook and dropped it into the bucket, which ignited the gasoline and the vest. Terry then left the circle of the Libertines and went behind the bar. He bent down behind the bar and could be heard stirring around as if he was digging through a cabinet or a box. After a few seconds, Terry came from around the bar holding a brand new vest with the full patch set of the Libertines sewn on the back.

Terry made his way around the other members and arrived behind Connor. Terry then put the vest on Connor. A tremendous sense of finality and accomplishment overcame Connor as he felt the weight of the patches now on his back. Terry then embraced Connor and kissed him on the lips. Each member took their turn doing the same.

Jackal, finishing up the ceremony, slammed the black gavel on the table, and then said, "Welcome, Brother Libertine."

Connor said, "Thank you, brother. Man, it feels good to call all of you 'brother' now. I won't let any of you down."

"That's good to know," said Jackal. "Now, let's put this shit up and get the patch in party started."

Bill and Jackal took the skull and the liquor bottle into the Church meeting room while Cobbler walked over to the door, awaiting the signal to open up the clubhouse for the party. When Jackal and Bill returned into the room, Jackal nodded at Cobbler, who motioned and Connor to come over toward the door and Cobbler opened up the door.

Cobbler then gave Connor a slight nudge moving him outside the clubhouse and said, "Get out there and show your new brothers your cut."

Various members of the other charters of the Libertines came up to Connor and congratulated him on his patching in as they filed inside the clubhouse and started to drink. After all of the members entered, the guests in the parking lot filed into the clubhouse as well, offering their congratulations to the newest Libertine.

As everyone entered the clubhouse, Connor took his cell phone from his pocket and sent a text to Julie: "I'm now a full-fledged Libertine. I just got my vest! I love you!"

Connor looked down at the front of his vest, realizing in all of the excitement he did not see what name the club had given him. As he looked as his vest where his name patch was sewn on, he noticed his new name, "RUB."

"Rub?" he thought. "Those bastards. It figures."

RUB was typically a derogatory term used in the motorcycle world for a "Rich Urban Biker." Seeing as Connor was the only member of the club that truly had a high paying job and a career, he understood why they would call him a RUB. Now, they had made it official.

A few seconds later, Julie returned the text: "Good for you. I will see you later tonight. Going to have drinks with the gals."

Chapter Fourteen – The Party Ensues

Wearing his shiny new leather vest complete with the full patch of the Libertines, Connor, who now bears the road name "RUB" walked back inside the Libertine's clubhouse to join the party held in his honor. Connor knew that every person in there wearing that same cut as he were now his brothers. They would go to the ends of the earth for him and in turn he would now do the same for them.

Connor would gain the total respect of the community surrounding the club and the general public, who would now not only respect him, but fear him. Now that he had full patch status, he knew that his perks had grown and his responsibility had as well. The first thing that Connor decided he needed to do was to begin dissolving the doubt in Cobbler's mind about him.

As he walked past the door, where Cobbler always stood, he stopped and stuck his hand out to shake Cobbler's, saying, "Brother, I hope you have no ill will toward me. Now that we are brothers, I want to get rid of any doubt that you might have."

Cobbler responded, "Look bro, I signed your card, I didn't vote against you getting your patch. You have nothing left to prove to me as far as wearing that cut. It's on you. There ain't shit I can do about it now. You just remember, the work hasn't stopped. It's just now starting. You had shit pretty easy as a prospect. Don't coast."

"I got you, bro," replied Connor, "Can I get you a beer?"

Cobbler responded, "Hell no. You're not a prospect. It don't work that way. Let the bitches take care of that for me, and for you. You don't fetch beer. You don't do bitch work. Look, you haven't been in this clubhouse as anything but a prospect, and now a member. You will see tonight how shit works."

Connor nodded at Cobbler and began to walk across the room to the bar to get a beer. After a few steps, Connor felt a hand reach under the back of his vest in an all too familiar sort of way and a voice which he soon recognized began to speak.

"Hey honey. Can I get you something?"

Connor turned around and verified his suspicions. It was Sally, whom Connor had done a good job warding off her advances over the past six months. Sally had not made this easy for Connor, especially since the club life had become his primary life and his home life had become secondary. Julie being with Lisa for the wedding plans much more over the past month, as well as Julie hanging out with her new friends for the past few weeks, had made their marriage a bit distant and Connor was feeling lonely.

"Sure," said Connor, "I need a beer, and so does Cobbler."

Sally replied, "I'll take care of it"

Sally sashayed off in her normal fashion and went to attend to Connor's immediate need for thirst quenching. As she walked off, Terry came up to Connor and embraced him once again, except this time; Terry had a tear running down the left side of his face.

Connor said, "What's up man?" in a concerned tone.

"Brother," replied Terry, "I am so glad to call you that. From the day that I became a prospect in this club I was hoping that one day you would get back on two wheels and be a member here with me. I missed us hanging out like we used to. Until I became a member of this club, you were the only true friend that I have had."

"I appreciate that and I am glad you got me into this. It has been life changing. I had no idea what I have been missing the past several years."

"Well," continued Terry, "you know that this is just the beginning. The club will be having a sit down soon about a new project that we are taking on to make money for all of us."

"Yeah," replied Connor, "I know that I have heard some stuff about something new and I have a feeling that is why I got thrown in here so quickly."

"Nothing gets past you, RUB!" said Terry with a chuckle.

"So," said Connor, "What exactly is this project?"

"Honestly," replied Terry, "I don't really know. I know that it is complicated and it is going to take a smart mother fucker like you to pull it off, and that's about it."

"Well," said Connor, "It can't be any worse than some of the shit that I have already done, so I'm up for it."

"Let's not worry about that shit right now, man. Let's worry about getting all kinds of fucked up. Tonight is your night, brother."

Sally walked up to the pair and handed a beer to Connor. Connor and Terry clanked their beer bottles together and embraced once again. Sally then wrapped her arms around Connor underneath his vest and gave him a firm squeeze as well. She then ran her right hand down the small of his back and put it in the back pocket of his jeans and winked at him.

"I will come back and check on you in a bit, honey," said Sally as she walked off to assist the bartender.

Terry looked at Connor and said, "Man, when are you going to tap that?"

"Tap it?" said Connor, "Bro, I can't tap that. I'm married. I love Julie too much to cheat on her."

"Hey," retorted Terry, "It ain't cheating if it's done in the clubhouse. The clubhouse is kind of like Vegas, man. What happens here stays here."

"Easy for you to say," continued Connor, "You ain't married and you don't have an ol' lady to answer to. It's been hard to fan her off, man. She keeps on trying and trying and it's getting harder and harder to tell her no. Problem is, if I do it, I will regret it, and I don't know if I could even face Julie afterwards. The guilt will just plain eat me up."

Terry decided to use a little bit of Connor's logic to sway his thinking as he said, "Well, let me put it to you this way. Did you tell Julie about what you and Knuckles did, or what you and Pepper did, or what you and Nutcase have done twice?"

Connor raised his eyebrow at Terry, realizing where he was going with his logic, replying, "That's totally different."

"No, it isn't," responded Terry, "Do you really think Julie would want you to be a Libertine if she knew some of the things you have done. I mean, to be in this club, you had to prove that you were willing to break the law of the man for this club, which you did on more than one occasion. So, how would Julie feel if she knew that?"

"Well," Connor said with a laugh, "she would be pissed to say the least."

"Exactly," said Terry, "she would be pissed. Now, she hasn't found out about any of that shit and that was some gruesome shit. If she didn't find out about that, how would she find out about you tapping some club bitch?"

"I guess she wouldn't," said Connor, as he was running out of arguments with Terry about sleeping with Sally.

Terry finished his argument, stating, "Well, just think about it. I would hate to see you pass up a nice piece of ass like that over your fucking morals. Remember, you're a Libertine. That shit doesn't apply to you anymore."

"I'll drink to that," replied Connor as he raised his beer bottle to his mouth again and took a drink.

As he lowered his beer bottle, he noticed that he had almost finished that beer, when Sally arrived with another beer. She took the almost empty beer bottle from him and gave him the fresh beer, smiled, winked, and walked off again. Connor began to drink that new beer and began to ponder whether or not it was worth messing around with Sally. He knew that no one would find out, and figured that Sally could keep her mouth shut also. Julie would never come around the clubhouse in the first place. She didn't care for the biker lifestyle. She wanted to go to higher priced places, where smoking was not allowed, and where all the drinks had fancy names.

Connor did miss Julie not being there to celebrate him patching into the club, as he ranked this higher than graduating college, or even landing his high paying job. Since Connor and Julie had known each other for so long, they have had their ups and downs before. Connor just assumed that this was another period of downs with all the wedding plans and his new involvement in the club. Now that he had patched in, he didn't have to hang around all of the time to fetch beer and clean bikes. He could now spend more time with Julie, and Connor was looking forward to that. He did miss his wife, but the matter at hand was enjoying his patch in party.

Connor continued to drink throughout the night, having conversations with both members of his charter and other charters. All of the guests there wanted to also make sure that if they had not met Connor before, that they introduced themselves to Connor. Many of the male guests there wanted to be invited to prospect for the club, and of those, there were some that were quite jealous of the fact that an unknown had come into the fold of the Libertines and had basically bypassed the hang around period and patched in so quickly.

One of these individuals was Scott. Scott had been hanging around the shop for about 3 years and had been hanging around the clubhouse now for over a year. Scott was at the clubhouse every Thursday night for the after Church party. Connor had seen Scott at least twice a week, sometimes 4 or 5 times. When the club would go to a bar, Scott was there.

Since Connor was a prospect at the time, he would not dare ask anyone from the club why Scott had not been asked to prospect. Connor did not want to bring down the mood of the party, but seeing Scott at HIS patch in party, Connor decided it was finally time to solve the mystery.

Connor looked around the room and tried to decide who he was going to approach with this question. He figured that the safest person would be Terry, but now that he was a member, he could ask anyone, but who was it going to be? Jackal was busy talking to three different women at the time, Cobbler was standing at the door talking to Sampson, and Pepper was busy flirting as usual.

There sat Ratchet, who, for some reason, was sitting by himself, sipping on a beer. Connor walked over to Ratchet's table and tapped him on the shoulder.

"Hey, brother, can I borrow you for a minute?"

Ratchet looked at his wrist as if he was staring at a watch that was not there, turned around and said, "Yep, looks like I have a few minutes."

Connor and Ratchet walked toward the door of the clubhouse, which was opened by Cobbler, and the two of them walked outside. Ratchet walked behind Connor in his normal swagger, which was leaning forward a bit with both of his hands behind his back, fingers interlaced and gripping his beer bottle. The two walked out of ear shot of anyone outside and Connor stopped, leaning on a light pole as Ratchet stood there.

Ratchet asked Connor, "What's on your mind?"

"Ratchet, I got to ask you something. What's the deal with that hang around, Scott? He's always here, and he's been here a lot longer than me. He's obviously interested in being a member, but he hasn't been tapped to prospect."

Ratchet took a drink of his beer and stroked his beard as he said, "Ol' Scotty, huh? He's a fucking mess, man. You're right, he wants to prospect, he wants it bad. Thing is, man, just because someone wants in really bad like him doesn't mean he's getting in.

"Look around that clubhouse, man. There are tons of guys in there who want to prospect. They want to be a bad ass, and we know that. They are of more use to us not being in the club."

Connor looked confused as he asked, "How can they be more use to us not in the club?"

Ratchet laughed again and said, "I guess Big T never explained this to you. Think about this. Look how small our charter is. Not that many folks, but all good folks. Even you. You're a pretty good mother fucker, and the club knows it, and the club has a use for you.

"We don't need any more Billy Badasses. We got Knuckles, Cobbler, and Pepper. That's enough bad asses for any charter. Everyone seems to think that to be a Libertine they need to be able to kick everyone's ass single-handedly, and that just ain't true.

"Fuck me; look at me, I would be lucky now to beat my way out of a wet paper bag. In my day, I could, but now, fuck me, I'm too tired. I would rather just drink beer and tell jokes."

Connor immediately interrupted Ratchet, saying, "Ratchet, you're a good mother fucker and you know that."

"Thanks, bro," replied Ratchet, "and now you are starting to get it. Those hang-arounds in there are all trying to prove something, either that they are a bad ass or a kiss ass, and we don't need any more bad-asses and we sure don't need any kiss-asses."

Connor laughed at said, "I get it, Ratchet. That makes sense, but how can they be of use to the club?"

"They can do shit for us and they aren't members, so it can't come back on us. We haven't had to do that for a long time, but you never know when the time might come where we need to be able to have that. Don't sweat it, bro. You are over thinking shit again. Let's get back in there. I need another beer."

Ratchet started walking back toward the clubhouse and Connor stood there for a minute. Connor thought back on some of the bad shit that he had done as a prospect and wondered what kind of things the club would need to be done that they wouldn't want to have traced back to them, but as the beer began to take over Connor's thinking, he dismissed it and made his way back into the clubhouse as well.

As Connor walked into the clubhouse, he saw Pepper heading to the back rooms with a woman on each arm, while his hands were on the butt cheeks of both women. Connor just laughed to himself and thought what a lucky guy Pepper was. Connor wished that he had just half of the looks and charm that Pepper did, but he had Julie, so it didn't matter.

Connor then turned and saw Knuckles and Sampson sitting at a table, drinking beers and laughing. Nutcase and Terry had bellied up to the bar alongside Jackal, who sat on his usual barstool. Bill was standing over to the side with three of the guests talking to him. Connor decided to check on Bill and see what he was up to, so he strolled over towards Bill, when Sally came from across the room, with two beers in her hand.

Sally stopped Connor and handed him one of the beers and she kept the other beer. Sally looked deep into Connor's eyes as she took a drink from her beer. She took the end of the longneck beer bottle and slid it into her mouth slowly and then pulled the bottle back just as slow, as to mimic oral sex, and set the bottle on the table next to her.

She then looked at Connor and said, "I wish that was something else."

"You do?" replied Connor as he let out a nervous chuckle.

"You know that I do," replied Sally. "You know that I have wanted you from the first time you walked into this clubhouse. Come here."

Sally took Connor's hand and without hesitation Connor followed behind Sally as she took him over to one of the couches on the far side of the clubhouse, and it just so happened to be the couch that she attempted her first pass at Connor. Sally sat down on the couch and Connor sat down next to her.

Sally then took Connor's left hand with her right hand and twisted his wedding ring with her fingers as she said, "Look, honey, I know that you are married. I have no problem with that, but I know you do."

Connor opened his mouth to begin an explanation, but before he could, Sally took her index finger of her left hand and gently placed it on his lips, as to silence him so she could finish.

Sally continued, "Wait, honey, let me finish. I don't know your wife, and I don't want to know her. What you do with your wife is between you and her, and what you do with me is between you and me. It's that simple. Besides, I'm sure that I would do some things to you that you wife won't."

Connor laughed as Sally giggled and Connor began to explain his reasons why he couldn't, as he tried to make coherent sentences under his now growing blood alcohol level, saying "Sally, my home life ain't as good as I would like it, but if I hooked up with you, I don't think I could live with the guilt. Even if my ol' lady never found out, I don't think I could face her."

Sally responded, "Well, you won't know if you can and you definitely won't know what you're missing until you try and I really want you to try."

At this moment, Bill came up to Connor and said, "Hey RUB, come here for a second, I want you to meet someone."

Connor thought to himself that Bill was his savior. Sally knew that Connor would have to go since a member needed him, so she let go of Connor and he rose to his feet and followed Bill, who took him outside, where there was no one for Connor to meet.

Bill then began to preach to Connor, "Look, there ain't anyone for you to meet. You need a fucking education here, brother."

Before Bill could finish, Connor interrupted, as if he knew what Bill was about to preach, saying, "Bill, I know. It's one of the perks."

"Are you going to let me finish or are you going to stand there and run your gator?" said Bill, who was a little bit mad that Connor had interrupted.

"Sorry, continue," replied Connor.

"Okay, now, here is what I got to say about this shit, so listen," continued Bill, "You do whatever the fuck you want. It's your life, but if you nail that little tart in there you are going to regret it.

"Look, bro, I have had so many opportunities over the past to nail whatever bitch arrived in that clubhouse, and I passed on all of them. That way, I can look my ol' lady in the eye and without hesitation, tell her that I love her and she's the only one. I don't have to lie. You have to think with the big head and not the little head.

"If you love your ol' lady, then keep your promise. I'm not saying anything bad about our other brothers who do, but you won't find me doing it. If you do it, fine by me. I'm not going to bust your balls about it, but, I said my piece. Now, you got to do what you got to do."

Bill went back inside the clubhouse, not allowing Connor to offer any kind of retort to his speech and Connor began to weigh his options. Julie and Connor had not had sex in quite a while and Connor was allowing this pent up sexual frustration sway his thinking. Connor thought to himself that he needed another beer and went back inside the clubhouse to join the party.

Chapter Fifteen - Hangover

Connor awoke in the middle of the night. He looked over at his alarm clock and saw that it was 2:36 in the wee hours of the morning. He glanced beside him and noticed Julie was fast asleep. Feeling the urge to urinate, Connor crawled out of bed and stumbled into the bathroom. At this moment, Connor realized that he didn't even remember coming home, but he had obviously made it.

After he finished going to the bathroom, Connor walked into the garage just to make sure his bike was there. He opened the pass-through door and saw his prized bike sitting in its usual spot.

"Well, I guess I made it home on my own," Connor thought, "and that's a surprise. I'm still drunk. But, I can't remember if Julie was here when I got home or if we fought about me getting home late, or being drunk. Shit! Oh, well."

Connor wandered back inside and decided to take two aspirins and have a nice big glass of water to help aid him in his eventual hangover he knew was coming in a few hours. He reached into the cabinet and took out two aspirins and filled a very large plastic glass full of water. He tossed the pills to the back of his throat and began to drink the glass of water in large gulps at a time until there was very little water left in the glass. The remaining water in the glass was poured down the sink.

As Connor put the glass into the dishwasher, he noticed that Julie's cell phone was on the kitchen island, which was extremely odd. She had forgotten to put it on the charger. He picked up her phone and started to carry it to the bedroom when his curiosity overtook him.

Connor opened up her phone and decided to see who she had been talking to. The call log looked unsurprising, containing several calls to and from Lisa over the past few days. Then, Connor changed over to the text message menu and noticed a text from Chrissy. The text message thread was as follows:

Julie: Hey

Chrissy: Hey back.

Julie: Lisa and I are going out to the usual tonight.

Chrissy: Cool. I will be there

Julie: I can't wait. See you then.

Chrissy: See you.

Julie: Thanks again.

Chrissy: Can't wait until next time. Hopefully it can just be us.

Julie: I don't know. That's risky. Maybe.

Chrissy: Ok. See you.

Connor thought to himself, "What the fuck is this all about?" but he closed the phone and continued on into the bedroom, where he plugged her phone into the charger and crawled back into bed. He looked over to make sure the alarm was set and went to sleep.

A few hours later, Connor awoke to his alarm. To his surprise, the aspirin and water didn't do the trick. Connor was hung over and hung over bad. He pulled himself out of bed and began his normal routine of morning preparation.

As Connor got dressed, he glanced over and admired his new set of colors and his full three piece patch set. Even though his head was killing him, Connor thought to himself that the night before was worth it. All he had been through was worth it. This was his first full day as a full patch Libertine.

And Connor was also especially proud of himself that he had not done anything with Sally the night before. Now that his intoxicated state had become a hung over state, the pounding headache he was suffering from would have been worse from the guilt of cheating on Julie with Sally.

Connor went out to the garage and opened the garage door, started his bike, and proceeded on to work, sporting his brand new cut. As he was overcome with pride and happiness as he felt the weight of the patch on his back, he couldn't help but think about the text message thread that he read the night before on Julie's phone.

"Why," Connor thought to himself, "would Julie think it would be risky to be with Chrissy. Of course, I haven't met Chrissy yet, but she must be ok if Julie is hanging out with her now."

Connor never did really keep up with any of Julie's friends, even the ones that he knew. He just didn't care much for any of them, and especially the last six months during his prospecting period, everything that Julie said to him was met with a cordial response, as Connor didn't really care about anything but the Libertines.

And now that his patch was sewn firmly on his back, Connor had no reason to care about anything else. He had done it. He had made it. He was a no shit, fully fledged outlaw biker. He knew that his patch alone would instill fear in most and those that it did not would feel the unfortunate retribution from his new brothers should they step out of line.

Connor arrived at work and did his normal change of clothes and started his boring work day. However, Connor was at least a little bit pleased that it was Friday, and he would be able to hopefully relax this weekend. Since Connor and Julie had not really done anything, he thought he would surprise her and take her to dinner that night.

Connor waited until he figured that Julie was up and around and gave her a call.

Julie answered, "Hello."

"Hey, babe. I was thinking," said Connor, "why don't we go do something tonight?"

"Like what?" asked Julie.

"Well," answered Connor, "how about we go have dinner and a few drinks afterwards. Maybe we could go out in a group with Lisa and her fiancé and your group. I mean, hell, I don't know any of them really except Lisa."

"I don't think so," responded Julie, "The wedding is drawing really close now and Lisa really needs my help. Why don't you just go to the shop after work today and I will see you at home later on tonight. I have a call coming in on the other line from Lisa. I will see you tonight."

Julie hung up the phone. Connor had mixed emotions about her response. On the one hand, he actually wanted to do something with Julie and tries to pay her some attention; while on the other hand, he now had a free pass to hang out pretty much all night.

So Connor decided to let it go and cut out of work early to head to the shop. He figured since it was Friday, he could slip away a few hours early, but since he had done maybe too much sneaking away, he decided to run it by his boss.

Connor walked down the hallway and knocked on his boss' door, which was partially opened, and walked into his boss' office. Connor's boss was sitting at his desk reading a news story off of the internet about new technology products coming out that year.

"Hey, Frank" said Connor, "you got anything big you need me to do today? If you don't, I was going to cruise out of here a little early if you don't mind."

"Connor," answered Frank, "shut the door and come in here for a second if you would."

Connor shut the door behind him and walked into Frank's office and took a seat on the other side of his desk. Frank leaned back in his chair and propped his feet up on his desk and put his hands behind his head.

"Connor," began Frank, "I'm in a tough spot with you right now, and I have to be honest. You are a great employee, and I have never had any problems with you or your work. In fact, between you and me, you are the best guy I have in your department. My problem is I don't want that to change."

"Don't worry about that Frank," replied Connor, "I'm making sure that I get everything done."

"I know you do," continued Frank, "but here's the issue that I have now. What am I supposed to do if your work starts to slip? I don't want any trouble."

"Trouble?" asked Connor.

"You know what I mean. I don't want any trouble from your new friends."

Connor laughed and said, "Frank, you know first off my work isn't going to slip and second off if it did slip, it would be all on me. My so called friends won't do anything about me not getting my work done."

"You know," said Frank, "there are quite a few people around here now that are concerned about you being in this motorcycle gang."

"Wait," said Connor, "it's not a gang. It's a motorcycle club, and that's it. I'm not a criminal. Frank, you have been watching way too much cable TV."

"Well," said Frank, "as far as I am concerned, as long as your work is done, and you are readily accessible, I am putting you on a self-controlled schedule. You set your hours as long as your work gets done, and I am also giving you a raise."

"Wow," said Connor. "Thanks Frank. I won't let you down. I will not let this be a problem for you."

Frank continued, "This stays between you and me. In return, I don't want any trouble showing up here at the office. I have had to assure people that there will be no problems. In fact, some people are just flat out scared of you now. I need your assurance that all will be well."

"Consider it done," responded Connor. "You can rest easy. I will make sure that everyone feels safe here. Thanks again."

Connor left Frank's office and went into the men's room to change his clothes as was his normal after work practice. He folded his work clothes neatly into his duffle bag and took out his t-shirt and jeans, put them on, and took his vest out of the bag. He carried his vest from the men's room, through the office, and put it on outside while he stood next to his bike.

As he threw his colors on his back, he noticed three of the female office employees watching him through the window with varying looks of fear and attraction on their faces. As they watched him throw a leg over his bike and start the motor, they walked away from the window.

Connor began his ride to the shop from his office. That Friday was a beautiful Kansas day, with temperatures in the mid 70s, and not a cloud in the sky. The wind rushed through Connor's hair and the sun on his face was a welcome feeling from being cramped in his office. Connor felt that his first full day as a patched Libertine could not get any better, with a raise at work, a now open work schedule, and a pass from Julie to hang out with the club.

Connor arrived at Bill's shop and dismounted from his bike. Bill was standing outside his shop door, with a beer in his hand and his trademark cheap small cigar hanging out of his mouth. Bill's only company so far that day was his little dog, Chief, who was lying down outside on the asphalt taking in the sunny day as well.

"There's the cleanest patch in the club," remarked Bill about Connor's arrival. Bill made this reference to Connor's patch as still being shiny from its newness, since the other members of the club's patches were a bit worn due to the sun fading the original color and the wear of taking the vest on and off, not to mention some other activities that can cause premature patch wear.

Connor laughed at Bill's greeting and said, "Everyone had a clean patch once in their life, brother."

Bill replied, "So, what the hell are you doing here so early?"

"Well," responded Connor, "I decided to get the hell out of Dodge a bit early today and I don't really have shit to do. Julie's got more wedding shit that she is doing so I have a kitchen pass."

Connor and Bill spent the next few hours working on a few of Bill's projects around the shop, including an old basket case shovelhead that Bill had received as a gift from a current client. Over the past few months, Connor had been increasing his knowledge of working on motorcycles by watching and helping Bill with his work.

After a few hours of just Connor and Bill working together in the shop, they both looked up from the lift they were working from as a bike pulled up. The owner of the bike was Scott, the same hang-around that seemed to always be at the clubhouse. Scott noticed that Bill and Connor were at the lift by themselves, and although neither one of them were wearing their colors, Scott knew not to approach them without permission.

Scott waited for a few seconds until Bill called out to him from across the shop saying, "How you doing, Scott?"

Scott walked up to Connor and Bill and said, "I'm good. I'm doing real well. How are you guys doing?"

The three men exchanged pleasantries for a minute and then Bill handed Scott a $20 bill and said, "I buy, you fly."

Scott took the $20 bill and headed across the street to the convenience store to fetch beer. Connor had a nice feeling of relief, knowing that his trips across the street to fetch beer would now be few and far between as long as there was someone around other than a patched member.

As Scott made his way across the street, Bill looked at Connor and said, "So, what do you think about prospecting Scott?"

Connor was surprised that Bill was asking his opinion about this, but offered his solicited advice as he explained, "Well, if you ask me, Scott loves this club. He's been hanging around longer than I have and I know that he wants the tap. However, I'm not quite sure what he has to offer the club. The brothers didn't tap me because I'm a bad ass, which I'm not, and there seem to be plenty of bad asses wanting the tap. I don't have a single problem with him, but that's my take."

"That's interesting," responded Bill, "See, it's good to have smart mother fuckers like you around to over think this shit. If I tap him to prospect, will I have your vote at Church?"

Connor scratched his chin and responded, "You would have my vote, but I don't think that you will have a unanimous vote on Scott."

"And just why the fuck not?" asked Bill.

Connor replied, "I know that there is at least one member who feels that there is no need to bring in any more 'tough guys' so to speak, so you might hit a hurdle there."

"Who the fuck thinks that?" asked Bill.

"Well, since this wasn't really said to me in confidence, I guess I can tell you. It was Ratchet."

Bill laughed and shook his head, saying, "Fucking Ratchet. He doesn't know what the fuck he is thinking half of the time. Sometimes his head gets as fucked up as a nigger checkbook."

Bill and Connor laughed and realized that they now had to change the topic of conversation as Scott was making his way back into the shop with a cold case of beer in his hands. Scott placed the beer into the refrigerator and extracted three beers from the case. Scott carried the beer over to Bill and Connor and placed a beer in each one of their hands. The three men cracked open their beers and began to drink.

After a refreshing gulp was enjoyed by all, Bill broke the silence as he looked toward Connor and said, "Hey, brother, I need to go on a parts run. Can you watch the shop while I'm gone?"

Connor answered, "No problem, brother. I got it."

Bill guzzled down the rest of the beer that Scott had brought over to him and as he walked outside to get in his pickup truck, he stopped by the beer fridge to grab one for the road. Bill hopped into his truck and whistled at Chief to come along for the ride, who jumped up into the truck with Bill, and the both drove off.

Connor continued to drink his beer as he leaned against the lift where he had been working. This was the first time that Bill had left him in charge of the shop, but not the first time that Bill had left someone from the club in charge of the shop. Bill's parts runs usually only took 30 minutes, so Connor knew that he would not be away from Bill for long.

However, the fact that he was alone in the shop with Connor bothered him. Connor had spoken to Scott on several occasions, but it was either at the shop around several people or at the clubhouse during a club party. Connor knew that it was not his responsibility to entertain Scott and decided that he was just fine with standing in silence, drinking his beer and enjoying the nice weather, but Scott had every intention of talking.

Connor could tell that Scott was searching in his for something to break the ice and spark up a conversation. Scott was pacing around the shop and his eyes fell on Connor's vest as it hung next to the lift.

As Scott was looking at Connor's cut, he said, "Hey man. Congratulations again on patching into the club last night."

"Thanks man," responded Connor, as he realized that he was not going to be able to continue the silence, "it was one hell of a party."

"It sure was," said Scott, "I'm pretty sure that I am still a bit hung over from last night, but it was worth it. Hey, switching gears, I just want you to know if there is anything that I can do for you or the club, don't hesitate to give me a call."

"I appreciate that," responded Connor as he took another drink from his beer, wishing that his uncomfortable conversation would end, but Connor's mind took over as he responded and he wondered to himself if there was a real reason that Scott was there.

His curiosity overtaking him, Connor could not help himself but ask, "So, what brings you up to the shop today?"

Scott replied, "Nothing really. Just hanging out I guess."

The awkwardness began to grow as Connor knew that this parts run was going to turn out being one of the seemingly longest he had ever witness unless something happened. Connor decided to stand there in silence and enjoy his cold beer. He drank the beer a bit faster than he usually did and drained the final sip from the can.

As he lowered the empty can from his lips, and before he could move toward the fridge to obtain another, Scott spoke up with his hand outstretched as if motioning to take the empty from Connor, saying, "Here, let me have that. I will get you another."

"Thanks," replied Connor.

As Scott walked back over to Connor with a fresh cold beer in his hand, Ratchet and Cobbler pulled up outside the shop. Then, as they were dismounting from their bikes, Pepper pulled up right behind them, parked, and dismounted from their bikes. Connor felt a sense of relief that he no longer had to be at the shop alone with Scott.

The four club members exchanged their typical greetings as Scott watched. Connor kept an eye on Scott as he watched the members greet each other and noticed that Scott was not doing a very good job hiding the jealousy on his face. Scott glanced at Connor and noticed his stare, but not realizing why Connor was looking at him, he walked over to the refrigerator to grab a beer for each of the members who had just arrived.

Scott passed out the beers to the members as they finished their greetings. As the members all opened their beers, Bill arrived back at the shop with a brown cardboard box full of assorted motorcycle parts to complete repairs on the various motorcycles in his shop.

Bill exited his truck and looked over at Scott as he said, "Hey Scott, grab that box out of the back of my truck and take it into the shop."

Scott obeyed as he always did and took the box of parts into the shop. As he did, Bill joined the circle of club members outside his shop as he finished the beer that he took with him on his parts run.

Pepper then said, "So, I say we head to Bubba's when Bill closes up."

Everyone nodded in agreement.

Pepper continued, "Cool. Hey Rub, text the guys that aren't here and tell them that we are headed to Bubba's after Bill closes up."

Connor answered, "Will do" and proceeded to send the text as the other three members continued to drink their beer. Connor also added a note to the text of who was at the shop and invited them to come up there before they headed to Bubba's.

Connor then sent a text to Julie to inform her of what he was doing: "Going with the club to Bubba's for dinner and a few beers. See you later on tonight."

As the time drew near for Bill to close up shop, the whole club except Terry had shown up at the shop to ride over to Bubba's, and Connor had not received a response from Julie.

Chapter Sixteen – Friday Night at Bubba's

Friday night was always a good choice in nights to visit Bubba's, if you were into drinking, women, and live music. Bubba's was always going to deliver that on a Friday night, and Connor knew that and was looking forward to his arrival at Bubba's for a few reasons.

For one, Connor liked live music and since his introduction into the club, he had grown much fonder of drinking. Secondly, this would be the first opportunity for Connor to walk into an establishment with his brand new full patch on his back. And finally, Connor was getting to go somewhere with the club and not have to perform his prior prospect duties such as fetch the waitress, watch the bathroom, or constantly check on the motorcycles parked outside.

Bill closed the doors to the shop after he moved his bike outside and parked his truck inside. He walked into the retail portion of his shop and retrieved his colors from behind the counter, set the alarm and locked the door.

All of the members of the charter were there, except Terry. Terry had not shown up to the shop nor had he responded back to Connor's message. Connor figured that Terry would just meet the club members at Bubba's, and Connor also knew that Terry could be a little bit flaky at times and could possibly be passed out as his house from drinking by himself.

The members began to fire their bikes to life, one by one, similar to the beginning of a car race. The roar of so many loud Harley Davidson motorcycles was deafening. The pack of bikers walked their bikes backwards to the street and one by one lit up the throttle as they roared down the street toward Bubba's, which was only about a 5 minute ride from Bill's shop. As Connor was the newest member of the club, he was the last bike in the pack, at least of the members.

Connor looked in his rearview mirror and noticed that Scott was following about 5 bike lengths behind the pack. Connor thought to himself that he was not surprised that Scott was tagging along. After all, Bubba's was a public place and the Libertines were not going to stand at the door and bounce people out that they didn't invite.

The club arrived at Bubba's are all parked their bikes together, backing them it adjacent to the building as was their custom. As they all dismounted, Scott pulled into the parking lot and parked his bike a few parking spaces away from the club, as he knew not to park next to them. There was also 4 motorcycles parked a few spots away from the club.

The club walked into the bar single file straight passed the bouncer, who did not bother to check their IDs or accept a cover charge from any of them. However, as Scott walked in behind the club, he was subject to the cover charge, as well as a check of his ID.

The club found themselves a table and began to sit down. Bill motioned to Scott to join them. Before anyone could get relaxed, a waitress came over with beer bottles for all of the members, as well as Scott.

She said, "This round is on me," as she smiled at everyone and gently rubbed her hand on Pepper's neck, which once again was typical.

As each member took their first drink from their respective bottle of beer, Jackal spoke up, saying, "Hey Rub, where the hell is Big T at?"

Connor responded, "I don't have a clue. I sent him the message and haven't heard from him."

"Maybe you should call him," suggested Jackal.

"Okay," responded Connor as he stood up from the table and began to walk outside. There was no way for Connor to hear due to the volume of the band getting ready to begin their set.

"Scott," said Bill, "go outside and watch his back."

Scott followed Bill's instructions and followed Connor outside. Connor took his phone out and called Terry. The phone rang and rang and finally went to Terry's voicemail. Connor then sent another text to Terry: "Hey Bro. Where the fuck are you? Call me or text me." Connor went back inside and Scott followed.

Connor sat back down at the table and shared the news, "Well, no answer. I sent him another text."

Knuckles said, "Big T is probably getting him some or he is passed out drunk. After all, it is Friday."

Everyone shared a laugh at Terry's expense. The club sat at their table enjoying their beer and all of the members could tell that Scott was enjoying his time hanging out with the club. As they sat, Connor noticed that there were 4 men sitting a few tables over from them who obviously were the owners of the 4 bikes outside due to their apparel. As far as Connor could tell, no one else had seemed to pay any attention to them or acknowledge their presence.

One of the 4 men caught Connor's eye as he was glancing over at them. The man made eye contact with Connor and raised his beer bottle into the air as to offer a toast to Connor from across the room. Connor returned the gesture.

The man arose to his feet and approached the table of Libertines. He introduced himself to the club and explained that the bikes outside belonged to him and his friends. Connor seemed to be the only one of the club that was interested in the man's conversation, as the rest of the club seemed to basically ignore him.

Connor said, "Good deal, man. Nice to meet you."

The man, who said his name was Andy, said, "I just wanted to come over here and say hello. Your next round is on me. You fellas have a good evening," and then he retired back to his friends.

The band that was playing that night was called "The Gamblers" and played a mix of southern rock and outlaw style county music, which was a favorite of all of the members of the club except Connor, who was beginning to like that form of music due to being surrounded by it at nearly every club function or outing. The Gamblers had been playing at Bubba's every other Friday for the last few months and began to grow a descent size following, so there were quite a few people in Bubba's that night.

The next round of beer came, as promised, from the 4 men at the table from across the room. The club, along with Scott, enjoyed their second round of free beer. Connor wondered to himself if they would finally have to start paying after this round, or if there would be another free round coming. Connor was hoping for a free round.

Connor felt that the night was damn near perfect. There was great music, cold beer, and he was hanging out with his club. The only thing missing was Terry, but Connor decided that he would not let Terry's absence get to him. Connor figured that if Terry wasn't going to call him back or return his texts that he was in fact busy, so Connor let it slide.

After the second round of beer had been consumed, the waitress brought a third round to the table. Behind her was the manager of Bubba's, who explained to the club that the rest of the night their beers were on the house. The manager knew that as long as they were in the bar, there would not be any trouble out of anyone, and if for some odd reason trouble came up, there were not any others that the manager would rather have in there than the Libertines.

Three more rounds of beers passed through the members and the band finished their set. Bubba's was now clearing out with the exception of a few people who were regulars sitting at the bar and the club, along with Scott.

Jackal stood up from the table and said, "Well guys, I'm tired and old. It's time for me to go home."

Knuckles, Cobbler, and Ratchet stood up along with Jackal and all seemed to be in agreement. Seeing this, everyone else stood up from the table as well. Pepper walked over and thanked the waitress for bringing the club their beer as only Pepper could, with a hug and a hand on the waitress' ass.

Everyone from the club, and Scott, walked outside and said their goodbyes. They all got on their bikes and rode off in their separate ways.

As Connor rode, he rounded the corner and headed onto his street. He approached his house and noticed that there was a motorcycle parked in his driveway. Upon arriving closer, he recognized the motorcycle as Terry's bike and saw Terry sitting on his front porch on the ground right next to the door of Connor's house.

Connor pulled into the driveway as he pushed the button for his garage door opener and pulled his bike into the garage. After shutting his bike down, Connor walked back outside to meet Terry, who had stood up from his prior resting place on the porch and met Connor on his sidewalk in front of his house.

Terry then said, "Man, where have you been? I have been waiting here forever."

Connor replied, "I called you and texted you. You never got back to me."

"That figures," said Terry, "my stupid piece of shit phone broke today. I'm going to have to go get a new one tomorrow I guess."

Connor said, "That's a relief. We were all hanging out at Bubba's and I was a bit concerned about you. I'm glad to see you are ok."

Terry replied, "Yeah, I'm ok, but I have a problem. Actually, we have a problem, I think."

"Well, Terry," said Connor, "What's the problem?"

"It goes like this. See," continued Terry, "I took the day off of work today and I met Sampson up in Missouri. He wanted some help working on his bike and it was a nice day so I told him I would come up there.

"We were working on the bike and shit and we got to talking about the club and he told me that I needed to get a message to the charter down here. It seems that the charter up there in Missouri is having problems with the police, and maybe even the fucking Feds. Since they have some members who are doing some illegal shit, they are trying to pin it on the whole club.

"Some government asshole up there has a hard on for motorcycle clubs. It looks like the state of Missouri is going to try and ban motorcycle clubs."

Connor, who was extremely surprised, said, "They can't do that. There's no way it will pass."

Terry continued, "Well, apparently all of this has been flying under the public radar until today, when a law passed that allows police to profile anyone who belongs to an organization or club that a convicted felon belongs to.

"Basically, if I got caught doing something and was convicted, then the cops have the right to arrest you and search your house and shit without getting a warrant."

"Terry," said Connor, "there's no fucking way that has happened."

"I wish I was lying to you," continued Terry, "but I'm not. The charter in Missouri is nervous because they have some brothers in lockup right now and they think the cops are going to come busting into their clubhouse and their homes any day now."

"Well," answered Connor, "I guess I better call Jackal."

Chapter Seventeen – Bad News

Connor hung up the phone with Jackal. In keeping with the rules of the club, Connor had not gotten into details about Terry's visit or exactly what had been said. Connor never really understood that rule from the beginning since he had no reason to believe that his phone was tapped, and with the exception of a few vigilante type "crimes," Connor felt that the club really had nothing to hide.

Jackal told Connor that he would get in contact with some of the Missouri charters as well as the club's charter in Topeka, which had some government ties. Connor thought to himself that this was the absolute worst time to get into this club. He knew that there were quite a few individuals that had anywhere from a questionable to a shady past but it didn't quite seem to him like there were any in his charter, as far as he knew.

Connor took the second to last beer from the 12 pack that Terry had sitting on his porch and Terry took out the last one. The only thing they could do was wait for a return phone call from Jackal. The two finished their beer and decided to part ways for the night. Connor told Terry that if he heard from Jackal and there was something that Terry needed to do, he would go to Terry's house.

Terry fired up his bike and began his journey home as Connor went inside. Even though it had become quite common over the last few months of Connor coming home alone, he had not gotten used to it. He would have much rather walked into the house to find Julie sitting on the couch watching TV or talking on the phone as he was more used to.

Connor jumped in the shower and washed the cigarette smoke smell off of him from being at Bubba's. After his refreshing shower, he went back into the living room and decided to turn on the TV and watch something as he waited for Julie to come home. Connor changed the channel over to the cable sports channel and was watching the daily highlights when he decided to text Julie to let her know that he was home.

Several minutes passed and there was no return text from Julie. Connor felt that was odd, as she usually had her phone very close to her, but Connor just figured she might be on the phone or wherever they decided to go was a bit loud and she didn't hear her phone go off.

The highlight show finished up and Connor felt his eyelids getting heavier and heavier and was becoming more and more unable to fight off the need to fall asleep. He debated with himself if he would just lie down on the couch or go on to bed. However, before he could come to that conclusion, he heard the garage door open. Julie was home.

Julie came walking into the house talking on her phone, presumably to Lisa, as she finished her conversation.

Connor looked up at Julie and said, "Hey babe. How was your night?"

"It was pretty uneventful. Just the girls talking about the wedding stuff."

Connor replied, "Don't you ever get sick of talking about Lisa's wedding? All of the days and nights that you two are together, I would have thought that all this stuff was figured out by now."

Julie retorted, "Don't you ever get sick of your dumb friends and their motorcycles?"

Julie always had a way to flip any question of Connor's back on him. Rather than starting a fight, Connor decided to switch around his line of conversation.

"So," continued Connor, "where did you guys end up going?"

"We were at Lisa's place most of the night, and then we decided to go have a drink at Turnover's."

Connor didn't care too much for Turnover's. Turnover's was a fancy yuppie bar in town that was typical of the pretty boy type bar where everyone wore expensive clothes and tried feverishly to impress everyone. As an added characteristic of dislike, Turnover's had quite a restrictive dress code, part of which would not allow motorcycle club members to wear their colors inside.

"Glad you went there and not me," said Connor with a slightly harsh tone in his voice.

"I just like the drinks there and they don't allow smoking inside so I don't come home smelling the same way you do when you go out with your loser friends."

Connor then asked, "Why do you have to be that way?"

Julie answered, "I'm not being any way. You are just being a little too sensitive. I guess you can dish it but not take it."

After this comment, Julie headed into the bedroom. Connor sat on the couch a bit stunned, but didn't think too much into it for two reasons. For one, he was tired and bordering on drunk. Secondly, Connor figured that he would rather have Julie hang out with her friends in a seemingly safe bar such as Turnover's rather than some of the rough hole in the wall type pubs that he frequented with the club.

Connor arose from the couch and headed into the bedroom where he found Julie had already made her way into the bed and was reading a magazine. Connor crawled into bed and rolled onto his side, facing away from Julie, and faded off to sleep.

\#

The next morning Connor awoke to the sunlight peeking through the blinds. As his eyes made focus on the alarm clock, he realized that it was after 10:00 in the morning. He reached up and rubbed his eyes to begin the awakening process. He swung his legs from under the covers and sat up on the side of the bed.

"Hey babe. What do you want to do today?" asked Connor as he stretched his arms above his head.

Silence filled the room. Connor turned around to look and see if Julie was still asleep and noticed that she wasn't in the bed. Julie was not one to usually sleep in so Connor hoped that she was in the kitchen or the living room. Connor wandered out into the living room and did not find Julie. He then wandered into the kitchen and once again did not find Julie.

"Julie!" yelled Connor almost at the top of his lungs. He waited, and heard no response. Connor walked back into the bedroom and noticed that both her cell phone was removed from the charger and her purse was missing from the nightstand.

Connor walked over and removed his phone from the charger and called Julie.

After a few rings, Julie answered, "Hello."

"Where are you at?" asked Connor.

"I have some things that I need to do this morning. I will be back around noon."

Connor replied, "Rather than come home, why don't we meet somewhere for lunch?"

"Ok," responded Julie, "Where do you want to go?"

"You pick," replied Connor.

"How about the little café downtown?" suggested Julie.

"Sounds good to me. I will see you there at noon."

Connor hung up the phone and went through his normal morning ritual of getting ready. Seeing that it was now only 10:30 and knowing he had a little over an hour to kill, he decided that he would visit Bill at the bike shop.

Connor hopped on his bike and rode down to the shop. There were no bikes parked outside that morning. Not to his surprise, Bill was all alone in the shop. Connor figured that everyone else from the club was still sleeping off the booze from the night before.

Connor walked into the shop to find Bill wrenching on a bike with Chief lying down at his feet, chewing on a bone. Connor reached down to pet the dog and then greeted Bill.

Bill said, "You are here kind of early aren't you?"

"Yeah," answered Connor. "I'm meeting the ol' lady for lunch around noon and I have an hour to kill so I figured that I would come up here and bullshit with you a bit."

One of Connor's favorite activities now was what he called "Bullshitting with Bill," which was basically going to the shop and drinking beer while Bill and him told jokes and Connor would every once in a while help Bill with bike repairs.

While Bill was continuing his work on the bike he was repairing, Connor explained to him the conversation that he and Terry had the night before. Bill appeared to be perplexed at the notion just as Connor was.

After Connor had completed his explanation, Bill asked, "So, smart guy, what do we do from here?"

Connor replied, "I guess this is something that we are going to have to talk about at Church on Thursday."

"No shit Sherlock," responded Bill, "but I think we had better get some talking going before Thursday. My ass was going to be taking off work early today to go to my cabin and do a little bit of gut stuffing, but I guess that might get called off."

Bill had a cabin in the woods about an hour's ride from his shop as a nice little getaway for him and his wife. The club usually would go camping there once or twice a year, but it was typically a private retreat for Bill to unwind and be alone, since his shop tended to always be full of people watching him work all of the time.

Bill then told Connor, "I want you to send a text message to everyone to be here at the shop around 2:00 so we can figure out what we need to do."

Connor complied and sent a text message to everyone. Connor then remembered that Terry's phone had most likely not been replaced. Connor explained to Bill the situation about Terry's phone and said his farewell. Connor then headed over to Terry's house to inform him of the 2:00 meeting at Bill's shop.

Time was now running short for Connor and he did not want to miss his lunch date with Julie. After a brief conversation with Terry, he headed to the café for lunch. Connor pulled up outside the café with just a few minutes to spare. He thought to himself that he had gone from having a bunch of time to kill to almost being late.

Connor walked inside the café and looked around but did not see Julie anywhere. He asked the hostess for a table for two and explained that his wife would be arriving shortly and that he would wait at the table for her. The hostess agreed to seat Connor without Julie.

Shortly after noon, Connor saw Julie walk into the restaurant, and as almost always, she was talking on her cell phone. She finished her conversation right as she approached the table where Connor was sitting.

The couple had a nice lunch together. Connor spent the entire time listening to Julie go on and on about the wedding while he ate his soup and sandwich. Connor did find himself enjoying his time with Julie, even if it was only over a quick lunch and having to listen to more about Lisa. When Julie finally gave Connor a chance to switch the subject, he did, informing Julie that he had to return to Bill's shop to take care of some club business. Julie didn't seem to mind and said that she had some errands to run anyway and told Connor that he could take his time.

The couple finished their lunch and departed upon their separate ways. This sudden shift in Julie's attitude toward the club made Connor quite confused as to how to accept it all. For most of their relationship, Julie had basically told Connor what he could do, when he could do it, and who he could do it with. Now, Julie was allowing Connor to do pretty much whatever he wanted, whenever he wanted, and with whomever he wanted to do it with, which typically was members of the club.

Connor watched as Julie entered her vehicle, put her seatbelt on, started the engine, and very Julie-like, dialed her cell phone and began a conversation. Meanwhile, Connor mounted his bike, started the motor allowing it to warm up for a few minutes while he checked his phone for the time and noticed that the meet up time at the shop was a little less than an hour away.

Connor then watched Julie drive away. He rocked his bike up off of the kickstand and headed toward Bill's shop. As he pulled up, he noticed that there were still no visitors to the shop, which Connor thought was odd since it was a Saturday and that was when most of the shop hang-arounds would come up to the shop on their day off and basically play biker.

Now that Connor was a patched member of the club, he was looking forward to the shop hang-arounds being there to see him and basically see to his every need, offering him a service similar to a servant in the court of a king. After all, the Libertines were the kings of the city in a certain way.

Connor walked into the shop and found Bill still working on the same motorcycle that he had been wrenching on before, and saw Chief was fast asleep, finally finishing his bone. As the time of the called meeting approached, bikes from the club started to appear one by one outside Bill's shop. Upon the arrival of Jackal, who was the last member of the charter to arrive, Bill walked over to the door and pulled it closed so that the club would be uninterrupted for their impromptu meeting.

Jackal began, "I'm sure all of you know by now a little bit of what is going on. I made a ride up to Missouri this morning with Cobbler and we both heard from the horse's mouth that this shit is true. We all know that the governor of Missouri is good buddies with our governor here, so our primary concern is stopping this bullshit law from passing in Kansas. We already have a message out to the puppet clubs to start writing letters to the government saying that they oppose this, but I think it's not going to work this time.

"So, believe it or not, that's the good news and now, the bad news. Squeaky over in the Topeka chapter told me that there is someone who is feeding information direct to the governor's office from our charter. He doesn't know who it is, and he said that it is definitely not a member, but it is someone who is close to a member. We need to be careful right now and keep our mouths shut around anyone who doesn't have a patch on their back. I don't have a fucking clue where to begin in finding out who this person is, and I am not blaming anyone in this room. You guys just need to be careful, and this is a reminder for all of you, don't fucking talk about any club business around anyone outside the club."

Everyone from the club nodded their heads in acknowledgment and collectively started thinking whether or not it was them who had the possible rat in their presence. Connor felt he was completely in the clear since he had only been patched in a very short while and never said anything about the club. Most of the club members suspected that it was probably Pepper who tended to have so many girlfriends it was hard to keep track of.

Bill interjected, "You boys need to start thinking about who the fuck this person could be that would have some kind of connection to the state. We don't need any heat on this chapter. Things are nice and quiet and that's the way that I like it, nice and fucking quiet, unless I'm banging my ol' lady, then I tend to get loud."

The club all laughed, but at the same time realized that Bill was right. Things have been quiet and there had been no entanglements with law enforcement since before Connor became a prospect, and with their new endeavor waiting on the horizon, they needed to stay squeaky clean.

Jackal then concluded, "We have one more quick item of business to discuss, and I don't want to wait for Church. I have already spoken to Knuckles about this, and he is in agreement with me. Knuckles would like to step down from the office of secretary. He said he just doesn't have the time or the patience to do it, and now that we have a new member, who I think would make a good secretary; I think we need to make Rub our secretary. Anyone opposed?"

Connor stood there in a bit of shock. Jackal had not run this past him and Connor had no idea how to be the club secretary. Before Connor could even respond to Jackal's idea and try and talk him out of it, Jackal beat him to the punch.

"Done," said Jackal. "Congratulations Rub. You're the fucking secretary."

"Better you than me," responded Knuckles.

Everyone patted Connor on the back and offered their congratulations, which sounded more like condolences. Connor began to worry about being able to fulfill this position, but figured that if he had the support of Jackal, he had the support of the club.

Bill walked over to the shop door and opened it back up. The sunlight filled the shop and hurt everyone's eyes as they had been standing is relative darkness during the meeting in Bill's shop, which only had one fluorescent light fixture burning at the time. The members repaired to the beer fridge and retrieved a beer each and began talking about things of a much lighter nature, except Jackal, who motioned Connor to follow him outside.

Jackal and Connor stood by themselves outside and Jackal began to explain to Connor his new duties, saying "Ok, you need to swing by the clubhouse a bit early at every meeting. I will meet with you before Church so we can go over what needs to be talked about. You will take down the minutes and they need to stay at the clubhouse. Got it?"

"Got it," responded Connor, "and what else do I need to do?"

"Well," explained Jackal, "you will figure it out as you go along. Just make sure that shit runs smoothly and you will do fine."

Jackal handed Connor a piece of paper and continued, "Here is the phone number for the secretary of the Topeka chapter. His name is Butter. You might want to set up a time to meet with him. He is a damn good secretary and knows his shit. He will be able to guide you."

Jackal hopped on his bike and left as it was his common practice not to hang out at Bill's shop for very long. Connor took out his cell phone and stored Butter's number into his contact list. Connor then made a phone call to Butter and explained to him about his sudden rise to the office of secretary and made arrangements to meet with Butter in a couple of hours to have a sit down and discuss how to be a good secretary.

Connor then went back inside the shop and found Terry, who was wandering around drinking his beer, and said to him, "Hey man, feel like making a quick ride to Topeka to talk to Butter?"

Terry replied, "Sounds good to me. I ain't got shit to do today."

Chapter Eighteen - Topeka

Connor and Terry hopped on their bikes and began to head towards Topeka. Connor had discussed with Butter that he wanted to meet somewhere that they could talk club business openly and Butter said that the best place for that to take place would be the Topeka charter's clubhouse. Terry knew the way to the Topeka clubhouse so Connor was able to lean back in his seat, follow beside Terry, and enjoy the ride.

Connor was a little bit excited to see another charter's clubhouse as he had only been inside his home charter's clubhouse and was curious to see what another clubhouse would look like. He wondered if it would be just like his or if it would appear completely different.

The ride to Topeka didn't take the two club members long to get there and the ride turned out to be fairly uneventful. The usual looks came from their one gasoline stop that they made from the patrons at the convenience store, but no comments and no drama. The pair rolled into Topeka and made their way to the clubhouse with a few minutes to spare, where they found Butter standing outside, smoking a cigarette and holding a beer.

Butter introduced himself to Connor and greeted Terry as they already had met. The three men walked inside the Topeka clubhouse, which was a dilapidated building in the industrial part of town that stood alone. No fence, no large parking area or party zone as Connor's home chapter had. The inside was dismal and dark, with old cloth furniture covered in beer stains and cigarette burns. Connor was highly disappointed; as it appeared that the Topeka chapter had not cleaned their clubhouse in about 10 years.

Butter sat down at a table in the center of the room after retrieving a beer for Terry and Connor as they pulled up a chair and joined Butter.

Butter began the conversation, saying, "Well, you drug me down here Rub, what do you want to know?"

Connor replied, "Apparently I am the new secretary of my charter and I have been told that you are the man to talk to about being a good secretary."

Butter laughed and replied, "That's a good one. Sounds to me like Jackal thinks a bit more about me than he really should. It's not fucking rocket science, but I will tell you that you have to keep good records. You never know when you are at Church and someone says something about a decision that was made forever ago and everyone disagrees on what was decided. That shit you need to have right there at your fingertips.

"You have also got to keep track of who has paid their dues or not, and make sure you keep that up. It will fall back on you if someone doesn't and they don't know.

"The main thing is you have to keep all of this shit where no one else is going to be able to see it, just in case there is some shit in there that we don't want anyone reading. You know what I mean?"

Connor replied, "Yeah, that makes sense to me," while it didn't really make any sense to Connor at all. There had not been anything discussed at Church so far that Connor didn't feel like he couldn't tell anyone, but maybe, he thought, that was going to change.

Butter continued, "It's pretty simple, man. I wish I would have known that this was the club business you wanted to talk about. We could have done this over the phone and saved you two a trip over here."

Connor said, "It's no biggie. Besides, Big T didn't have anything to do today, and my day was fairly open. It was kind of nice to get out for a ride, you know?"

Butter responded, "Yeah, I heard that. So, while we are talking, what's up with this Missouri shit I'm hearing about?"

Connor explained the situation to Butter. Butter sat in amazement that something like this could even possibly happen. After Connor's explanation, Butter sat in silence, as if he was taking everything in. Butter reached into the pocket of his colors and retrieved a cigarette, which he put up to his mouth and lit. After taking a large drag, he tilted his head back and blew a smoke ring above his head and shortly after released the rest of the smoke from his lungs.

He then looked at Connor and said, "So do you guys have any idea on who the informant in your charter might be?"

Connor and Terry were taken aback by this question. Connor had not made mention about this in his explanation to Butter.

"Since you brought it up," responded Connor, "no. We don't have any idea. We know it's someone connected to one of us, but no one seems to have a clue."

Butter explained, "Well, I will tell you what I have heard, which I don't know whether or not this is true, but apparently it is someone's ol' lady or side project that has a friend in the fucking governor's office."

Connor looked Butter straight in the eye and said, "You have got to be shitting me?"

"No bullshit. I don't know anything about this chick, but the story around the campfire is that someone's chick is getting friendly with some asshole in the governor's office. Problem is, no one has a clue who in the governor's office has the info. We have a few of our boys from the support club keeping an eye on the local dudes here."

Connor asked, "How did you find this out?"

Butters answered, "We have a friend of the club in the governor's office also. He was the one that brought us that info, but he doesn't know who in the office is getting the info. The governor's office knows that we have friends in high places, so they are being cautious. This bullshit that is going on in Missouri is most likely going to come over here as well, and we are pissed about it. The two governor douche-bags are like Frick and fucking Frack man. One dipshit does something and the other follows. With the elections coming up next year, the Missouri governor is looking to really make a name for himself so he can be the president. Can you just imagine if this shit goes nationwide and the whole MC world gets put underground?"

Connor replied, "There is no way that would ever, ever happen. No way."

"Don't be too sure," replied Butter, "I have seen some strange shit come down the pipe in my day and I just don't get too surprised about anything I hear anymore."

"I guess," said Connor as he finished his beer. "Well, Butter, thanks for the advice. I guess we need to start heading back."

"Hey," said Butter, "anytime. Look, if you have a question about secretary shit, just call me. As long as it's not specific to club business, we should be fine, especially if it is just some general book type question."

"I will, and thanks again."

Connor and Terry walked outside the clubhouse and Connor breathed in a deep breath of fresh air, which he had been looking forward to. Connor looked at his phone to see what time it was and calculated in his head how long it would take him and what time it would be when he arrived back to his home turf.

Connor and Terry mounted their bikes and hit the road. The sun had begun its path into the western sky and the day was beginning to be much warmer than when they arrived. Connor followed beside Terry on the ride back, taking in all of the scenery along the way. The trip back into town was just as uneventful as the trip to Topeka and Terry and Connor arrived back into town fairly close to the estimated schedule that Connor had figured in his mind.

As the two pulled into town, they arrived at a stop light, where Terry turned to Connor and said, "Let's go by Bubba's and grab a beer. You game?"

Connor thought for a second, and realized just how thirsty he was, and said, "That sounds like a plan to me, bro."

The two bikers made their way through the town to Bubba's, where they noticed that Pepper and Knuckle's bikes were parked. Terry and Connor parked their bikes next to Pepper and Knuckle's bikes and walked into Bubba's, where they found the two club members sitting at a table next to the bar.

The four club members greeted each other and Terry and Connor took a seat at the table where Knuckles and Pepper were sitting. A waitress who was unfamiliar to Connor brought Terry and Connor a beer each along with a refill for Knuckles and Pepper.

After clanking their beer glasses together, and after a quick gulp of beer, Pepper broke the silence and asked, "So, how was Topeka?"

Terry replied, "Well, Connor met with Butter up there and he told us some interesting shit. Turns out, they have someone in the governor's office who confirmed the shit that Jackal told us this morning. So I guess now we have to figure out who it is."

Connor added, "Yeah, and that's going to be tough as far as I am concerned. I don't think any one of us has done it on purpose."

Everyone nodded in agreement as they sat in a collective pondering, trying to figure out not only who could be the culprit, but if the culprit was doing this by accident or on purpose. Terry, Knuckles, and Pepper all had looks on their faces as if they were trying to make sure in their own minds that they were not the guilty party. Connor was the only one at the table that felt safe in knowing that it couldn't be Julie, and the only other girl that had any connection to him was that tart, Sally, whom Connor had not done anything with and definitely had not said anything to, so he satisfied himself that he was in the clear.

As the other three club members sat in their deep thought, Connor took his cell phone out of his pocket and sent a text to Julie: "Having a few beers with the club. What are you doing?"

After a minute or so, a response came back from Julie which read: "At home, fixing to go over to Lisa's. Be home late. Have fun. Don't get drunk."

Connor thought, "Another kitchen pass," as he put his cell phone back into his pocket.

He then leaned over to Terry and said, "Well, it looks like the ol' lady is doing more wedding shit with her friend, so I got me a kitchen pass. What's your plan for this evening?"

Terry replied, "Man, I ain't got shit to do. Looks like I'm drinking beer with you."

Connor then turned to the table and spoke to Knuckles and Pepper saying, "You two got anything going on tonight or are you up for a beer run?"

The club tended to go on what they called "Beer Runs" a few times a week. Basically, a beer run was going from bar to bar, drinking a few beers at each bar, so as to make a presence around town that the Libertines were here and that they were watching. To most citizens in the town, they welcomed them due to the fact that the only trouble that ever arose with the club being around was not started by the club, but it was always finished by the club.

Knuckles and Pepper nodded their heads as if to affirm that they were in on doing a beer run. Connor figured that he would invite Ratchet and Nutcase to go along as well. He sent a text to both of them informing them to meet the rest of the club at Bubba's and upon their arrival they would head out and hit the town. Ratchet responded to Connor's text message fairly quickly and said he would be there in about 30 minutes. Nutcase had yet to respond.

As promised, after 30 minutes, Ratchet came strolling into Bubba's, announcing his entrance to the club members with his usual, "What's Happening?" greeting. Although, to Connor's disappointment, he was followed along by Scott.

Connor thought this was a bit unusual. He had determined in his own mind that if someone from the club was not going to be in favor of Scott prospecting, it would be Ratchet, and now in walked Scott following behind Ratchet, and it was obvious that they had ridden to Bubba's together.

After Ratchet and Scott took their seats at the table, Knuckles spoke up, "Well, since you guys just got here, let's have one more and move on to the next stop."

The waitress brought every member another beer and within a few minutes the beer was consumed. As was typical, the club attempted to pay the tab and was refused by the management. Connor loved this part about being in the club. Even though his alcohol intake had more than tripled since he became a part of this group of bikers, his monetary expenditure on beer had dwindled down to almost nothing.

The club filed out of Bubba's and had decided to go just a few miles down the road to another tavern. Everyone hopped on their bikes and fired them up. The roar of all of the motors could be heard inside Bubba's and a few of the patrons peered outside the window to watch the club roll away.

As they made their way onto the main thoroughfare of the town, they approached an intersection, complete with a stop light. Upon their approach, they noticed several police cruisers with their red and blue lights flashing, a fire truck, and an ambulance. It was obvious that there had been an accident. The members put their kickstands down and sat up off of the seats of their bikes to catch a glimpse of what was in front of them.

It was at this moment when Connor noticed a horrific site. He rubbed his eyes and looked again; just to be sure that he was not imagining something. Unfortunately, Connor's eyes were not playing tricks on him and he was not witnessing a mirage.

Chapter Nineteen – Protected Left

As Connor began to realize what he was witnessing, so did the rest of the members of the club. In the middle of the intersection were the remains of what was once a motorcycle. The police had a man in custody, complete with his hands cuffed behind his back and was sitting on the edge of the curb on the opposite side of the intersection from the club. However, the rider of the motorcycle was nowhere to be found. The club in almost perfect unison shut their bikes down, dismounted, and began to approach the scene of the accident.

Ratchet turned to Scott and said, "Stay here and watch the bikes. If the cops come and say we got to move them, you tell them to come talk to us."

Scott nodded his head and the 5 men walked toward the remains of the smashed up Harley-Davidson.

"Oh my God!" exclaimed Pepper, "That's Nutcase's bike!"

It was at that moment that Connor looked across the intersection and saw a body lying in the grass adjacent to the intersection face down and plain as day the Libertine colors on the body's back. The body was not moving and none of the paramedics seemed to be doing anything to assist the injured man.

The members of the club walked past the police on the scene, who realized that there was nothing that the police were going to be able to do to stop the club members from attending to their fallen brother. The club members approached the body and all at once saw the bloody mess of the remains of Nutcase. It was evident that he had been thrown violently from his bike.

Knuckles and Pepper began to cry and Ratchet followed within seconds. Terry fought to hold back tears a bit longer, but was quickly consumed with grief and lost it as well. Connor held himself together, as he did feel the loss, but had not became all that close with Nutcase, so it was easier for him.

Connor decided to call Jackal and inform him of the incident.

Jackal answered, "Dammit Rub, you better not be in trouble, cause my ass is in bed."

Connor responded, "Sorry Pres, I got some bad news. Nutcase was in a bike wreck down the way from Bubba's. It looks like it wasn't his fault, but that doesn't really matter. Nutcase is dead."

Silence filled the air between the two club member's phones as Connor awaited a response from Jackal, which never came. Jackal simply hung the phone up on the other end. Connor then made a similar call to Bill, and the exact same thing happened. Bill hung up on Connor after hearing the news.

After these two brief phone calls, Connor decided not to call Cobbler and attend to the situation at hand. Knuckles had made his way to one of the police officers standing by a fire truck and it was apparent that Knuckles was determining what exactly had happened. After a few minutes of what to Connor appeared to be a negotiation of some sort, Knuckles returned to the semi-circle of club members who were standing over the tattered remains of their brother.

Knuckles said, "Brothers, it was like this. According to some witnesses, Nutcase was stopped in the left hand turn lane waiting on the green arrow. He got the arrow and started around the intersection when that asshole over there in handcuffs came flying through the intersection, running the red light, and creamed him. And if that ain't bad enough, that dumb mother fucker over there is drunk. The cops are arresting him for drunk driving right now."

The entire circle of men turned and watched as a police officer placed the intoxicated man into the back of a squad car and closed the door. The intoxicated man was looking through the windshield of the squad car at the club members as they stared him down. It didn't take long for the drunk to realize now that his vehicle had hurt one of the members of the Libertines.

At this point, Knuckles lost control. In a full sprint to rival the speed of Carl Lewis, Knuckles ran furiously toward the patrol car housing the drunk. Before anyone could react, Knuckles was pounding on the window of the squad car in hopes of trying to get his hands on the man in the back seat. The drunk, who was safely inside the steel cage of the back seat of the squad car, urinated in his pants in total fear of the crazy biker pounding away on the car.

It took about 10 seconds for three police officers to finally pull Knuckles away from the squad car and subdue him. After this incident, a police officer entered the squad car and took the drunk away to jail, which in this case was clearly safer for him than at the scene of the crime.

After this brief display, the sound of a motorcycle was heard pulling up. It was Jackal, who had Cobbler with him. The other members motioned to the pair to join them around where Nutcase's body lay. Jackal and Cobbler approached the scene and upon arriving, Cobbler reached down and removed Nutcase's colors from his lifeless body. The colors were soaked in blood from the massive injuries that Nutcase had sustained from the accident, but that did not seem to deter Cobbler from removing his colors.

Cobbler rolled the colors up into a tight roll and placed them under his left arm, similar to a man carrying a newspaper on his way to using the restroom. Jackal them embraced each member of the club, including Connor, telling each one that he loved them.

Jackal looked at Terry and said, "Is that Scott over there by the bikes?"

Terry responded with a nod acknowledging that it was.

Jackal then said, "Ok. Big T, take Scott with you and go to the clubhouse. Knuckles, you and Cobbler go by the store and get some food and take it back to the clubhouse. Pepper, you stay here and you follow the body to the morgue. Once it gets there, head over to the clubhouse. Rub, you head over to the funeral home with me.

The members of the club departed and went their separate ways as Jackal had instructed. Connor followed behind Jackal as best as he could, as Jackal was riding like he was literally going to a fire. The two arrived at Rodger's funeral home and went around back.

As the two shut down their bikes, the interior lights came on and a man in a white shirt and black slacks met them at the back door. The man's name was Charles Rodgers, and he was the owner of the funeral home, and also lived there.

Charles and Jackal shook hands, and it was evident that Charles and Jackal had known each other before. Jackal explained to Charles what had happened and Charles offered his condolences. Charles further explained to Jackal that he would do whatever the club needed and would take care of everything for the club so as to not bother them with the arrangements.

Jackal then looked at Connor and said, "Text Pepper and tell him that Rodger's is going to be picking up Nutcase from the morgue and as long as the body has made it there, he can head to the clubhouse."

Connor did as Jackal had asked. After the message was sent, Jackal then motioned to Connor that they were heading out. They mounted their bikes and it was evident that they were headed toward the clubhouse now.

Upon arrival at the clubhouse, Connor saw that Scott was standing outside the clubhouse door overlooking the motorcycles of the entire chapter, including Bill's. Connor and Jackal sat down around a table inside where the other member's were sitting in complete silence. The members were waiting for someone to break the silence, and then it was broken by Bill.

"I can't believe that this fucking happened. Who knows if Nutcase was even drinking, and I guess it doesn't matter, but this fucking pisses me off. What the fuck are we going to do about this?"

Jackal responded, "Calm down, brother. We are all mad right now, but this is not the time to make rash decisions. What we have to do is figure out the next move once we get our brother in the ground."

"Next move?" asked Connor.

Everyone turned toward Connor after he asked what he assumed was a simple question as Jackal responded, "Damn right next move. We can't let this shit go unpunished."

"I think there will be enough evidence to convict this asshole of at least intoxicated manslaughter," responded Connor, "so what is there for us to do?"

Jackal quickly retorted, "Let's put it this way, Rub. Say your ol' lady got creamed by this douche bag and was charged with some bullshit intoxicated manslaughter crime and got 5 years in jail and was out in 2, would you consider that justice?"

"When you put it that way," responded Connor, "I would have to say no."

"Then," continued Jackal, "it's all the same. We lost a brother tonight, and we are going to get some fucking justice for our family. Cobbler, I want you and Pepper to come up with something. Rub, I want you to monitor this shit and find out when and if he gets bail. You might need to call Jackson tomorrow. He will be able to help you."

"Who is Jackson?" asked Connor.

"Jackson is the club's attorney. He should be able to tell you when and if he gets out. Now, did we get the license plate?"

Cobbler responded, "Yeah, I wrote it down."

"Good deal," said Jackal. "Rub, give this to Jackson so he can get us an address."

Connor responded, "Shit, I can get that done. I just got to get to a computer."

"Well, then get it done. I want this fucker's address yesterday. Now, I'm going home and I'm going to try to get some sleep. I suggest that you guys do the same, but, before I go, a toast to Nutcase."

Everyone raised their beer bottles in toast to Nutcase and took a drink. As the members of the club finished their beer, they all slammed down the empty bottles and said their farewells to each other and departed in their own separate directions. Connor and Jackal were the last two remaining inside the clubhouse.

Connor noticed that Jackal appeared to be in a complete state of disarray. Connor had not had any meaningful conversations with Jackal and was used to either being told something to do or getting an explanation of what Connor did not understand. However, the unavoidable discomfort of Jackal made Connor want to attempt a fulfilling conversation with the president.

"Jackal," started Connor, "you ok?"

Jackal glanced at Connor with a blackening somber look and replied, "No. I'm not ok. In the last few days so much bad shit is coming down on this charter and this club that I can't believe any of it. So much is going to have to be put on hold.

"When we patched you in, you were patched in for a purpose, a single purpose. Most of us thought that you were a descent enough guy, but your sole purpose of being tapped has to be indefinitely put on hold, and that just plain fucking sucks.

"When I look at you, I have to know that you are prepared to get into some really bad shit, because with this death at our feet and the fucking dumbass government trying their bullshit out on us, we are going to have to get loud. No more quiet shit. I have to know, brother, are you going to be down for that?"

Connor swallowed a deep lump in his throat and thought about it for a split second. Thoughts of things he had seen, heard about, and even done for the club started to race through his mind. Connor realized the tight knit brotherhood that he was now a part of and that it was time to show that he was willing to continue to earn the right of wearing that patch on his back.

"Jackal, my brother, I will do whatever you and this club needs me to do. No questions asked."

"Well," responded Jackal, "that's good to know brother. I don't like being in the dark about anything. I will take you at your word as my brother that you are in this shit as deep as the rest of us."

"Consider me in," replied Connor.

"What I need for you to do is find out whatever you can on the douche bag that killed Nutcase. I want to know addresses, girlfriends, where he hangs out at, who he hangs out with. I need to know everything."

Connor answered, "I will get to work on that right away."

"Last thing, and then I'm going home," continued Jackal, "I need you to text everyone and tell them to be at the clubhouse in the morning."

Connor replied, "Will do."

Jackal left the clubhouse and Connor sat there alone for a while, gathering his thoughts about all of today's events and realizing that upon his awaking tomorrow, his life would change forever.

Chapter Twenty - Research

Connor returned home from the clubhouse late that night to find Julie fast asleep. Since he had some alone time on his hands, he took out his computer and began to do some research on the culprit of Nutcase's death.

Searching various sites on the Internet, Connor found his name and address, as well most of his personal information such as his date of birth and social security number. Connor began to make a profile of the guy on the computer so he could print it out and show it to everyone at the clubhouse in the morning.

From either the clicking of the keys on the computer's keyboard or the noise of the cheap ink jet printer producing Connor's document, the noise woke Julie up. She came into the room where Connor was using the computer.

"What are you doing?" asked Julie.

"Nothing, just getting some shit done for the club," replied Connor.

"Who is that?" Julie asked as she picked up one of the pieces of paper that Connor had printed.

"That guy just ran a red light tonight and killed one of the guys from the club."

"Who?" asked Julie.

"Nutcase," replied Connor, knowing that Julie had no real idea who anyone was with the exception of Terry.

"Sorry to hear about that," said Julie in a reverent tone. "I am going back to bed."

Julie retired back to the bedroom and Connor finished printing his documents, shut the computer off, turned out all of the lights, and climbed into bed.

#

The next morning came in what seemed like an instant. Connor felt as if he had not gotten any sleep whatsoever. He got up and went into the computer room to gather up the paper to take to the clubhouse and decided to see if there were any news articles on the Internet about last night's crash.

Within a few seconds he had found one. The police had already released the name of the driver and said that he was under arrest for suspicion of driving while intoxicated, but there was no mention of murder or even manslaughter. Knowing that the press typically made mistakes in his little town and also knowing that the story was not really old enough to develop, he didn't think too much about it, but did decide to print the article off to take with him to the clubhouse.

Connor got all of his stuff together and got dress, throwing his colors on his back and heading out of the house on his bike towards the clubhouse. During his ride, he noticed that there were several people in the town who seemed to give Connor looks as he rode towards the clubhouse as almost an offer of condolences. Connor nodded to all of them in a slight show of appreciation while trying to keep his outlaw game face on.

Connor arrived at the clubhouse about 30 minutes before the scheduled meeting time only to find that everyone was already there, and much to his surprise, so was Scott, outside standing by the bikes. Connor thought to himself that he was afraid it was only a matter of time before Scott became a prospect.

Connor parked his bike along side of the rest of the club, leaving the keys in the bike as was standard practice for all of the club members. He gave Scott a polite wave hello and entered the clubhouse with his documents in had prepared to give a presentation of his findings.

"It's about time, Rub" called out Cobbler as Connor entered.

"Damn Cobbler, I'm 30 minutes early."

Everyone laughed as Cobbler spoke up, "No shit, Rub. Just busting your balls. Calm the fuck down."

As Connor entered, Jackal instructed Cobbler to tell Scott to pull the gate closed outside and lock it, and Cobbler did as he was told. Jackal also instructed everyone to go to the church room and all followed.

Once Cobbler entered the room, the door was shut and silence filled the room awaiting Jackal to begin, when Jackal said, "Alright. I see that Rub has some shit on this guy, which is good. What have you got, brother?"

Connor passed out the documents to everyone which included a picture of the offender. Among all of the pertinent information, the club noted the man's name, which was Seth Allen. As everyone read the papers that Connor had handed out, Connor also explained that he saw in the news article this morning that there was no mention of murder or manslaughter.

This infuriated Cobbler, as he yelled, "This fucking nigger. This nigger is going to pay. I fucking know who this is."

Everyone turned and looked at Cobbler wondering how he knew Seth Allen.

Without hesitation, Cobbler continued, "This fucking nigger runs with the Sixers. He's a fucking gang banger."

"If that's true," announced Jackal, "then we have a bigger problem than we initially assumed. What's your thoughts V.P.?"

Bill replied, "I'm torn. We have to enact revenge. My feeling is that if we know this asshole is running with the Sixers, then they must know that they killed one of us last night and most likely are having them a little nigger pow-wow trying to figure on their next move. We can't wait too long, though. I don't want to show weakness."

Now, the Sixers were an African-American gang that was based in a small town about 30 minutes east of Clark named Creston, Kansas. Creston was a notoriously violent town, riddled with crime, drugs, and prostitution, most of which was overseen by the Sixers.

The Sixers did not have any rivals in town, and there was not a presence of Libertines in Creston. The Simmons chapter was the closest to them and they were located in the next town over from Creston. However, the Simmons chapter was a probationary chapter and had only been in existence for almost a year.

According to the rules of the club, a probationary chapter could be formed with at least 3 existing Libertines, they could prospect new members, but they were not granted full charter status unless all of the clubs across the county voted unanimously to accept their charter. If not, they would all be stripped of their patches.

One of the reasons for the creation of the Simmons chapter was to facilitate a closer communication line with the Sixers. The Libertines did not deal drugs as a club per-say. The Libertines did have members who dealt drugs as a way of making side cash, but due to other club business the powers that be had decided to stay away from dealing drugs. Those that dealt drugs did it without the knowledge of the club, and did not under any circumstance do any drug dealing with their colors on.

Jackal continued the conversation, "I spoke with the president of the Simmons chapter this morning and told him the news. They are watching activity around Creston right now. If we need to get a message to the Sixers, we can use the Simmons chapter."

"We need to get a message to them, and we need to get that shit done now," exclaimed Bill.

Cobbler, who was noticeably still perplexed, spoke up and said, "God damn niggers. We should just roll up in force and fill their nigger bodies full of holes."

"Cobbler!" yelled Jackal, "Enough! I know you are pissed. I'm pissed. You have to control your anger here. Let's not make a decision that we are going to regret."

As Jackal finished calming Cobbler down, a loud banging was heard at the front door of the clubhouse. The members looked up at the closed circuit TV which had a camera stationed above the front door and noticed it was Scott.

"Rub, go see what he wants," said Jackal.

Connor knew that this had better be important. Scott should know not to interrupt anything going on inside the clubhouse while the door was locked. Connor reached out and unlocked the door to find Scott standing there.

Scott said, "I'm sorry, but there is a Mr. Jackson here who said he is an attorney and he needs to speak with Jackal."

Connor yelled, "Jackal, Jackson is here."

Jackal replied, yelling as well, "Get his ass in here."

Connor told Scott to unlock the gate and have Jackson pull his car in and then send him inside. Connor waited at the door of the clubhouse for

Jackson to enter the compound, as he did, and welcomed the attorney inside the clubhouse. Before Connor could explain to Jackson where everyone was, Jackson began walking into the church room as if he had done so many times before.

Connor locked the door behind him and followed Jackson. Jackson entered the room and placed his briefcase on Jackal's desk.

"Well, fellas," began Jackson, "Mr. Allen made bail this morning. It wasn't done through a bondsman either. It looks like someone from the Sixers had their ol' lady put up the cash in her name so as to not show any association. I did a background on Mr. Allen and he has no priors, and not only that, I called in a favor and it turns out he wasn't even over the legal limit, so a DWI conviction isn't going to happen.

"I'm afraid that this is being looked at as an accident, and nothing more. Best case scenario on this one is going to be some kind of 'failure to control vehicle' or something of that nature, unless you want to go with civil charges, and without you answering that one I know how you feel about that.

"I have this gut feeling that someone has been paid off. I know this isn't the kind of news that you want to hear, but unfortunately that's how this one has come out. Do you fellas have any questions for me?"

Jackal looked and Jackson and said, "I don't think so. Thanks counselor. We will call you if we need something."

As Jackson left the room he turned back and said, "I'm so sorry for your loss."

Jackson was led out of the clubhouse by Cobbler, and upon Cobbler's return, Bill spoke up and said, "Well, there you go, fucked again by our justice system."

Knuckles followed, "I tell you what, that nigger was drunk or high or something and when I looked at him sitting in the back of that squad car, I knew he was fucked up."

Connor was shocked at the word "nigger" being floated around the room. Connor was not a racist and grew up in a world where that was not a part of everyday language. He held no disdain for the guilty man simply because he was black, and Connor was also not convinced that this was even his fault. Connor was the only man in the room that was giving Mr. Allen the benefit of the doubt, and with that, Connor knew to keep his mouth shut about his opinion.

However, this placed Connor in a tough spot. He knew that he was going to be involved in some form of retaliation, he was just unsure as to the level, whether it would be focused on just the individual, or this entire gang, which placed a level of fear inside Connor he had never felt. Connor knew that it was gut-check time with himself, to see if he had the balls to get in the middle of what seemed to be an inevitable bloodbath, with losses possible on both sides of the fence.

Pepper, who had been noticeably quiet during all of this, spoke up, saying, "What are the possibilities of having a sit down with the Sixers? I mean, they have to be shitting in their pants right now with the thought of us bringing down the heat on them hard core. If we could set up a meeting with their boss on neutral ground somewhere, we might get this problem solved without an all out war erupting."

The entire room thought about Pepper's proposal for a minute and then Bill offered a response, saying, "There ain't no way that they are just going to hand over their nigger buddy to us so we can execute him."

It was apparent to Connor that violence was going to be the answer, and that is when the solution hit Connor. Without putting too much thought behind his proposal, Connor stood up.

Connor announced, "Let me throw something out there. If I'm wrong, tell me and I will shut the fuck up."

The group listened attentively as Connor began to explain, "I know that I haven't been around long enough, but this unfortunate event has me upset as much as all of you. I don't want us to bring any more heat on us than necessary if we have a way around it, and I think we do.

"If we are dead set on retaliation, then I think that we have a way to get this done and not involve any one of us. Scott wants the tap to prospect so fucking bad. What if we task him with the retaliation?"

Before anyone could respond, Jackal took the floor immediately, "I have already considered that. However, I won't bring anyone into this club that I don't believe will patch out, and not only that, if he is not in deep, there is a good chance he could tuck tail and run."

Connor replied, "I have a pretty good feeling that Scott wants in, and even though he would not contribute anything to this club other than the fact of being an enforcer, we need an enforcer type to carry this out."

Connor could not believe the words coming out of his mouth as he said them. Connor had an underlying problem with Scott from the first moment he met him, and now he was basically giving his opinion out that he should be tapped as a prospect.

Jackal then put Connor on the spot, saying, "Well, Rub, if that's your solution, and everyone else is in agreement to accept Scott as a prospect, then you are going to have to sponsor him."

Before Jackal finished his sentence, Connor knew where he was going, what he was about to propose, and dreaded the inevitable vote that was about to come. In a time of club disarray and losing a member who was a true bad ass, it became a no brainer to most of the members that a bad ass replacement needed to happen.

Jackal announced, "Anyone got a problem with Scott being a prospect?"

No one said anything or raised their hands in opposition. Connor's stomach turned. Not only did the club have the death of a member at their feet, the government coming up with a possible law to rid the country of MCs, he now had a prospect to sponsor, and this was only after being in the club a few short months.

Chapter 21 – RIP Nutcase

The following Thursday at Church, Scott was officially brought in as a prospect and it was announced to him that Connor would be his sponsor. Scott was extremely happy at the notion of beginning his journey toward becoming a patched member of the Libertines, but Connor did not share his level of enthusiasm.

As the members left the Church room and entered into the main section of the clubhouse where the normal party was ensuing, Scott was congratulated by several of the hang-arounds as well as some members from other charters who were there for the funeral. Even though there was some aura of happiness for the charter to bring in a new prospect, the looming funeral for Nutcase the next day was well on everyone's mind.

The members of the Libertines from around the country would be showing up in town and the population of Clark, Kansas would soon swell due to the influx of bikers. The news of the funeral quickly made its way outside the circle of the Libertines and had made the papers and had circulated around message boards on the Internet. Official condolences had been received from other MCs around the country at this time of sadness from the death of a patch holder.

The news of the funeral had also caused the police department in Clark to call in additional help from the county sheriff's office and the state as well. Typically, biker funerals would not cause any legal issues other than random noise complaints and a few attempts at drunken driving stops. With the government sticking their nose into the club, all of the rank and file Libertines was on high alert to basically be on their best behavior.

Scott was unaware of the heightened amount of responsibility he would be given to care for basically all of the needs of the patch holders coming in from around the county. Connor had instructed Scott that his primary job was to ensure that the needs of all of the patch holders were met and not to concern himself with anything else. The other members of the Clark charter knew that Scott would have his hands full with this task and decidedly would leave him alone until after the funeral, knowing that the next task at hand would be not only more important, but much more difficult.

The gathering at the clubhouse was nearing the twilight times, were drunk people were staggering into the parking lot and getting into their cars or on their bikes. Many of the out of town club members were passing out on couches inside the clubhouse or sleeping in rooms along the back. Scott was busy sweeping up the clubhouse floor and the only other remaining members who had not yet passed out were Connor and Cobbler.

Connor knew that Cobbler would be retiring to bed soon now that all of the noise had departed and that he was waiting for Scott to finish cleaning up.

Cobbler barked at Scott, yelling, "Prospect, that's enough. I'm fucking tired so it's time for you to hit the bricks."

Scott put the broom away after completing about half of his cleaning duties and left. The look of sheer exhaustion on his face was amusing to Connor as it had not been that long ago that he was at the end of that broom. Connor decided that it was his time to go as well so Cobbler could go to bed. Connor followed about 10 steps behind Scott toward the exit where Cobbler was in his usual place guarding the door.

As Scott exited the clubhouse, Cobbler closed the door before Connor could make his escape, and turned to him, saying, "Well, Rub, you got a shit load on your plate, and thanks to you, Scott is now a prospect. Looks like you are getting in balls deep."

The look on Cobbler's face as he spoke to Connor was a bit troubling to Connor as he had yet figured out exactly how to take Cobbler's incessant commentary towards him.

Connor responded, "All I am trying to do is what I think is best for the club, whether it be right now or 10 years from now. Before Nutcase died, I would have never supported Scott as a prospect or a member. However, we have a need right now in the club and I feel that he is a good solution to that problem."

Cobbler then said, "You know, I have been around this place for years, I've seen good times and I've seen bad. I have seen brothers leave, brothers die, and brothers go the wrong way. The fact that Jackal listened to you, who hasn't been around that long, and went along with your plan shocks the shit out of me, but he's the president, and it's his call. No one voted against it, not even me, but I will tell you one thing, if this idea of your fucks up, and there is a good chance that it will fuck up, this will cost you, brother."

Cobbler then opened the door and waved his hand in a motion as to show Connor the way out. As Connor's mind was digesting the flurry of thoughts just handed to him, he decided to test not only himself but Cobbler. Rather than walking out of the door, Connor took his right hand and closed the door back.

Connor looked up at Cobbler, who outweighed him by at least 75 pounds of muscle, and whose knuckles bore the scars of more fights than Connor had even seen in his life, and said, "Look, brother, I still don't get the beef between me and you. We are in deep shit right now, and I am getting in balls deep, but you seem to fucking question me every fucking time I do something. What the fuck is it about me that you just fucking can't get past?"

Cobbler looked at Connor and gave him a sinister go to hell grin and said, "Well done, Rub. That right there is what you fucking needed. You need to get fucking angry. You are all right in my book. Lock the door on your way out."

Cobbler turned around and headed to bed. Connor felt as if he could shit in his pants at any second, but also felt quite proud of himself for standing up to Cobbler. Of course, Connor knew that Cobbler probably would not have assaulted him, as it was against the rules of the club to strike another member without a third member present to witness the fight and the cause of said fight, a rule that Cobbler was well aware of.

Connor returned home that night and once again came stumbling in a little bit drunk and much later than he should of. Julie was fast asleep in bed and probably had been for at least a couple of hours. Due to the fact of Connor's continued tardiness and use of alcohol, Julie and Connor did not really talk as much, and much to Connor's surprise, Julie didn't seem to care what he was off doing.

Connor didn't have second thoughts about staying out late that night. He had taken the next day off of work for Nutcase's funeral, which wasn't until 4:00 the next day, so he knew he would be able to sleep in. He went into the bathroom and took a shower and then went on to bed, all of which never stirred Julie from her slumber.

\#

The next morning, Connor awoke to find that Julie had already left. As he rubbed his eyes from the horrible night's sleep that he just left, he leaned over and looked at the bed side alarm clock and much to his surprise it was already a bit later than 1:00 in the afternoon.

Connor could not remember exactly what time he arrived home the night before and also couldn't figure out exactly why Julie getting out of bed didn't at least stir him to a semi-conscious state. Since there were only a few hours left until Nutcase's funeral, Connor arose and began getting himself ready. Even though the funeral was at 4:00, Connor had to be at the clubhouse prior to the funeral for the ride over there, and he didn't have much time.

Connor threw on a plain black t-shirt and a clean pair of jeans, his Libertine colors proudly on his back, and tied a black bandana around his forehead, leaving his hair visible from the top. He mounted his motorcycle and began an uneventful ride to the clubhouse.

Upon arriving at the clubhouse, he found Scott, standing outside watching after the bikes. Now that Scott had received his prospect vest, Scott walked around and carried himself much differently than before towards non-members of the club, but still seemed to act the same way toward patched members, with one exception; Scott was now kissing ass, especially Connor's ass.

Connor knew that this was an integral part of the prospect process, meaning that you did whatever another patch holder told you to, but Scott was doing it much different than Connor did. Scott seemed to be asking questions of many of the patch holders, which Connor never would have dreamed of doing. Scott seemed to really pay no mind to the "Shut the fuck up prospect" rule, and since there was so much going on, it didn't seem like anyone was doing anything about it.

Knuckles walked outside of the clubhouse and met Connor as he dismounted from his bike, and placing his hand in a brotherly way upon Connor's shoulder, Knuckles said, "Rub, I need a minute."

Connor and Knuckles walked off to a secluded part of the Libertine's compound and Knuckles began, "Hey Rub. I know that you are new at this; you haven't even been patched for a year. Now you are the secretary, we have all this shit going on, and on top of that, you are a sponsor.

"It's a lot of shit to keep track of but we all know that you are a smart motherfucker and that you can handle it, but you are slipping."

Connor asked, "I'm slipping? How so?"

Knuckles continued, "You need to reign in your fucking prospect. He is going around talking to patched members from not only our chapter, but from others as well. Hell, I think he even pissed of Sampson by talking to him. Everyone is in a state of mourning right now and we don't want to rock the boat, so pull him aside and set him straight."

Connor nodded to Knuckles in understanding. Connor realized that he was not doing his job properly as Scott's sponsor and unfortunately Scott becoming a prospect was half of his doing and all of his responsibility.

Connor walked up to Scott and began his instruction, saying, "Prospect, I need to go over a few things with you.

"First off, you need to shut the fuck up. Only speak when spoken to. You aren't a hang-around anymore, who can just fucking shoot the shit with people, and you are a prospect. And since you are a prospect that means do as you're told, and I am telling you to shut the fuck up.

"Secondly, if you have a fucking question, I am the one to answer it. You only ask me questions, not Jackal, not Knuckles, not Cobbler, not anyone but me.

"And while we are at it, the third thing is, stop marching around this place like you just got a fucking kung-fu lesson by putting that cut on your back. You got me, prospect?"

Connor was proud of himself for speaking like the bad ass that he definitely was not.

Scott replied, "Yes sir!" in an almost militaristic kind of way.

Connor immediately responded, "Don't fucking patronize me prospect. I will yank that cut right off of your fucking back and kick your ass to the curb. You got me?"

Scott, now tucking his proverbial tail between his legs, responded, "I got it. Sorry."

"Don't be sorry, just get it done right. When you fuck up, I get shit for it, not you. So if I get shit, I'm going to bring that shit down on your tenfold."

Connor stormed off in a fit of rage, impressing on Scott that even though Connor appeared smaller and weaker, Connor could definitely hold his own. Knuckles overheard the conversation, as Connor did not attempt to be quiet by any stretch and before Connor could enter the clubhouse, Knuckles stopped him.

"Holy shit, brother! Why did you stomp a mud hole in his ass? A simple 'speak when spoken to' would have most likely worked."

Connor replied to Knuckles, "Perhaps, but my method worked as well."

Connor also was unaware that Cobbler was listening in from the porch of the clubhouse. As Connor opened the door he looked over at Cobbler and nodded hello. Cobbler returned the nod with that same devilish grin. It was apparent to Connor that he and Cobbler were now good.

Connor entered the clubhouse to find the rest of the members of his charter to be present, as well as approximately 100 or so members from other charters who had come to show their support. Greetings were being continually exchanged and Connor could overhear stories about Nutcase being told. The amount of food and booze in the clubhouse was about 4 times that of a normal day or night for that matter, as there would be a giant party that night after the funeral, and Connor was looking forward to that.

It had now become time to ride to the funeral home. This would be Connor's obvious first time to ride a motorcycle in a funeral procession, which was a two-by-two ride from the clubhouse to Rodger's funeral home, which happened to be only a few miles away.

Connor was surprised that the service at the funeral home was extremely similar to every other funeral he had been to. There were the typical spiritual songs and hymns, a local preacher delivered a sermon, and Jackal delivered the eulogy. The only thing that seemed different than a normal funeral was the amount of motorcycles parked outside and the lack of formal attire inside the funeral home.

In fact, Connor saw nothing that was remotely close to anything different, until he arrived at the grave site for Nutcase. It was at that moment when he witnessed a rare show of brotherly love. After the casket was lowered into the grave, all of the full patch members who were in attendance took a shovel and began to cover the grave, one shovel full of dirt at a time.

Connor took a shovel as everyone else did and noticed that each member placed anywhere between 10 and 20 shovels full at a time and passed their shovel to the next person. Once Connor placed 15 shovels full of dirt into the grave, he handed his shovel to Sampson, but before he turned loose of the shovel he leaned over to his ear and asked why they were performing the fill in of the grave.

Sampson replied, "It's an old tradition. No one, and I mean no one, throws dirt on my brother's face."

Sampson then began his turn. Connor was astounded. The job of filling in the grave took about 15 minutes. After all of the dirt had been deposited into the grave, a cooler was brought to the grave containing several beers. Each full patched member of the club removed a beer from the cooler and opened it. They took a large drink from the can which amounted to approximately half of the beer and then poured the rest on the newly filled grave.

As the members finished their beers they all walked toward their bikes and Connor did as well, although, no one started their motors. The last patched member to mount their bike was Jackal.

As Jackal mounted his bike he held his pointer finger of his left hand in the air, as if he was pointing into heaven and started his bike. The remainder of the bikes then fired up their engines as well. Everyone began to rev their motors, high into the redline. Jackal was the first to pull away, spinning his back tire leaving a streak of black rubber on the street. More than half of the other members did as well. Unsure of his burn-out ability, Connor refrained from doing so.

Chapter Twenty Two – In Memory of Nutcase

The club, along with a few guests, retired back to the clubhouse, and upon returning, saw that some of the regular hang-arounds were waiting with baiting breath, knowing that a tremendous party was about to take place.

As the bikes were parked in their normal fashion, Connor instructed Scott to keep watch over them as prospects had to do. Connor then entered into the clubhouse and much to his surprise was met at the door by none other than Sally, who had a beer waiting for him.

Sally put her arms around Connor and said, "I have missed you darling. I'm sorry I haven't been around as much as I should have."

Connor honestly didn't even realize that she had not been there and had basically put her completely out of his mind. Sally was dressed in a tight black leather mini skirt and a low cut white top, which left fairly nothing to the imagination. It was apparent to Connor that she had already had a few beers, most likely one past what her limit should be due to the manner in which she stumbled toward him, and the length of the heel or her stiletto heel didn't help her gate as well.

Connor withdrew from the embrace politely and responded, "Yeah, it's good to see you to. Thanks for the beer."

He then walked over to Terry as if there was something important that he had to talk to him about. Terry had seen this display from across the room and could tell from the look on Connor's face that he was trying to get away.

Connor finished his quick journey across the clubhouse and arrived in front of Terry, saying, "Man brother, that tart is going to get me into trouble one day."

Terry laughed and replied, "She sure is, but what the hell? You should just nail that bitch, go balls deep, and get it over with."

Connor responded, "There ain't no fucking way. I can't do that to Julie. I couldn't live with myself. Besides, Julie wouldn't do that to me."

Terry retorted, "Are you sure about that, brother?"

Connor was taken aback by Terry's question. He was well aware that Julie didn't care much for Terry to begin with and was also aware that Terry knew of Julie's disdain for him. However, this was the first time that Terry had ever said anything questioning Julie's commitment to him.

Connor then inquired, "What the hell are you talking about?"

Terry replied, "Think about it. Julie has kept you under basically lock and key for so long, ever since you two got engaged. She didn't even like the fact of you eating fried foods or much less drinking a beer.

"Now, all of a sudden, you buy a motorcycle and within a few months are in deep with a MC, you show back up home whenever you please, and Julie has absolutely no problem with it.

"I'm no fucking fortune teller or Albert Einstein, but I'm thinking maybe she has something going on to keep her attention now, other than you."

Connor rubbed his fingers through the stubble on his chin and thought for a minute, then replied, "Dude, there's no fucking way Julie is cheating. Think about it. Some dude hits on an ol' lady from our club, his clock would be cleaned quick."

Terry added, "Maybe the dude she's fucking doesn't know who you are or who you roll with."

Connor laughed and said, "This is getting too heavy. I trust her. She ain't doing shit."

Terry laughed and said, "I'm sure she isn't brother. I'm just trying to get you laid."

The two both laughed and Connor shrugged the conversation off as normal banter between friends and continued to celebrate the life of Nutcase. A picture of Nutcase standing in front of his bike was now hanging on the clubhouse wall with a black ribbon glued to it diagonally. Several people would go up to the picture and evidently would say a few words to the picture as if they were talking to Nutcase and tap their beer bottle against the glass of the frame to mimic a toast.

The mood of everyone in the clubhouse had now changed into a joyous party type mood. People were drinking and bullshitting with each other. Stories were being exchanged back and forth about Nutcase between patch holders and non patch holders alike.

Connor decided that it would be a good opportunity to go pay his prospect a visit outside and see what was going on. Connor walked past Cobbler as he was standing at the door of the clubhouse in his usual spot and went outside to find Scott standing post, watching over the bikes parked outside in the parking lot and the remaining area of the Libertine compound.

"You got everything under control out here, prospect?" asked Connor.

"It's being handled," replied Scott.

"Good deal. So how well did you know Nutcase?"

Scott replied, "I didn't know him much outside of the clubhouse. He seemed like a great fella. I'm sure he will be missed."

"You are right about that, prospect. He will be. Let me ask you a question, and I want you to tell me the God's honest truth."

Scott replied, "Ask me anything. I'm not going to lie to you. I have no reason to."

Connor continued, "Good. That's one thing that we will not tolerate around here. So, are you really sure that you want to be a Libertine?"

Without hesitation, Scott answered, "Absolutely one hundred percent sure. For the longest time, that's all I have wanted, was just the chance to be a part of this club."

"Why?" asked Connor.

"You know, I thought that someday you or someone else would ask me. I have two reasons. First, I think that I would be a good asset to the club. I will do whatever the club needs out of me or asks of me.

"The second reason is honestly selfish. I want that patch on my back. I want to have that immediate respect that comes along with being a member of this club, but, in doing that, I want to make sure that I earn that respect that comes along with the patch."

Connor continued, "You do realize that you are really going to have to earn this patch that's on my back? And when I say, 'earn', I mean you are really going to have to earn it."

Scott answered, "I completely understand."

Connor, content with Scott's response, began, "Let me tell you a story about one of my experiences with Nutcase.

"When I was a prospect, I got a call from Nutcase one night. He said that he had received a call from a member of the Bucs that they were having issues with protection money collection and needed some assistance. He wanted me to go along for the ride and watch his back, so I agreed.

"Anyways, we arrive at a tattoo parlor where the guy running the place was standing outside smoking a cigarette. Turns out, this guy was the one giving the Bucs their problems.

"Now, even though most people think that we handle everything with violence, such is not the case. Nutcase decided that the best play here would just be to talk to the guy. So that is what we did. Nutcase walked up to the guy as I stood just behind him and to his right and proceeded to tell him that he should not be giving the Bucs issues with the protection money and that he would have issues with us if he did.

"Well, little did we know that this dumbass was tweaking on something and decided that neither one of us was going to tell him what to do. His response was basically to fuck off and go back where we came from.

"Usually, that would be a quick ass kicking, but Nutcase somehow kept his cool. He told the guy that there was no reason for him to get belligerent with us and that we were only there to square up the business of the Bucs and ensure that things would continue to run smooth.

"So this dumbass doesn't take the second hint and starts trashing the Bucs and calling them a bunch of worthless pussies and that we were just a couple of pussies hiding behind a patch and acting like we were tough.

"And that is when I saw it. I saw the unbelievable wrath of Nutcase, a side of him that I would not wish on most people. Before you could blink your eye, Nutcase dropped him flat on his back with one solid punch to the chest. Why he didn't hit him in the face I guess I will never know.

"The dude was lying there on the pavement flat on his back with his wind completely knocked out of him. When he tried to come back to his feet, Nutcase kicked him in the chest again, completely removing any breath that he had in him. The dude gasped for air and put his hands out in front of him in a feeble attempt to beg for mercy, but Nutcase wasn't having any of that.

"Nutcase then put his steel toed boot right on top of the guy's crotch and leaned in with all of his weight, crushing the guy's junk. The dude screamed in pain and even my stomach turned a bit just thinking about the pain this dude was going through.

"What I didn't know was that Nutcase was trying to make the guy pass out, which after what seemed an eternity, but most likely was only a few seconds, the dude finally did.

"So I'm thinking that we are done, and once again I'm wrong. Nutcase tells me to grab the guy's feet and he grabs his arms and we carry him into the tattoo parlor. Nutcase told me to pull the blinds and lock the door, which I did. He then strapped the guy into one of the tattoo chairs with duct tape where the guy couldn't move a muscle.

"And no shit, Nutcase looked me straight in the eye and asked me what my favorite color was. I couldn't believe it. So, I thought for a minute, since I don't have a favorite color, and told him blue.

"Nutcase leans over to the tattoo equipment and pulls out the tattoo gun and dips it in blue ink. He then tattooed 'cocksucker' on the guy's forehead and drew a penis on each one of his cheeks. He spun him around in the chair so when the dude came to he could see it in the mirror. He then looked at himself in the mirror and gazed at his work and said 'Maybe I should have been an artist' with a no shit serious tone.

"Nutcase then looked at me and asked me what kind of tattoo I wanted. I was no shit nervous when he asked me that. I thought to myself that I was going to have to get a tattoo now and how was I going to explain this to the wife. So I told him that I really wasn't sure and he just laughed and told me he was kidding, but that he wanted a smiley face on his forearm, which was pretty much sleeved out already.

"He took the tattoo gun and drew a little smiley face in a bare spot on his left arm, looked at it and told me that he was very proud of his work. Then he looked at me and asked me where I wanted to go for a beer, as if none of this had happened.

"I thought to myself, no wonder they call him Nutcase, because this dude is freaking crazy. We ended up going to a beer joint in that town, which I can't even remember the name, and we sat down at the bar and had a couple of beers.

"After about an hour or so, the tattoo parlor dude had come out of his state of unconsciousness and must have had a friend show up and cut him loose. He must have driven around town and lucked upon the fact that our bikes were parked outside.

"So in this fucker comes with three friends and he yells at the top of his lungs 'I'm going to fuck your shit up motherfucker.'

"Recognizing the voice we turn around from the barstools and see that he has three friends with him. Of course, there is still some blood running down from Nutcase's ink work that he had done to the dude and Nutcase said to the other patrons of the tavern in a loud voice, 'Hey, anyone want a blow job, because there is a cocksucker.'

"The guy starts to barrel across the bar towards us and now I know that I am about to have to fight, with the odds stacked against us 2 to 1. Before the dude can get to Nutcase he yells 'STOP' really loud and the dude does.

"Nutcase then tells the guy that he realizes that he is probably a little bit upset that his ink work was not quite as good as what he could have done and promised him he would try harder next time. The dude was so taken aback by what he said, I mean, he just couldn't comprehend it at all.

"Before the dude could provide some form of retort, Nutcase clocked him right in the jaw and dropped him. He told me 'let's get them' and we both charged for the other three. They threw their arms up and told us that they didn't want any trouble and ended up apologizing and left.

"We walked back over to the tattoo guy who was getting up while realizing that his friends had left him and now he was facing 2 to 1 odds. He told us that he didn't want any more trouble and then Nutcase told him that was a good thing, because next time he would bust his teeth out of his mouth so he would become the world's greatest cocksucker.

"We finished our beer and left. It was quite a night."

Scott, who was enamored with the story, responded, "Holy shit. I guess Nutcase was kind of a nut case, huh?"

"Not exactly," replied Connor, "but you definitely didn't want to see his crazy side, that's one thing I am certain of.

"So, the reason I told you that story was this; you never know when you are going to get a call from a patch telling you that you are needed and you better be ready to participate in some rough ass shit. If you aren't ready for that, tell me now and hand over that cut."

Without hesitation, Scott answered, "I'm ready. I will be there, day or night."

"Good," replied Connor, "because very soon I am going to be making that phone call to you. There is already something brewing and the way that you handle this problem is going to be a major test for you."

"Got it," answered Scott.

"Ok. Now, keep a close eye on all these bikes out here and I will see if I can get one of the prospects from another charter to relieve you in a bit so you can come inside and have a few beers."

"Thanks," responded Scott as he turned and continued watching his post as instructed.

Connor walked back into the clubhouse to grab himself a beer and found that Sally saw his entrance and noticed his empty hand and brought him one. Connor thanked Sally for the beer and saw Knuckles give him a wave from across the room.

Connor approached Knuckles and said, "What's up?"

Knuckles replied, "Not to bring a downer on the party, but we just got a line on who is feeding the governor's office information."

"No shit?" replied Connor. "What do we know?"

"Well," continued Knuckles, "we don't know a whole hell of a lot, but we know his name and where the guy hangs out."

"That's a start," said Connor.

"True," said Knuckles, "The guy likes hanging out at yuppie type places like Luke's and Turnovers and his name is Chris."

Chapter Twenty Three - Chris

"So, that's pretty much all we know, huh?" asked Connor of Knuckles.

"Well," continued Knuckles, "that's pretty much it. Our contact didn't know his last name, but the good news is, turns out that the dude is at Turnovers right now."

"Man, I don't want to go to that fucking yuppie bar," said Connor, "but I think we need to pay this asshole a visit and maybe we can squelch this shit real quick. You want to roll over there?"

Knuckles thought for a second and responded, "Sounds good to me. We need to keep this kind of low key, so just you and me. Deal?"

"Deal. Will we know him if we see him?" asked Connor.

Knuckles replied, "Let me make another phone call to an associate who is there so we can get a description."

Knuckles disappeared for a few minutes as he walked away dialing his phone. In the corner of the compound, Connor watched as Knuckles was nodding his head in understanding, making mental notes of what to look for. After a five minute phone conversation, Knuckles returned to where Connor was standing and explained the plan and then told Connor he was going to fill Jackal in with the plan.

Knuckles entered the clubhouse and ran the plan by Jackal, who agreed to the idea that Knuckles had proposed. Knuckles then came back outside and told Connor to get ready to roll. Both of the Libertines mounted up and headed towards Turnovers.

Upon arrival, both of the men noticed that Turnovers was packed. There were only two parking spots remaining in the parking lot and it was apparent from looking into the windows that there was quite a crowd inside. Turnovers was not a typical spot for a Libertine to walk into and the crowds of young rich folks were typically uncomfortable around bikers, especially Libertines.

Knuckles explained to Connor what the plan was, stating, "Okay Rub, here's the plan. We have an associate inside who is supposed to be standing close to the bar that we will approach. He will buy us each a beer. We will shoot the shit with him for a minute or so and he will go to the pisser.

"His ol' lady is waiting outside to take him home, under the presumption that he is drunk. She is on board with the plan, by the way. Anyways, this 'Chris' character is sitting on the opposite end of the bar from our contact. On his way back out of the pisser, he is going to 'accidentally' trip against the guy's barstool as if he's drunk so we know who he is.

"He is then going to stumble out and get in his ol' lady's car and leave. The rest is up to us."

Connor replied, "I got it. So what's the plan when we ID this guy?"

Knuckles said, "We are going to have to play that one by ear. These fools inside Turnovers are going to be quick to call the cops if we resort to violence. Depending on the layout around the bar, we could just pull up a stool next to him and make him uncomfortable, or we could meet him outside. I guess we are just going to have to make that decision on the fly based off of what is going on."

Connor shook his head and said, "I got you, brother. Let's get this done."

The two Libertines were met at the front door by the bouncer, a large African-American man who outweighed both Connor and Knuckles and looked like he could stop a freight train. However, the bouncer was very familiar with the Libertines in town, as well as their lack of attendance at Turnovers.

The bouncer said to Knuckles and Connor, "Hey fellas, you two are welcome here, but we don't want any trouble. Can you behave in here?"

Connor laughed and said, "There won't be any troubled started out of us, but I can't guarantee that if trouble is started that we won't finish it."

The bouncer let out a chuckle and said, "I expected an answer like that from you. You both know this isn't exactly your kind of place, but I like you guys. You two have a good time."

Connor and Knuckles entered the bar and Knuckles immediately made contact with the associate who was standing next to the bar toward the far end as he had described. The pair made their way through the crowd of yuppies, all dressed in their polo shirts and khaki pants, which parted the floor as if Moses was parting the red sea. Connor could feel the eyeballs staring at them and the collective deep breaths as they walked in.

Rather than being forceful, as they well have could done, Connor followed Knuckles through the crowd as he used his manners, saying "excuse me" and waiting split seconds as he passed. After strolling over to the bar and upon meeting the associate, the two received their beers as promised. Connor began scanning over the bar, trying to determine who this 'Chris' was before the associate could identify him, and to Connor's surprise, he found a couple of familiar faces. It was Julie and her friend Lisa.

Julie and Lisa had not noticed that Connor had entered the bar with Knuckles. They were completely involved in their conversation and the building could have been on fire and they would not have noticed.

Connor turned to Knuckles and said, "Hey brother. That's my ol' lady over there with her friend. I will be right back."

Before Knuckles could respond to Connor, Connor had already begun making his way toward Julie. When Connor had made it about three people away from Julie, he saw Lisa look up and him and whisper something to Julie. Connor could not make out what Lisa had said, but it was enough to make Julie choke on the gulp of her cosmopolitan that he had just sipped.

Julie turned around and saw Connor, who was now within arm's reach from her. Instead of a kind greeting that Connor expected upon this pleasant surprise, he was met with a phrase that might accompany an intrusion.

Julie said, in a callous tone, "What are you doing here?"

Connor replied, "I'm here with Knuckles from the club. We are just checking in on someone that has some business with the club. How are you two ladies doing tonight?"

Lisa, who spoke before Julie could, told Connor in a suspicious tone, "Just having a couple of drinks in *our* bar," insinuating that Connor and his club were not welcome there.

In any other circumstance, Connor would have immediately replied in a 'bitch-slapping' retort. However, since Lisa was there with Julie, he decided not to ruffle any feathers or cause him undue stress at home. Connor let the remark slide.

He then told the ladies, "Well, we won't be here long. I guess I will leave you two alone."

Julie said, "We were on our way out anyways. I guess I will see you at home when you are done playing with your motorcycle friend."

Julie and Lisa arose from their seats and made their way out of the bar. It was a bit suspicious to Connor that they had both left more than half of their drinks in the glasses, but it was getting late according to Julie's internal clock.

Connor watched as the two women made their exit from the bar. The patrons of Turnovers watch as they made their exit, quite possibly assuming that a Libertine had just hit on them and they became uncomfortable. After Lisa and Julie walked out of the front door, Connor made his way back over to the other end of the bar where Knuckles was now standing by himself and the associate was nowhere to be found.

Connor approached Knuckles and said, "Where's our friend?"

Knuckles said, "Let's go."

Knuckles did not allow Connor to argue with him, as the entire purpose of their visit was to make contact with the supposed informant, and they haven't even taken a look at him. Knuckles walked outside and Connor followed a few steps behind. The pair jumped onto their bikes and before Connor could ask Knuckles what the problem was, Knuckles fired up his motor and proceeded out of the parking lot.

Connor hurriedly followed behind Knuckles and it was then apparent that they were head back toward the clubhouse. Knuckles ran two red lights and three stop signs on the way back to the clubhouse and in order to keep up, so did Connor.

The pair arrived back at the clubhouse and parked their bikes. Once Knuckles had silenced his motor, Connor took advantage of the brief state of silence and looked at Knuckles.

"Dude, what the fuck happened? Why the quick exit, and what happened to our contact?"

Knuckles looked at Connor with a glazed look in his eyes and said, "Inside brother."

Connor followed Knuckles back into the clubhouse, wondering to himself exactly what went wrong while he was talking to Julie and Lisa. As the duo entered the clubhouse, Knuckles motioned over to Jackal and Bill in a suggestion towards the Church room. Terry saw the motion as well and followed Jackal and Bill toward the back and Connor followed in tow.

Upon the five men entering the church room, Knuckles closed the door. They all took a seat as Connor was about to be completely overcome with his curiosity. Connor could hardly sit still waiting on Knuckles to explain just what the hell had happened inside Turnovers, and then Knuckles finally broke his silence, but not to satisfy Connor's interest.

"Brothers, I saw this Chris tonight, and I have some information on him. However, I want to go this one alone."

Connor said, "Dude, what happened at Turnovers? I turned around and you were…"

Before Connor could finish his thought, Knuckles interrupted him, saying, "Don't worry about that. It will all be understood soon. Jackal, do I have your permission to handle this?"

Jackal looked down at the floor and scratched his head in thought, and after a few seconds looked at Knuckles and said, "I trust you brother. If you want to handle this and go at it alone, I have confidence in you that this situation will be handled."

Knuckles replied, "I'm on it."

Knuckles then stood up and left the room. Terry and Bill looked at each other with a stare that they were more in the dark than Connor was.

Terry looked at Connor and said, "What happened over there?"

Connor answered, "I don't have a fucking clue. We walked in and met with the associate. I saw my ol' lady in the bar with a friend of hers and I walked over to speak with them. I wasn't over there for more than two minutes and they left. When I went back over to Knuckles he didn't say much other than we were leaving and he didn't say a word to me at all. What you heard him say was the first thing he spoke since telling me we were leaving."

Bill, who had smoked his cheap cigar almost down to the nub, raised an eyebrow at Connor and said, "Well Rub, maybe if you would have left Knuckles standing there by himself with the contact then you would have known what happened."

"I guess you have a point there," replied Connor.

Jackal concluded, "I guess we can go back out there and have a few more beers. Knuckles is a big boy and he can handle himself. If he wants to go it alone, then I respect that wish."

The remaining four went outside the Church room and returned to the party. They walked over to the bar and took another beer from the bartender. Jackal assumed his normal post at his barstool, which everyone in the building knew not to take, even upon Jackal's absence. Bill reached into his back pocket and took out a new cigar and lit it. Terry wandered off in his normal attempt of finding a wife for a night.

Connor looked across the room and noticed that Cobbler was standing in his usual spot by the door, but he appeared to be holding a set of Libertine colors in his hands. Connor made his way across the bar towards Cobbler, but before he could reach him, he was stopped by Sally.

Sally said to Connor in a flirty tone, "Hey babe, where did you go? I missed you."

Connor responded, "I had something I had to go take care of. I will talk to you in a little bit."

Connor shrugged Sally off and continued his pursuit toward Cobbler on the other side of the clubhouse. As he finally arrived where Cobbler stood, he noticed that indeed Cobbler was holding a set of Libertine colors, and those colors belonged to Knuckles.

Before Connor could ask, Cobbler beat him to the punch, saying, "Man, what the fuck is up with Knuckles. When he was leaving he said that he had something to do, and he had to run incognito. He tossed me his colors and hopped on his bike and left."

Connor said, "I don't know. Something happened earlier and

Knuckles has been acting strange ever since. We went to Turnovers to follow up on the lead about the informant in the governor's office and we left rather quickly. Knuckles didn't really explain himself other than he knew what to do and was going at it alone."

Cobbler said, "Well, Knuckles can be a bit strange at times. Hopefully whatever he decides to do, he will think it out while he rides.

Connor then replied, "I hope he knows what he is doing. I started this thing out with him and then he just abandoned my help real fast.

Cobbler explained, "Sometimes Knuckles likes to do things by himself his own way. When he gets that wild hair up his ass, you best just let him do his thing. He hasn't been wrong yet."

Connor decided to take a minute and check in with Julie and try to figure out exactly why she also disappeared so quickly. He walked outside where he would be able to hear her on the other end of the phone and dialed her number.

After a few rings, she answered, "Hello?"

Connor responded, "Hey babe. I was just making sure you made it home and I was wondering why you left so quickly?"

Julie answered, "We were pretty much ready to go when I saw you and Lisa is a bit uncomfortable around you when you are all dressed up like a biker."

Connor said, "I didn't know that. So, was it just you and Lisa tonight?"

Julie replied, "Yeah, pretty much. There were a couple of people in the bar that we have seen before and talked to, but Lisa was the only one that could make it out tonight and since you were doing your biker thing with the funeral I told her I would meet her for a night out."

Connor continued, "Well, okay. I just wanted to make sure that everything was fine. I shouldn't be too much longer. Things are beginning to wind down here so I will see you in a little bit."

Julie concluded, "I'm tired and I am getting ready to go to sleep. Don't be too loud when you get home. I will probably be asleep. Bye."

Connor heard the tone through his phone of the cancellation of the phone call by Julie. Connor returned his phone to his pocket and walked back toward the entrance of the clubhouse. He noticed that another prospect from one of the visiting charters was watching over the bikes now, which had allowed Scott to take a break. Connor felt that this was well deserved.

Connor spent the remainder of his night trying to fend off the relentless pursuits of Sally, and as the time passed farther into the night, and Connor's alcohol intake increased, the pursuits were getting more and more difficult to resist. It was apparent that Sally had now made it her mission in life to cause Connor to have an affair. Nevertheless, Connor was able to fend off all of her advances.

The clubhouse had now grown much quieter and there were only a few out of town members there along with just a few of the Clark charter there, when the clubhouse door opened, revealing Knuckles.

Knuckles walked in and appeared to be exhausted, almost as if he had ran a marathon, but everyone knew that Knuckles had not been doing that. He found a seat on the nearest couch to the front door and plopped himself down, stretching his legs out onto the other side of the couch and placed his hands behind his head. He let out a loud breath of air and closed his eyes.

Connor hurriedly approached Knuckles and had to be the first one to hear what had happened, saying, "Well, where have you been and what did you do?"

Knuckles looked up at Connor, making devilish eye contact with him and said with utmost sincerity, "Doing you a favor."

Chapter Twenty Four – Two Fifty One

Knuckles walked out of the clubhouse after the quick meeting in the church room and headed out the door with Jackal's blessing. The information that he had gathered at Turnovers was blowing his mind. How someone could do this to a brother of his was beyond his imagination.

Knuckles walked up to Cobbler and said, "Brother, I need you to keep in charge of my colors. I have to go do something and I need to run incognito. I also need the keys to the van."

Without question or hesitation, Cobbler took charge of Knuckles' colors and reached behind the door to grab a set of keys for the old white van that Cobbler had. Cobbler rarely drove it as it had no air conditioning or radio. Cobbler tossed the keys into the air towards Knuckles.

Knuckles grabbed the keys from midair and headed toward the van. He put the key in the ignition and fired up the old beast. As he reached for the radio to turn it on, he had forgotten that it was broken, but the silence would allow Knuckles to clear his mind for the mission that he had at hand.

Knuckles reached into his pocket and pulled out a wadded up napkin that his contact he had met at the bar had given him. The napkin read:

Montcliff

Blue F150

#251

As Knuckles was beginning to formulate exactly what his plan would be, he realized that since the number of the apartment began with the number 2, he assumed it would be on the second floor.

Knuckles hated stairs. His knees bothered him if he had to walk up stairs due to the several incidents of laying his bike down over the years. Although Knuckles was a seasoned rider, he had his share of mistakes as well as near misses, and most of them were due to his state of inebriation at the time. The last drop had left him with a little bit of a limp, especially on colder days or if he had been riding for a while.

The Montcliff Apartments were not very far from the clubhouse so it only took Knuckles about 15 minutes to arrive. After entering the complex, it became necessary to scope out the buildings and try to locate apartment number 251. It took Knuckles a couple of circles around the complex until he located the apartment and he also had located the vehicle that he was looking for, a late model Ford F150, which was blue in color.

Knuckles had remembered that his contact told him there was a small sticker in the lower left hand corner of the back glass of the truck, which Knuckles had also located and thereby convinced himself that he was not only in the right place, but he was also there at the right time.

Before Knuckles exited the van, he gave himself a brief pep talk. He would not have the immediate intimidation of the sight of his colors on his back or the roar of his old Harley-Davidson shovelhead as he approached, but what he did have was the element of surprise.

Knuckles got out of the van, which he had decided to park two buildings over from apartment number 251, and began walking toward the building. He ascended the flight of stairs and arrived outside of the door of the apartment. Instead of knocking on the door immediately, Knuckles decided that he needed a few seconds to allow the throbbing in his knees to subside.

Knuckles reached down and rubbed his knees in a vain attempt to make some of the pain go away, but he felt the adrenaline beginning it rush through his veins and his muscles began their light spasms as he readied himself for the task at hand. He walked up to the door of the apartment and offered a few polite knocks on the door.

Much to Knuckles surprise, the tenant in apartment 251 opened the door without asking who was there or even peering through the peep hole. The door swung open all the way and a man stood there in the doorway. This man was Chris.

Knuckles asked, "Excuse me, sir, but do you know who I am?"

Chris replied, "No, I don't. Can I help you?"

Knuckles grinned at Chris and said, "Probably not. It's you that will need help."

Knuckles then grabbed Chris by the throat with both hands and walked him backwards into his apartment. Knuckles kicked the door closed behind him and Chris grabbed a hold of Knuckles' wrists in a futile attempt to free himself from the powerful grasp he was under. Knuckles released one of his hands and gave Chris a nice pop from his fist in the nose to cause it to bleed.

The blood started running from his nose and collecting on Chris' lips and Knuckles' wrists. Chris was now in a substantial amount of pain with his newly broken nose and was trying desperately to remain conscious from the lack of air entering his lungs. Chris made a feeble attempt to strike Knuckles defensively, but his blow glance off of Knuckles' cheek barley disturbing the whiskers on his unshaven face.

Knuckles let out a girlish giggle after Chris' attempt at a strike and punched him in his broken nose again, and then he released him. Chris fell to the floor, still gasping for air, unable to scream for help. Knuckles took aim with his boot and kicked Chris in the stomach, which caused the remaining air to escape Chris' chest. Chris began to turn blue.

Knuckles then looked at the tattoo that Chris had on his leg, which was an anchor in some sort of Merchant Marine motif in an attempt to make Chris seem more of a man than he was.

Knuckles bent down and looked Chris in the eyes and said, "I am going to ask you again, do you know who I am?"

Chris did not understand why he was receiving this beating or who Knuckles was. Even if Knuckles would have been wearing his colors, Chris still did not know why he would be receiving a pounding from a member of the Libertines.

Chris shook his head no and said, "No, I don't know! Please stop! What did I do to you?"

Knuckles replied, "It's not what you did to me, it's what you did to my brother, which means you might as well have done it to me, and you better be glad that my brother didn't show up with me."

Chris pleaded back, "Please, tell me. I'm sorry. I don't know what I have done."

Knuckles said, "You know what you are doing with the married chick. That married chick is a brother's ol' lady. You don't fuck around with a

Libertine's ol' lady."

Chris said, "Who? I don't know who you are talking about."

Knuckles said, "You damn well know who I am talking about. You shouldn't be messing around with married women anyway. If you knew half of the bad shit that my brother is capable of, you definitely wouldn't be barking up that tree."

Chris replied, "I'm sorry. I'm really sorry. I won't do it again."

Knuckles grabbed a hold of Chris by the neck once more and drug his body toward the back door of the apartment. Knuckles then opened the sliding glass door and went out on the balcony, carrying Chris in tow. He then proceeded to hang Chris over the balcony with both hands by his neck. Chris grabbed onto Knuckles' wrists, trying to support his weight as his feet dangle below the balcony's porch.

Knuckles then looked Chris in the eye again and said, "Well, now you know me, and now you know not to be fucking around with married women. Furthermore mother fucker, if you ever see me again, at any point in your life, I promise you that my face will be the last living memory you have. Got it?"

Chris, gasping for the oxygen to speak, said, "Got it!"

Knuckles dragged his body back over the ledge of the balcony and with his elbow hit Chris in the face once again. The force of this blow completely knocked Chris into a state of unconsciousness. Since Chris had not put up any kind of struggle or fight to his liking, Knuckles had not become satisfied with the outcome.

Knuckles decided that Chris would also have to pay for his requirement of walking up a flight of stairs to deliver the message. Chris took his 4-D Mag-Light flashlight from his belt and began to repeatedly hit Chris on his left knee until he heard Chris' patella crack from the continuous strikes. Knuckles was now satisfied that Chris had received enough of a beating, but wanted to leave one final message.

So, in one last dishing out of embarrassment to Chris, Knuckles pulled down his pants and defecated into Chris' mouth. Unluckily for Chris, Knuckles had already consumed quite a bit of beer and liquor that night, so the feces that entered his mouth were of a soupy consistency. Knuckles then used Chris' shirt to wipe his backside with and left him lying there on the floor of the living room of his apartment.

Knuckles then went into the bathroom and washed his hands of the blood that was on him and exited the apartment. He then walked down the flight of stairs, pausing when he had made it to the bottom floor in a minor amount of pain to his knees, and then proceeded to walk toward the van he had borrowed from Cobbler.

Knuckles then hopped into the van and drove back to the clubhouse, stopping first at a drive-thru fast food restaurant for a cheeseburger, which he ate on the way.

#

"What favor, brother?" asked Connor.

Knuckles, as he let out a loud belch from the cheeseburger that he had just finished a few minutes beforehand, "I took care of your little problem."

Connor, still confused, probed further, asking, "What fucking problem?"

Knuckles, now realizing that Connor had no idea, told him what the contact at Turnovers had told him, explaining, "You know our associate that we met up at Turnovers? Well, when you wandered off to talk to your ol' lady, he let me in on a few things about this Chris character."

"So, I took from what he said that this Chris fucker likes to hang out at Turnovers. I guess the dude is going through a divorce and is living in an apartment close by while all the shit gets settled over who gets what and all that bull shit. In his spare time at night, he likes to hit on women, just like any other red blooded American male would. However, he isn't very smart in the ones that he chooses to hit on.

"When you went over there, our contact asked me what you were doing. I told him that you went over there to talk to your ol' lady. You should have seen the look on his face. He told me that she has been in there at least twice a week with usually a friend or two and she spends most of the night flirting with Chris."

Connor's heart sunk. He was devastated. Julie and Connor had not been exactly getting along well, or speaking all that much, but he never thought, in a million years, that she would do something like that. Connor could feel his stomach beginning to tie itself into knots, but he knew that he had to hold it together in front of his club.

Knuckles continued, "When I heard our friend explain this to me, I thought for certain that you had some idea that your ol' lady might be running around on you. From what he said, they never come in together or at the same time even, but they always, always leave at the same time. He would not have known this if he wasn't keeping an eye on this Chris fellow for us."

Connor asked Knuckles what he had done about it and Knuckles told the story of where he had been for the last hour or so.

Connor said, "Brother, that was my problem and my beating. Why did you do that?"

Knuckles replied, "Plausible deniability, brother. He now knows that she is off limits and he also knows that I'm not her old man. I doubt that we see anything from this fucker again. Two birds with one stone as they say."

Connor was enraged and pleased at the same time. Pleased that this Chris guy got a good beating at the hand of Knuckles, but enraged that Julie would do such a thing.

Connor then said, "I need to get my ass home. Looks like I need to have a talk with the ol' lady."

Knuckles corrected Connor, stating, "Wait. Remember, it takes two to tango as they say. This is as much her fault as it is his. Now that you know what happened, I would wait until you have a clear head and make sure that you play your cards right."

Connor replied, "That's good advice. I need to sleep on this."

Connor then mounted his bike and rode home. Rather than going on inside to bed, he went outside on the back patio with a bottle of whiskey and contemplated his next move. After the bottle of whiskey was just about empty, Connor had finished formulating his plan, which would begin the very next morning.

Chapter Twenty Five – Damage Control

Connor awoke the next morning with the worst hangover he had ever experienced. Combining the late night whiskey binge, the beer, and the lack of sleep was wearing him thin. Connor thought to himself that he would never do anything like that again.

However, the late night thought session, even though clouded in a drunken stupor, had clarified what he had to accomplish in his plan. Connor set two goals. The first goal was to make sure that he rectified his position in the club. From what he gathered, it was his ol' lady that was providing information to this Chris character who was in turn providing information to the governor's office. Connor was unsure as to what exactly Julie could have been spilling, but it must have been something.

The second goal was to let Julie know that he knew about the affair, and whether or not he was willing to forgive, forget, and move on. Whether or not Connor was willing to forgive, he was unsure. For Connor to forget and move on would be twice as hard as forgiveness.

Connor decided that he needed to go for a ride to clear his mind. Since it was a Saturday, Connor decided to go out into the country for a few miles and swing by Bill's shop. As Connor let out the throttle on his bike, he felt the refreshing wind in his face helping to cure his hangover, but as his body started to feel better, his mind began to battle him.

He began to think about the worst that could have happened between Julie and this Chris fucker. Pictures in his mind became so graphic, like something from a hard core pornographic movie, which made his stomach turned. He imagined Julie doing things that he had only hoped she would do with him in his wildest fantasies. As the images became raunchier, Connor began to get angrier.

Then Connor's thoughts went toward his problem with the club. By now, Connor assumed that everyone in his charter was aware that his ol' lady was running around on him with the informant. Connor had decided how he would approach this issue with the club, but the one item that he could not nail down was what the reaction of the club members would be.

Connor felt that Knuckles was in his corner. Since Knuckles took it upon himself to enact revenge for the club and for Connor himself, he figured that Knuckles would stand shoulder to shoulder with him and support him.

Connor also assumed that Terry would stand behind him as well, since they were old friends long before he wore that patch on his back. Terry had been an integral part of his patching into the club, he was his sponsor, and had grown back into being Connor's best friend.

The wild card here was Cobbler. Cobbler had seemed to have made peace with Connor, but this situation could easy sever that peace that had been made. Cobbler typically had a good head on his shoulders, but he could easily be set off, and this was no small thing.

No matter what was about to happen, Connor knew that the sooner he got it over, the better. Connor pulled his bike over to the shoulder of the road and made a u-turn to head back into town towards the shop to begin facing the music. He might as well start with Bill.

As Connor pulled up to Bill's shop, he noticed that Terry's bike and Ratchet's bike were parked outside. Connor shut down his motor and took a deep breath as he set his jiffy stand and dismounted from his motorcycle. Hearing the noise of a bike pulling up, Terry and Ratchet peered outside, and upon recognizing Connor, began to approach him.

Before Terry could say anything, Ratchet grabbed a hold of Connor and embraced him with both arms, whispering in his ear, "We are here for you, brother."

As Ratchet let go, Terry embraced Connor as Ratchet had done, saying, "I love you, brother."

This exchange had made Connor feel much more comfortable. It appeared that he would not have to do any explaining at all. The three men walked inside the shop, and after Connor reached down to pat Chief on the head, he approach Bill, who was replacing a blown out rear tire on a customer's motorcycle.

Once the tire was mounted, Bill turned around and recognized that Connor was standing there. He put the tire on the ground and leaned it up against the lift next to his tire mounting machine and walked over to Connor.

Bill stood in front of Connor and said, "Hey brother. I know that you are going through some shit right now, but we are all here for you."

Connor replied, "Thanks, brother. That means a lot to me."

Connor then embraced Bill as he had done with Terry and Ratchet. It was now apparent to Connor that he had no problem with the club, and they did not blame him for the information escaping. Bill then asked Connor to text the remaining members of their charter and tell them to come to the shop for a quick meeting. Connor did as Bill asked.

Bill then walked over to the large door of the shop and pulled it closed. Terry, Ratchet, and Bill grabbed stools and sat down. Connor remained standing.

Bill began to notify the other three members of some new information, saying, "Well, we have some new intel that suggests that this Chris asshole, who is fooling around with Rub's ol' lady, is not exactly getting his information as we thought. He has got some information from her, but nothing more than our names and phone numbers, which I assume Julie took out of Rub's phone while he was sleeping.

"He has someone else that he is getting shit from. Now, since Knuckles took it upon himself to deliver a message, we are going to have one of two outcomes. Either this shit goes away, or we are going to get a hell of a lot more harassment.

"I spoke to Jackson this morning and so far there have been no reports filed about the assault last night. It won't take long for that Chris fucker to figure out who Knuckles is, but hopefully nothing comes of that. We don't need a member to go inside right now. This shit about outlawing motorcycle clubs has got to go away, and if Knuckles gets pinched for this assault, then the fucking news will have a field day."

The sound of motorcycles pulling up outside the shop could now be heard by the four club members and the door to the shop opened to reveal Jackal, Pepper, and Knuckles.

Bill announced, "There he is. How are those knuckles doing Mike Tyson?"

Everyone chuckled as the three remaining club members entered the shop.

Knuckles replied, "They are not nearly as bad as that mother fucker's face is doing."

Bill explained what he had said already to the now present members.

Jackal then said, "Ok, before we go any farther, I just want Rub to know that we are all behind you. Since Knuckles took this Chris bastard for a ride last night, I think as long as no charges are filed, the heat is off of us there for a bit.

"We need to shift our focus to the Sixers and what to do with that situation. Last we talked we decided to prospect Scott for one sole purpose, retaliation for Nutcase's death. I say we move on that."

Connor said, "I agree, brother. How about I get Scott up here and him and I make a ride out to the Simmons chapter. We know where the guy lives. I will see that this is taken care of without mistakes. I at least owe that much to the club after I fucked up my home life with the ol' lady and jeopardized us."

Jackal replied, "Rub, you don't owe us for that. It could happen to any one of us. Bitches get jealous. It's their fucking nature. So what if she looked around for some strange dick. That's not your fault. Put it out of your mind as far as the club is concerned. Your problems with your ol' lady are between you and her now."

Knuckles then said, "I don't want Rub taking the prospect alone. He needs someone else to go with him."

Connor retorted, "I appreciate the concern but I can handle this myself. He's my prospect."

Pepper then interjected, "Yeah, he's your prospect, but you are squeaky clean, and we need that to stay intact. I will take the prospect and see that it gets done."

Connor, now noticeably angry at what seemed to be a lack of confidence in his ability to produce a violent outcome himself said, "Fine. Pepper goes, but I am fucking going."

Jackal then said, "Done. Pepper, Rub, and the prospect will go pay that nigger a visit and take revenge for Nutcase. No mistakes. Before you do anything we need to prepare the Simmons chapter for a possible backlash. That nigger killed one of us, and we kill him, which should even the score, but those animals might start an all out war, and the first chapter in their crosshairs will be Simmons."

Cobbler then said, "I will visit Simmons and let them know to be prepared for war."

Bill continued, "All this sounds good, but we still will probably need to have a sit down with the Sixers after this to ensure that we don't get into a war."

Jackal replied, "Agreed. First things first, we go off that nigger. Then we will worry about our fried chicken and watermelon party. Pepper, you go ride over to the prospect's house and get his ass up here. Rub, you wait on them to return and head out to Creston."

Everyone stood up and parted ways. Bill then motioned at Connor to walk with him to the opposite side of the shop for a private conversation. Connor followed Bill as the remainder of the club stood by the main shop door which had now been opened and began to drink beer.

Bill stopped and turned around to face Connor. He reached into his pocket and took out a cigar from the pouch in his back pocket and lit it up. Bill then took a couple of puffs from his bent stogie and cracked his back.

He took the cigar from his mouth and said, "Look brother. You aren't the first person in the world to find out that your ol' lady is running around on you, but before you do anything rash to affect your home life, you need to think about what you really know and what you are just assuming to be true.

"As far as you know, an associate of ours has seen your ol' lady flirting with that guy in a bar several times. That's it. That's all you know. She could just be scamming the dude for free drinks for all you know. My point is, you don't know. That's what you need to find out. You need to find out what is really going on."

Connor said, "I agree, but my gut is telling me that there is a lot more to it that harmless flirting at a bar for free drinks. That shit might work once, but if he is meeting her up there several times, he's looking for more than just some broad to have a drink with, if you know what I mean?"

Bill answered, "I know. Just don't go jumping to any conclusions until you have some facts to back them up. If I were you, I would just sit down with your ol' lady and flat out ask her what's going on.

"You know, part of your problem is that you are not including her in this life. Because of that, you have that tart Sally rubbing up on you big time and you yourself are a breath away of cheating. Now that you think your ol' lady is, what's to stop you from hitting that? Think about it. You hit that and your ol' lady isn't doing anything. That fucks with you a bit, doesn't it?

Connor sighed and said, "Yeah, but I have no intention of hitting that slut."

Bill replied, "Whatever. You do what you got to do. I'm just warning you that you need to get your fucking facts straight it all. That's it. I got to get back to work."

Bill walked back over and picked up the tire leaning against the lift and began to install it. Connor walked over to the refrigerator and after grabbing a beer joined Terry and Ratchet outside the shop, where they were telling dirty jokes.

Two beers later, Pepper returned to the shop with Scott. As the two got off of their bikes, Pepper motioned for Connor to join them as they walked inside the retail portion of Bill's shop. The three entered inside, where no one else was, and Pepper closed the door behind him and locked it.

Pepper said, "So here's the deal, prospect. We know who killed Nutcase and today we get our revenge. This is going to be your test and what we are about to ask you to do might fuck with you a bit. So, before I tell you what you have to do, I want to give you a chance to hand over that cut and walk away, no harm, no foul. Understand?"

Scott replied, "I understand. I am ready to do whatever it takes to get my full patch and before you even ask me to do what you are about to ask me to do, I think I know, and to set your mind at ease, I will just come out and say it. As far as I'm concerned, that nigger deserves to die and I would be honored to do that for the club."

Connor then interjected, "This isn't the fucking movies, prospect. You

Page
198

do realize that you are about to commit murder, albeit a well deserved murder, but murder nonetheless?"

Scott answered, "I do realize that. I have no problem with that at all."

Pepper and Connor looked at each other and without saying a word, exchanged a glance which the two men understood as if to say, "Good enough for me!"

Pepper then said, "Okay prospect, go outside and wait on us. I need to discuss something with Rub here."

Scott obeyed Peppers request and went outside. After the door closed, Pepper walked over to it and locked it again. Pepper then began to detail out his plan.

He began, "Okay man, this is what I am thinking. I have someone from Simmons chapter tailing the guy today. My plan is to ride up to Simmons and wait until the guy goes home. Once that happens, our contact from Simmons will call me. They have a pickup truck that we can take from there out to Creston.

"We give Scott a gun with a silencer and let him plug the dude. After we shoot him, I am going to take a picture of him. Then we will take the truck back to Simmons and dump it in the woods. At the dump site will be a prospect waiting on us in a van to take us back into town, where we will hop back on the bikes and come home."

Connor asked, "Why the picture?"

Pepper replied, "We take the picture in case we need it for future bargaining power. After this dude gets what is coming to him, the Sixers are going to be just as pissed as we were when Nutcase died. Hopefully, the blood spilling ends there. We can't afford a war."

"So do you think we are still going to have a sit down with the Sixers after this?" asked Connor.

Pepper said, "We are going to have to have a sit down with them. If we don't, then they might just go digging trying to find out who took out one of theirs and it might bring heat on the Simmons chapter, and we can't do that to another charter."

"That makes sense," replied Connor.

Pepper then said, "You know what, man. You sure as shit have changed. When I first met you, I thought that you were nothing more than a paper pushing yuppie. Hell, that's one of the reasons we named you Rub for crying out loud. Now, you are willing to fucking kill someone for this club.

You have come a long way in a short time, from pussy to outlaw, damn near overnight. I'm proud of you. But, there is one thing that I have that you just won't ever be able to have."

"What's that?" asked Connor.

Pepper chuckled as he said, "a dick as big as mine!"

Connor laughed. Pepper always had to bring up the size of his package, and as far as Connor was concerned, he didn't want to have Pepper show him to prove it. Pepper then walked outside and prepared himself for the short trip over to Simmons. Connor decided that he would make one quick phone call before he left.

Connor placed a call to Julie. The phone rang and rand until her voicemail picked up. As Connor listened to her voice on the other end of the line, reciting her voicemail greeting, Connor took a deep breath and left her a message:

"Hey, it's me. I have to go on a run for the club and I should be back tonight. I'm not sure what time that I will be in, but hopefully it won't be too late. When I do get home, we need to talk."

Connor then ended the phone call and put his phone back into his pocket. He then looked around the shop and went over to one of the display cases which had knives in it. Connor took out one of the larger knives and fastened it to his belt on the back of his pants upside down, so the blade and handle both would be hidden by his colors.

Connor then walked back to the service area of the shop and handed Bill $40 for the knife as he showed it to him. Bill took the $40 from Connor and put it into his pocket. Connor then walked outside to find Pepper and Scott waiting for him. Connor sat on his bike and the three fired up their engines.

Connor gave a nod to Pepper informing him that he was ready to roll. Pepper looked at Scott and received the same nod back. The remaining members of the Libertines stood and watched as the three bikers left the shop, headed towards Simmons.

Chapter Twenty Six - Vengeance

The ride to Simmons had begun. Connor was nervous and excited all at the same time for what was to happen in the next few hours. Pepper was leading the ride and in typical Libertine fashion, going well past the speed limit. On the rural roads, it never seemed to be an issue.

Scott was positioned in between Connor and Pepper behind them, leaving only about half of a bike length away from them. Traveling at speeds in excess of 90 miles per hours and the rumbling of their three motor in sync was an impressive sight to other motorists who were quick to pull over to the side of the road to allow them to pass.

As most bike rides tended to be that Connor rode, this one was uneventful as well. It was just one more nice scenic ride that Connor went on, but the enjoyment soon ended as the group arrived at the Simmons chapter clubhouse, which was a detached garage building behind the president's house.

Four of the five of the members of the Simmons chapter were there, since one member, Rags, was tailing the Sixer, along with a prospect. The bikers from the Clark chapter pulled their bikes around to the back of the president's house and parked them in front of the clubhouse. Greetings between the two charters were exchanged and the prospect from the Simmons chapter grabbed a beer for the three travelers.

The Simmons chapter president was Bootleg. Bootleg was known for brewing his own beer and even though the name implied that he was a bootlegger, the name was misleading since everyone knew Bootleg was basically too cheap to buy his own beer, so he made it. Bootleg had moved to Simmons was originally a member in Topeka when he was given the ability to start the Simmons chapter.

Bootleg had met Pepper before, but this was the first time that he had seen Connor, or for that matter, prospect Scott. Bootleg and Pepper wandered off to talk by themselves, which left Connor and Scott there with the remaining four members of the Simmons chapter, and their prospect, whose name was Tim.

Connor began speaking to the Vice President of the Simmons chapter, whose name was Apache, saying, "Well, I wish we were here on just a party visit."

Apache responded, "It can't be all fun and games all the time. We just hope that what you boys are about to do doesn't erupt in a blood bath right here in our back yard."

Connor replied, "We are going to do what we can to avoid that. First and foremost is getting our revenge for a fallen brother. Then we can deal with the aftermath when it comes."

Apache then said, "You guys up in Clark are more equipped to handle situations than we are. We are still a young charter. Hell, we haven't even been approved by national yet. We would hate to have to call in the nomads before we even get blessed."

Connor, trying to pacify Apache, continued, "Like I said, we will do what we can. It puts you guys in a tough spot and I understand that, but it is what it is."

Apache had more time in the Libertines than Connor. He came down to Simmons with Bootleg to help establish the charter there and both Bootleg and Apache had been instrumental in keeping the peace between the Libertines and the Sixers.

Connor asked, "So, Apache, tell me about the Sixers. What do you know?"

Apache explained, "Well, they are an all black gang typical of niggers, riding around in their low riders. Their main gig is drugs. Fucking Creston is filled with meth heads and coke freaks and they make good money doing their thing.

"I would say there are probably 25-30 of them. They have tags sprayed all over that town and they also have a huge following of want-to-be Sixers that follow them everywhere. We stay out of their town and they stay out of ours. We have an agreement that they keep their shit in their own yard so we don't see much of them.

"We do have a neutral ground that we have met them at to talk, which is a gas station in between here and Creston just off of the highway. The owner of the gas station is a friend of the club. The only way to get between here and there is right by his business, so he keeps a watch for us if he sees low riders heading our way."

Connor replied, "That's good to know, brother. Good to know. Now, all we have to do it get this shit behind us and hope that there is no further retaliation."

After Connor had finished his comment, Pepper and Bootleg came back from their private conversation. Pepper explained to Connor and Scott that he and Bootleg were going to hop into a car a drive the route so they would know where they were going. Pepper told Connor and Scott to stay at the clubhouse and await their return. Pepper and Bootleg then got into a car and drove off.

Connor asked Apache, "About how long do you think this will take?"

Apache answered, "Not more than 30 minutes. It's not that far of a drive, but I know that Bootleg want to show him where the prospect will be meeting you later when you ditch the truck."

Connor inquired, "By the way, what is the deal with the truck? Why are we ditching it?"

Apache laughed and explained, "That old beater is just about done. It will get you there and back tonight with no problem, so don't worry about that, but she is on her last leg. We have already stripped all of the identifiers off of the truck and the plates are stolen. It's just time to put the old truck out to pasture."

Connor understood, as he looked at the truck and realized that it was basically a pile of junk, but he also knew that not everyone could afford the nicest rides and fondly thought of his old truck he used to drive to work every day, of course prior to the purchase of his bike.

Once 30 minutes had passed, as Apache alluded to, Pepper and Bootleg returned. They both exited the car and walked over to the clubhouse where Connor and Scott were awaiting patiently.

Pepper then advised, "Well, I know the route. It's not all that difficult. Actually, it's pretty straight forward. All we have to do now is wait on the phone call."

Time passed by slowly from that point. Patience grew into impatience and Pepper and Connor began to wonder if the guy would ever head home. After about three hours, and several phone calls from Pepper to Rags getting status updates, the call from Rags finally came in just after sundown.

Rags had informed Pepper that he had arrived home alone and he had been to a few bars throughout the day, but did not appear to be intoxicated. Since they were unaware if he was in for the night or not, the crew decided to head out right then and get this done. As they got into the truck, the three handed their cuts to Apache.

Bootleg then asked Connor, "Are you packing?"

Connor answered, "I've got just a blade on me."

"Here," replied Bootleg as he handed Connor a Glock 9 millimeter pistol. "You might need this."

Connor took the gun and placed it between his legs. He had no intention of using it, as they had brought a gun complete with a silencer for Scott to use. Pepper then drove off.

After a short 10 minute drive, the three arrived outside of Seth's house, which was located in a seedy neighborhood. The house looked like it was ready to fall down and there were no lights on inside. The porch was in shambles and there was trash and several empty beer bottles lying in the yard.

Pepper drove past the house and made one last phone call to Rags to verify that no one had showed up. Rags told Pepper that it was all clear and that he would see him back at the clubhouse. Pepper then went around the block once more and stopped just before Seth's street.

He handed Scott the silenced pistol and said, "Get it done. Connor, you run wingman and don't forget the picture."

Connor and Scott exited the vehicle and went around to the back of the house. They peered inside a window and could not see any lights on anywhere. Moving closer to the backdoor, they finally noticed a glimmer of occupancy in the house, the ambient light of a small television could be seen through the doorway of the back bedroom.

Scott then whispered to Connor, "Do we kick the door in and I go in blasting or what?"

Connor answered back, "Let's not get a head of ourselves. Check the back door first."

Scott reached over to the door handle of the back door and slowly began to turn it. Sure enough, the back door was unlocked. Scott pulled on the door very slowly, trying his best not to make any noise. Scott was able to get the door opened just enough for the two to slip inside.

As they entered the house, Connor became extremely nervous. He began to sweat profusely as it rolled down his face and he could begin to smell his body odor. Scott, however, seemed to be solid as a rock. In Connor's mind, Scott's stock just went up and in just a few more seconds, they would have an experience that would bring them closer together.

Scott crept a few steps in front of Connor towards the bedroom with the television on. The television program that was one was some kind of sitcom that Connor didn't recognize, especially since Connor had basically given up on television months ago. The volume on the television was not turned up very loud, but just enough where Connor could make out the laugh track from the program.

Scott had made it to just the other side of the door frame and peered around the corner, where he saw Seth lying on the bed watching the television. Before Connor could give Scott the nod to go ahead, Scott burst into the bedroom, catching Seth completely by surprise.

Seth reached into the waist band of his pants to draw a gun which he had. As Seth pulled his gun, Scott squeezed the trigger on the silenced gun. The shot hit Seth in the left shoulder. Scott fired again and hit Seth in the stomach, which caused Seth to buckle over and hit the floor. Connor and Scott watched as Seth lay on the floor, overcome by pain.

As Scott lowered the gun to take aim at Seth's head to finish him off, Connor put his hand on the gun. Scott glanced at Connor with a look of confusion on his face. Connor took the gun out of Scott's hands and handed him the cheap digital camera that Connor had in his back pocket to take the picture.

Connor then pressed the gun against the back of Seth's head and exclaimed to him, "This one is from me, for Nutcase."

Connor pulled the trigger. Seth's brains and blood splattered across his bedroom floor. It was obvious that Seth was dead. Connor then handed the gun back to Scott and turned Seth's dead body over. He then took the camera from Scott and took a picture of Seth with the camera. Connor pushed the review button on the camera and was satisfied with the picture. He then motioned to Scott that it was time to go.

Scott and Connor left the house just as they entered and closed the back door. The duo walked around to the front of the house and hopped into the truck where Pepper was waiting on them. Pepper then looked and Connor and without saying a word, Connor nodded his head "yes" and they left.

The three men arrived at the side of the road where they were to meet the prospect from the Simmons chapter, and he was there as promised with a black passenger van to take them back to safe ground. Pepper reached into the cab of the truck and pulled the transmission into neutral and the four of them pushed the truck into the woods. The truck rolled down a hill and smashed into a tree.

Everyone got into the van and Tim drove them back to the Simmons clubhouse, where the remainder of the chapter was waiting. Rather than sticking around, Pepper had already determined that they would head back to Clark immediately so they could report that all was taken care of.

Before Pepper, Connor, and Scott started their bikes, Pepper looked at Bootleg and said, "Hang tight, brother. Call us if there are any problems. We will talk soon."

The three fired up their bikes and rode towards their clubhouse, except this time, Pepper felt it was necessary to obey the speed limit, which they did. They arrived back at the clubhouse where they were met by Jackal, Bill, and Terry.

When they dismounted from their bikes, Jackal walked up and asked Pepper, "How did it go?"

Pepper replied, "It's done, and what a Kodak moment it was."

Connor tossed the digital camera to Jackal, who caught it and looked at the picture of the dead body. Jackal smirked and turned the camera off and then tossed it to Pepper, who put it in his pocket.

Jackal then suggested, "Let's go inside so I can buy you three a beer. That's right, even you prospect."

Connor replied, "I would love to, but I need to get home. There is some shit I have to do."

Jackal put his arms around Pepper and Scott as Connor walked away to get onto his bike. Bill walked up behind the three, smoking a cigar as usual. The men stood outside and watched as Connor rode off.

Bill then remarked, "That boy sure has come a long way."

Chapter Twenty Seven - Life

Connor left the clubhouse and began to ride home when he realized that he had coasted back into town on fumes. There was a gas station on the way from the clubhouse to Connor's house and he decided rather than risking it, he would swing in and stop to fill up.

Connor pulled up to the pump, swiped his credit card, and filled up his gas tank. As the tank neared capacity, Connor forgot to let go of the handle on the dispenser and gasoline spilled all over Connor and his bike. Fatigue from the ride as well as lack of good sleep from the past two nights finally caught up to him.

He took out some paper towels from the windshield washer box mounted to the side of the gas pump and wiped off as much of the gasoline as he could. He then took another paper towel out and attempted to wipe off his jeans, which had gasoline spots down both legs. Realizing that he now smelled like a Molotov cocktail, Connor went inside the gas station to wash up a bit.

Connor stumbled toward the convenience store in a state of near unconsciousness. He walked through the automatic door and headed toward the restroom. He pulled on the door and since it was locked he realized that it was occupied. He turned around and decided to pull on the door to the women's restroom to see if it was available, and it was empty.

Connor walked into the women's restroom and locked the door behind him. He went over to the sink and washed his hands in a futile attempt to rid himself of the gasoline smell. Once the scent of liquid soap overtook the petrol smell, Connor splashed some water on his face to attempt to awaken him. He reached over and took several paper towels from the dispenser and wiped his hands and face.

Then he gazed at himself in the mirror and began to talk to himself, saying, "You have got to get a hold of yourself. You know you have the balls when it comes to the club, now you need to man up and face Julie and call her on this bull shit."

Connor sneered at himself in the mirror and in a slightly psychopathic manner began to berate himself, continuing, "Don't be such a fucking pussy, you weak mother fucker. You know what you have to do. You know what you have to say. Man the fuck up and take your ass home and let's finish this fucked up day right."

Connor threw the paper towel at the mirror and gritted his teeth at his reflection. His crazy self pep talk had given him a temporary boost of energy and a small amount of confidence. Connor walked out of the women's restroom to find a lady waiting to use the facility. She looked up at Connor as he left the bathroom and flashed him a flirty smile. Connor did not pay any attention to her as he walked past as his mind was elsewhere.

He walked outside, leaving the convenience store, and approached his motorcycle, where he saw two men standing next to it, giving his bike a once over. Upon arriving next to his bike, the two men then realized that the motorcycle was owned by a Libertine. The two men looked admittedly afraid and without saying a word hurriedly walked back toward their vehicle. Once again, Connor paid no attention to them. He was focused.

Connor sat on his bike and fired up the motor. Revving his engine he dropped the transmission loudly into first gear and took off like a bat out of hell into the street. Connor raced towards home, disobeying all traffic laws, which he typically would only do when he was riding with another member of the club.

Connor then arrived at his house and pulled his bike into the driveway, and after raising the door to the garage, he noticed that Julie's car was missing. The absence of her car enraged Connor, as he had specifically told her to be home that night so they could talk. Connor pulled his bike into the garage and shut the door.

As he went inside he walked into the kitchen and noticed that he had a twelve pack of beer in the refrigerator that was just waiting to be consumed. He removed the entire pack and walked back into the front yard, where he pulled up a chair and sat down, cracking open a beer and waiting. Connor wanted Julie to see him sitting in the front yard, waiting on her.

Connor sat outside staring at the stars and the full moon, drinking beer after beer, trying to wind himself down from what had happened just a few hours before and preparing him for the confrontation that he would soon begin with Julie. Still, Connor was having an issue working up the courage to deal with the inevitable. After enough liquid courage, he decided to stick with his original plan.

After four beers, Julie's car pulled into the driveway. It was apparent that she saw Connor sitting in the front yard but she pulled her car into the garage as she always did, not slowing down to make eye contact with Connor. Connor heard the engine of Julie's car shut off, the door open and soon after close, and awaited her appearance from around the corner to speak to him.

Julie did as Connor had predicted and she walked out of the garage, around the corner, and walked up to Connor, saying, "Why are you sitting here in the back yard?"

Connor mustered up some courage to begin his case against Julie, saying, "Let me ask you a question. Why did you leave Turnovers so fast the other night? Was it because I was there?"

Julie said, "no, I told you that we were about to leave anyway."

Connor continued, "It was kind of strange that you and Lisa left your drinks half full and didn't pay the tab. It's not really like you to walk a tab or anything."

Julie hesitated for a second and then replied, "Lisa had a friend there who bought those drinks. We had already paid for the ones that we drank before."

Connor then inquired, "Really? A friend? And who might that be?"

Julie said, "I don't remember their name."

Connor responded, "Well isn't that convenient."

Julie then angrily said, "Connor, do you have something you want to say? If you do, then say it because I want to go inside and..."

Connor interrupted her, "You're damn right I do. I know what's been going on and I want you to confess."

Julie, a bit taken aback, replied, "I don't know what you are talking about."

Connor then yelled, "You know damn well what I'm talking about. Don't make me say his fucking name."

Julie then realized that Connor knew something, and said, "Who are we talking about?"

Connor, now growing more and more worn-out from tap dancing around the subject, came out with it, "Fucking Chris, that's who, mother fucking Chris. Don't act like there isn't anything there."

Julie said, "Oh, Chris. He's nothing more than a friend. That's it."

"Funny you are just now mentioning him," said Connor. "I thought I knew all of your friends, and you know what I have said about women with men friends. There isn't a man in this world who just wants to be your friend."

Julie now knew that she was caught, but was not quite sure how much Connor knew, so she carefully spoke to her defense, "Look Connor, nothing happened. Nothing at all. I have seen him like twice at Turnovers. That's it."

As the booze flowing through his veins now was fueling his rage, Connor replied, "So, you have seen the guy twice, and he is now your friend. That's fucking amazing."

Julie retorted, "Well, not so much a friend, just an acquaintance. You know, just someone that you say hello to at a bar or somewhere where people meet up."

Connor then inquired, "Do you ever talk to him outside of Turnovers?"

Julie replied, "No. Like I said, I just see him and talk to him while I'm there."

Connor, now extremely enraged at what he assumed was a blatant lie, screamed, "Let me see you phone!"

Julie asked, "What? Why?"

Connor then stood up and put his arm out in front of him with his palm turned up and commanded, "Give me your God damn phone, now!"

Julie delayed his request a second time, stating, "What do you want to see my phone for?"

Connor, now fed up with the delaying from Julie, said, "So help me

God Julie, if you don't hand over that fucking phone right now, there is going to be hell to pay. Give it to me."

Julie, now extremely nervous, handed Connor the phone. Connor opened up the phone and scrolled through her contacts, until he reached the name "Chrissy."

He then said, "Is this the same person?"

Julie, swallowing deeply and with an obvious amount of shame in her voice, replied simply, "Yes."

"So, now you have lied to me twice! Are you done fucking lying?"

Julie looked down at the ground and said, "Fine. Look, Lisa and I were at Turnovers one night with a couple of other girls, sitting at the bar having a drink and Chris came up to us. He offered to buy all of us a drink.

"We got to talking, all of us, and of course in the conversation he found out that Lisa was engaged and that we were there after a day of shopping. He asked me some general questions about myself, but he never asked whether or not I was married or had a boyfriend. We ended up talking for quite a while and he seemed like a nice guy, not forward or flirtatious or anything like that.

"So then about a week later we had a girl's night out and we ended up at Turnovers again. He wasn't there. I figured that after the first time I saw him I would not see him again. Well, he came in later that night when we were about to leave and Lisa and I stayed after the other girls left. I don't know why I did it, but I did.

"Of course, he came up to us since he remembered us and said that he had been in there a few times and we weren't there and that he had missed us. We hung out at the bar for a few drinks and Lisa told him about a joke picture that I had on my phone. He asked me to text it to him. I didn't even think that once I did that, he would have my phone number.

"He started to text me and I mostly ignored it. They were harmless texts, just asking what I was doing or how my day had been. He really seemed like a friend.

"Then you got so involved with your motorcycle friends, I became lonely. I started to text him more and more and things, well, I guess things started getting out of hand. This might hurt for you to hear, but I became emotionally attached to him and I think I started to fall in love with him, or at least the idea of falling in love with someone who was there for me emotionally."

Connor was taking in all of what Julie was saying and the more she talked, the harder the emotional knife was shoved into his back.

Connor decided that he had to prove himself back to Julie, saying, "You know, if there is one thing that I thought was a constant between us was trust. I never, in a million years, thought that you would cheat on me.

"Now, let me tell you something. Ever since I joined this club, do you know how many women I have turned away? Several. I mean, there have been so many women that want a piece of me, I could have easily cheated on you, but guess what. As many times as there were, and being able to keep it concealed from you, I never did.

"This patch on my back has made me a pussy magnet. I can't hardly keep them away. I tell all of them that I am married, and guess what? They don't care. They just want to be with a biker.

"But I had enough respect for you and our marriage vows not to ever do that to you. I knew that fucking Lisa would somehow fuck things up between us. I just fucking knew it."

Julie, trying to salvage Connor's feelings, said, "Connor, nothing happened. I mean, nothing physical happened. I have known that what has been going on was wrong but I just couldn't stop. The thing is, I know that what I have done is wrong, and I promise that I will stop it. I will not talk to him again.

"But, there is one thing you need to realize. You are not the man that I fell in love with anymore. The motorcycle, the club, your drinking; all of these things were not a part of you when we got married. I don't know why you changed. I never should have let you get that bike."

Connor was troubled by this statement in two ways. He remembered back to getting the bike for his birthday and it was set up as a surprise that Julie was supportive of his purchase. However, the other side of the coin that bothered him was now he realized how whipped he was before, and that he had allowed Julie to control him all of these years.

Connor then commanded, "Let's not try and turn this issue back around on me. This is all your doing. Now I know that I can't trust my wife. What a great feeling! All those fucking times I could have cheated and I never did. Fuck this and fuck you!"

Connor threw Julie's phone on the ground and started walking toward his bike. Julie came up behind him and grabbed his arm in a frail attempt to stop his progress. Connor threw his arm up in the air and continued walking.

Julie yelled, "Connor, please, wait! Don't go! Don't leave things like this!"

Connor replied, "This is all on you, bitch. I'm not going to live the rest of my life with a two-timing, cheating, no good slutty fucking cunt."

Julie began to cry uncontrollably. Connor had never said anything remotely that insulting to Julie. In fact, before this moment, Connor had not even called her a bitch.

As Connor walked his bike backwards out of the garage, obviously getting ready to leave, Julie pleaded with him once again, "Connor, babe, please, please don't leave. I'm so sorry. We can fix this. I promise. I swear. It's over. I love you. I am so, so sorry. Please don't do this."

Connor replied in a harsh tone, "Maybe you should have thought about that before you fucked the guy."

Julie whined back, "I didn't sleep with him. I swear. I didn't sleep with him. Please believe me."

Connor, who placed his hand on the starter of the bike, looked at Julie and offered her one more comment, saying, "I wish I could believe you, but once a liar, always a liar."

Connors finger pressed the starter button on his bike and brought the motorcycle to life. He started walking the bike backwards again to enter the street. Julie followed in front of the bike, in an obvious panic. Connor was ignoring her advance as she kept yelling at him to stop. Connor ignored her as he positioned his bike to leave. His foot pushed down the shifter and clicked the bike into first gear.

Connor started to let out the clutch, when Julie grabbed the handlebars and exclaimed, "Connor, I'm pregnant!"

Made in the USA
Lexington, KY
24 February 2012